Lydia's

Grammy Ta̶ ̶ ̶ ̶ ̶ ̶ ̶ ̶ generous one.
She gave of h̶ ̶ ̶ ̶ ̶ ̶, concern and her love.
She gave of herself—and it was the best gift
of all.

Grammy's spirit lived on—in the children who
played at Taylor House, in the mothers and
fathers who knew that their children were
happy and cherished. More than a day-care
center, Taylor House was the heart of the
community, whose steady beat could be heard
in the laughter of its children.

To keep Taylor House steadfast and
unchanging, to keep Grammy's spirit and
Katherine's dream alive, Lydia needed
courage, strength and wisdom. And love.

Now, more than ever before, Lydia hoped
for love.

ABOUT THE AUTHOR

Born and raised on Long Island, Leigh Anne Williams has now taken up permanent residence in Manhattan. Through her summers as a camper in the Berkshire Mountains, she came to know and love New England. This childhood love of small-town life in Massachusetts formed the basis of the Taylor House trilogy.

Books by Leigh Anne Williams

Lydia's Hope
Leigh Anne Williams

Harlequin Books

TORONTO • NEW YORK • LONDON
AMSTERDAM • PARIS • SYDNEY • HAMBURG
STOCKHOLM • ATHENS • TOKYO • MILAN

Published November 1988

First printing September 1988

ISBN 0-373-16269-3

Prologue

Bruce was determined to get that squirrel. He'd been chasing it all morning, his reddish-gold coat matted with autumn leaves from leaps and sprawls into the Taylor House bushes. This particular bushy-tailed rodent was giving him a hard time. It was up a tree now, perched on a branch too high for Bruce to scramble. He barked at it, annoyed, and the squirrel gibbered back.

"Bruce! Stop that racket!" Emily Atchins stood by the swings across the yard, the giggling children in her charge making enough noise to be heard in Greensdale proper, as it were. The dog looked back at her over his shoulder, tongue out and ears up. "Thank you," Emily called, then turned back to the nearest swing. "Michael! Stop pushing Melissa so hard. She'll fly right over the house."

"Wow, wouldn't that be great!" Michael grinned wickedly at her, but nonetheless took his hands off his sister's back.

"Michael, let's open the bakery again!" Carrie Lane was at his side, playfully batting him with a pie tin.

"Yeah, let's!" cried Melissa, hopping off the swing. "I wanna be the cookie maker today."

"First one down at the woodpile is the cookie maker," Michael said, and immediately took off, the girls scampering after him with squeals of protest.

Emily surveyed the yard, watching as Bruce joined the group of children climbing the little jungle gym by Mrs.

Taylor's vegetable garden. If the dog got into the arugula, Katherine would have a fit, but no, he seemed content to play with the children now, under Sadie Travis's watchful eye.

Sadie was monitoring the gym and the slide. Out of habit, she counted heads. "Where's Sarah Fine?" she called.

"Tucker took her to the bathroom," Emily called. "George, if you don't stop fighting with Roger you won't be allowed on the swings anymore." She shaded her eyes, following the trio of kids who had just gone running down to the fence that bordered the backyard. "Sadie, get Tucker, will you? Those mud-pie makers ought to have some supervision."

A wind rose, scattering colorful leaves over the lawn. An elderly elm that was rope-tied to the upstairs bedroom shutters made them creak loudly, adding another grace note to the cacophony of children's voices, squirrel diatribes and dog barks that was mixing with the country and western music from Tucker's radio on the back steps.

Katherine Taylor, standing at the window with a thermometer in her mouth, looked down at the yard, her head throbbing slightly from the constant din. Nonetheless, she smiled crookedly as she watched Emily gather up a batch of children from the swings below, herding them back toward the downstairs playroom.

In another moment, the house would resound with the sound of scampering feet and more raised voices. Even the thick carpets and the additional soundproofing that Peter had insisted on installing couldn't really shut out the presence of some twenty children, ranging in age from one and a half to five. Though Katherine wasn't feeling well, the noise was comforting. It was a reminder that dreams could actually come true.

When they'd opened the Taylor House Day-care Center nearly a year ago, she'd had no idea if the thing would work. They'd had a license, a small staff, good intentions—and that was about it. With ten children to start, three of them in the nursery, she'd hoped they could ease into the day-care regimen, finding out what worked as they went along. But their registration had seemed to double overnight, partially because the ConCo people had wasted little time taking over an old factory site in nearby Great Oaks, creating construction jobs for a number of Greensdale men.

The Taylor House was overrun in no time, and Katherine still felt as if the adults involved were just barely keeping each other alert and on their feet, while children—where did they get such energy?—swirled around them like a live, constantly revolving miniature hurricane.

Bruce was bounding across the lawn on the trail of a squirrel, headed for Grammy's garden. She rapped on the windowpane, trying to get Sadie's attention, but Sadie had her hands full with the Carter twins and three more kids. Fortunately the squirrel veered off at the wire mesh around the lettuce, and Bruce followed, leaving the vegetables unscathed.

Katherine stepped back from the window and took the thermometer from her mouth. When she saw how high a fever she had this early in the day, she sat down on the edge of her bed, annoyed and alarmed. There was no way she'd be able to make the trip back to Amherst this afternoon to teach her Nineteenth-century British Poets. She'd have to call Peter at his office. And Emily had better come up here for instructions.

The din from downstairs seemed to rise and fall in her ears like the pulse of a wahwah pedal in one of those old rock 'n' roll songs Peter liked to play. Before she did anything, she had to lie down.

Chapter One

"Now take it easy, we'll be inside in a minute. I'm going to put some food in your stomach and clean up that cut and give you a bath, and then maybe you'll realize it's your lucky day. Most derelicts don't get this kind of treatment," Lydia admonished him. "Especially those that were living in a pile of garbage."

"Miss Taylor!"

"Lydia, is that you?"

"Hey, boss!"

"I'm not here yet," Lydia answered all three voices, hurrying down the Pet Sanctuary aisle with the kitten cradled in her arms. Herbie, Elaine and Margaret could keep the place functional without her help for another five minutes. Tomorrow she'd be gone altogether, so the sooner they got used to relying on their own wits, the better.

"Shush," she told the kitten. She'd heard the poor black and white stray mewling piteously from beneath the lid of a Dumpster as she was passing Golden Gate Park on her way to work. He had a bad cut on his front right paw and might have starved to death if she hadn't rescued him.

Anyone else who ran a pet shop that was practically bursting at the seams with all manner of birds, beasts and fish might've thought twice about adopting another orphan, but not Lydia. Found pets made up at least twenty percent of her stock. It was how she'd gone into business in the first place. Her landlord had had her evicted for running a zoo in her apartment.

Unable to turn down any stray kitten, dog or parakeet that friends and acquaintances sent her way, Lydia remembered not being half as concerned with where she was going to live as where Scotty, Canhead, Tigger, Pug and all her other animal children would end up when she moved. Luckily, Mrs. Morris, her elderly friend at the Pet Barn across the bay had taken in the bulk of them, as well as hiring Lydia to replace her ailing husband behind the counter. The rest was personal and San Franciscan pet shop history.

"What kind of a world are we living in?" she asked Albert as she pushed open the swinging doors to the office in the back.

"I assume that's a rhetorical question," he said, looking up from an examination of a new pair of gerbils. "You tell me."

"People throw living animals out like they're empty beer cans," Lydia said grimly, opening up their medicine cabinet to take out alcohol, swab and bandage. "That's the kind of world it is."

Albert straightened up, sweeping his fashionably long bangs back from his forehead. "People throw out live-in lovers the same way," he said with a sigh.

"Don't get suicidal on me again," she warned him. "I have a wounded patient to take care of. Hold still," she told the kitten.

"Clearly more important, I agree," he said wryly. "You also have half a dozen phone calls to return, a telex from that lady in Boston to read, and an adorable Pekingese to inspect—when you have a moment."

"I don't have a moment," she muttered, shushing the kitten again as he yowled at her ministrations. "Fix me a bottle of milk formula, will you?"

"My, my, we're getting the royal treatment for a garbage pail baby, aren't we?"

"He can't stand and drink from a bowl in this condition," Lydia said. "Come on."

Herbie stuck his head through the door. "Yo, boss, Mrs. Kolker's on the line again."

Behind him, she could hear Elaine's singsong voice calling, "Ly-dee-ah, we're out of Kal Kan!"

The ringing phone, silent for a moment, beeped once. Margaret spoke through the intercom. "Miss Taylor, it's long distance for you on line two."

"Albert, you're going to be running this zoo while I'm gone," Lydia said. "I think you'd better get in some practice."

"I'm busy being a surrogate mother," he said, holding up the bottle of milk. "Okay, okay," he added, backing away from her exasperated glare. "Herbie, tell Mrs. Kolker we can't exchange poodles for the fourth time, it's store policy." Albert strode to the door, giving Lydia an exaggeratedly cheery thumbs-up on his way out. "Elaine, wasn't there a delivery this morning?"

"I don't know how I've done this for seven years," Lydia informed the kitten, who was now avidly sucking at the nipple of the bottle she held to his mouth, his newly bandaged paw batting at her hand in eagerness. With her free hand, Lydia reached behind her for the phone. "Lydia Taylor," she said.

"Lydia, it's Emily Atchins."

"Hi!" Lydia brightened, swiveling around in her chair, kitten in lap. "I was just going to give you guys a call. Do you know if Katherine's going to be able to pick me up at the airport?"

"That's just it." Emily's voice sounded worried over the long-distance static. "Lydia, your sister's in bed with 103 temperature."

"Oh, no." Lydia frowned, absently pulling her waist-length hair out of the kitten's reach. "When did this happen?"

"Just this morning," Emily said. "She had a sore throat yesterday but she thought it was only a little cold. Now it seems like we've got some kind of full-fledged flu on our hands."

"That's terrible. Have you called a doctor?"

"Hold on," Emily said, and in a moment Katherine's voice was in her ear, sounding woefully weak.

"Lydie, I'm writing my will," she said, and coughed.

"That's not funny. You poor thing! Where does it hurt?"

"All over. Listen, I want you to reconsider your game plan, okay? I'm in no condition for company—"

"Wait a second!"

"—and I'm probably contagious," she finished, coughing again. "Let's book you a room at some nice hotel in Boston for the time being, okay?"

"Wait," Lydia said. "There's no reason why I can't come to the house. It's still big enough for me to stay out of your way, and you could probably use some tea and sympathy."

"Emily's made tea," Katherine said, and cleared her throat. "Peter's very sympathetic. He's coming home from work early. So there's no need—"

"Sorry," Lydia said firmly. "You're not talking me out of it. I haven't seen the center in full swing since it opened! You're going to make me miss that?"

Katherine sighed. "No, you'd probably better see it while things are stable," she said.

"What do you mean?" Lydia asked, detecting something ominous in her sister's tone.

"Well, to tell you the truth…" Katherine's voice dropped in volume. "Hold on." Lydia could hear her cupping the receiver, her voice muffled. "Thanks, Em, I would." Then she was back. "Okay, we're alone. Lydie, something terrible's happening."

"What?" Lydia gripped the phone, ready to hear some horrific symptom of her sister's illness.

"We're losing Em," she said. "Her husband's got a job at the ConCo plant and they're moving to Great Oaks in less than a month."

"Oh, dear." The kitten, having finished off the contents of the bottle, was now attempting to climb onto Lydia's head. She gently disengaged it from her hair. "How can we replace Emily?"

"That's the problem," Katherine said, and coughed again.

"Kath, you sound terrible. And you probably shouldn't be trying to talk so much. You can tell me everything when I get there."

"Lydie, really, you don't have to—"

"I'm going to be in Boston tomorrow morning," Lydia interrupted. "And I'll be feeding you maple sugar trees by midafternoon, that's all there is to it, no argument."

Katherine managed a weak laugh. "Maple sugar trees!" she said. "You know, I haven't thought of those in..."

"Old family recipes work best," Lydia said. Those candies in the shape of miniature pines had always been their mother's indulgence when either girl was sick. "I'll call you as soon as I get in, to see how you're doing. Need anything from San Francisco?"

"Thanks, Sis," Katherine said. "But just you, that'll do fine. Dr. Harrison's taking good care of me."

Little hairs went up on the back of Lydia's neck, and she did her best to sound absolutely casual. "Jake Harrison? He's treating you for this?"

"Well, you know he helps out Dr. Knowles once a week in town. He answered Emily's first call, and he's been very attentive all week. He says ever since taking care of Grammy he's had a soft spot for the Taylors."

There might be more to it than that, Lydia suspected, but now wasn't the time to talk about it. "What's he giving you?" she asked.

"Just aspirin and plenty of bed rest," Katherine said. "There's not much else you can do for a flu like this except sweat it out."

For a moment, as Katherine described her various medications, Lydia wasn't listening at all. She was remembering Jake, not as he'd looked when she'd met him again so briefly last year; but how he'd looked that magical summer in Cape Cod so long ago—the way he'd appeared in the myriad romantic fantasies she'd had over the years....

Katherine had stopped talking. Lydia snapped to attention. "Wait a sec, here's Em," she was saying. "Take care."

"*You* take care," Lydia said.

"Lydia?" Emily was back on the line. "Do you think you can get out here under your own steam? We're kind of shorthanded."

"I'll arrange for a rental car right now," Lydia told her. "Take care of my big sister, okay? I'll see you both tomorrow."

When she got off the phone, she stared at it, unseeing. So Jake Harrison might be in Greensdale when she got there. She hadn't considered that possibility. It gave her a strange feeling, of both vague excitement and dread. Most romantic fantasies, especially those of an impressionable teenager, were probably best left as they were, fantasies. Still, it added another, provocative wrinkle to her trip East.

Albert was back, looking harried. "We have to call Larsen's," he said. "They screwed up the dog food delivery again."

"Fine," Lydia said, preoccupied. Her feelings about Jake were secondary, of course. The most unsettling thing was that he was concerned enough about Katherine to have stayed on the case, when he could've turned it over to Dr. Knowles. Lydia frowned.

It wasn't like Katherine to sound so weak, she mused, aware that the conversation had upset her. Ever since their mother's death, she'd been extrasensitive to even the slightest weakness in the family chain. When Katherine's daughter Clarissa had broken a thumb this past spring, trying to move one of her copper sculptures by herself, Lydia had worried over it almost as much as Katherine had.

"But I've got enough to worry about as it is," she told the kitten, who was happily sucking at the milk bottle in her hand. "I've got a new store to open three thousand miles away. What do you think about that?" The kitten pulled more vigorously at the bottle. "Think I can do everything I need to do in under a month?"

"Yo, boss!"

"Yo, what?" Lydia looked up at Herbie, who was peering through the open door again.

"Guy out front wants to know if we want a chimpanzee."

"Does he cook?" queried Albert.

"No more monkeys," she said. "Tell him to try Pets Are Us."

He indicated the kitten in her lap. "You want a cage cleaned for our new arrival, or what?"

"That's a good idea," she said. "Have Margaret hold all calls for a few minutes, okay?"

Herbie nodded, lifted the kitten gingerly from Lydia's lap, removed its claws from her skirt, and was gone. Albert pushed aside the gerbil cage to sit down on the counter opposite Lydia. "What's up?" he asked. "Worried about Boston?"

"Just tell me this place isn't going to descend into complete chaos while I'm away, all right?"

"The roof'll cave in the moment you walk out," he said, smiling.

"Thank you. Albert, if things don't go smoothly, I may have to stay there a little longer. I mean, three or four weeks could easily stretch into six."

He nodded. "It'll cost you."

Lydia made a face. "Seriously. The renovations at the store aren't finished yet and other than Grady I've got a whole staff to hire—"

"I'll survive," he said breezily. "Hey, don't come back. Up my salary another five thou and I'll take over, permanent."

"Careful," she said. "Your wish could come true. I'm getting a little weary of the beautiful Bay Area."

"You're just weary from meeting the wrong men," he said. "And believe me, I can sympathize." He put the back of one hand to his forehead in arch despair. "After my last experience, I'll be happy to lose myself in gerbils...bury my sorrows in parakeets...throw myself to the dogs...."

"Please," she said. "Albert, you call Larsen's. I've got to get organized." Lydia swiveled around to the medicine cabinet as a thought occurred to her. "How are we doing on vitamin C? I'd better start some preventive medicining...."

SHE HAD FORGOTTEN how brilliantly beautiful Massachusetts could look in early November. Though she'd missed the shimmering panoply of yellows, oranges and reds that made autumn's leaf-turning a tourist attraction, she almost preferred the subtler, stark display of bare trees against purple-gray hilltops, the vivid blue skies laced with smoky cloud banks that were a coming winter's trademark.

She was glad she'd packed some sweaters and long pants. After over ten years in the Bay Area she still hadn't forgotten how cold it would be here. Even the cat and kitten she'd brought with her were equipped with a warm shawl covering their carrier in the back seat. "How you doing back there?" she asked. The felines were still quiet, probably sleeping off the effects of the pills she'd had to feed them for the flight to Boston.

A familiar landmark, the old abandoned barn in the field to her left, alerted her to bear right for Greensdale proper. She was looking forward to this. On her last trip East, she'd found a perfect space for the store and grabbed it—as she so often did things—on impulse. The deal had closed so fast that she hadn't had time to visit Katherine and Peter. This time she'd be living at the house with them.

The commute into Cambridge could be done in under an hour, and she'd save a fortune on hotels. But the main thing was, she'd get a chance to be friends with her older sister almost in the way they'd been so many years ago. Lydia slowed, noting that not much seemed to have changed since her last visit. For that matter, not much had changed here in years, and that was comforting. She certainly wasn't as stable.

Maybe Albert was right. It wasn't so much San Francisco, her home for so long. No, her dissatisfaction with

where she was and how she lived went deeper than that.
After she'd broken up with James, she'd drifted from one
almost-but-not-quite-committed relationship to another.
And now, at the ripe old age of thirty-three, she was starting to wonder if she was destined to end up alone.

This depressing thought made her think, logically enough,
of the doctor's appointment she had in Boston tomorrow.
She wondered if this Dr. Newcomb would really have anything new to tell her, any hope to hold out that the doctors
on the West Coast hadn't already nipped in the bud.

The whole thing was getting academic, she thought ruefully. If she didn't end up involved with someone within the
next few years, the fact that she most probably wouldn't be
able to bear children wasn't really going to matter.

"Happy days," she said aloud, shaking her head at her
own maudlin frame of mind. She switched on the radio, relieved to hear a nice Beatle tune whose jaunty melody was
capable of quickly altering her mood. She hummed along,
concentrating on remembering her way into town.

There was Main Street. A new 7 Eleven had taken the
place of the old convenience store on Main and Elm, but
other than that, things looked comfortably familiar. Spirits
lifting as she drove on toward the house, she turned up the
radio volume, singing along now, sure that she was off-key.
But the cats wouldn't mind. She hoped they got along with
Kathy's cat, Winkie. Well, Grammy's was big enough.
Funny, but even though the place was officially the Taylor
House now, and had been her own home once, it would always be Grammy's to her.

And her mother would always be Grammy. She'd been
only seventy when she'd died last year, but for years before, Lydia and Katherine's mom had been nicknamed
Grammy. That was what Katherine's daughter Clarissa had
called her, and the children who had played on the grounds
in the days before the place became a real, licensed day-care
center. The people in town had taken to calling her Grammy
Taylor, too, a more affectionate title than "the professor's

wife,'' which was how she'd been known when the family
had first come to Greensdale.

So Lydia thought of her mother as Grammy, too. As she
drew closer to home, she remembered the feeling of sanctuary it had always given her. No matter what twists and
sometimes tragic turns fate had put the Taylor clan through,
the house had been there for them. When Father had died,
for example, the Taylor sisters had moved back in for a few
months while Grammy mourned and reordered her life. And
when Katherine had lost her first husband, the women had
gathered there again.

Lydia had retreated to Greensdale from California, too,
whenever she'd had troubles of her own. And the old but
eternally young grandmother and her big old house had
made a welcome shelter for Clarissa from time to time, in
the tumult of adolescence and growing pains. There it was
now, looming over the crest of the hill. Lydia felt that
unique pull, that nostalgic sense of returning to the roost
that she always felt when she saw the gables of the house
from the road. Even with Grammy no longer in it, the house
was still home.

It was a Victorian mansion dating from the late 1800s,
complete with sprawling front porch, porticoes, its facades
full of blueberry-blue shuttered windows. A pair of gables
facing out from the corners on each side of the gray slate
roof flanked the central one, where the roof edge trim
peaked to a little flat top over a small round window. It had
always made Lydia think of the house as a woman with an
old-fashioned hat setting off her lined white face.

The gable windows glinted in the afternoon sun as she
pulled into the driveway. The trees that hovered protec-
tively about the two-story house shimmered rust in the wind.
She could see that the bushes usually overgrowing the sides
of the front porch like a furry shawl had been cut back. A
new coat of white paint and the roof repairs had spruced the
place up. It gave her a warm feeling. She smiled, thinking of
the maple sugar leaves she'd found at a grocery store en

route. Not quite Grammy's "trees," but close enough. Katherine would be pleased.

She hoped that maybe, just maybe, Katherine was on the road to recovery. She killed the motor, knowing that was an unduly optimistic thought. Whatever her sister had, it was stronger and more debilitating than a common cold. She'd certainly sounded terrible on the phone that morning, when Lydia had called her from Sellars Street.

She'd met Bob Grady there, to see how the Pet Sanctuary East was shaping up. Bob was going to run the place for her once it was officially opened and functional. He'd been overseeing the renovations in her absence, and so far, things looked all right—behind schedule, of course, but not too far. Tomorrow, after her doctor's appointment, she'd start nudging the contractors more forcefully.

Lydia got out of the car, inhaling the crisp air. The subtle smell of pine needles made her smile with anticipation. This trip had been a good idea, a perfect change of scene. She hoisted her one trusty suitcase out of the trunk and shut the trunk with her elbow. She got the car's back door open and was greeted by some feeble meows from Dexter and Dumpster.

Dexter was a Pet Sanctuary alumnus she was bringing to Greensdale for Sadie Travis, who wanted a healthy male cat to help her take care of a domestic mouse problem. Dumpster was the black and white kitten she'd rescued and formed an attachment to, named of course for his place of origin, as well as for the euphonious combination with his traveling companion's name.

"Almost home," she reassured them, and reached for the carrier. It was when she had it in hand and was backing away from the car, ready to push the door shut, that she lost her footing. Just as the thought occurred to her that she hadn't managed this properly, she was suddenly sprawling into space.

The next thing she knew she was flat on her back with the wind knocked out of her, staring up at the sky. "Idiot," she mumbled, a pain throbbing in her left ankle. Her right wrist hurt, too, since she'd tenaciously hung onto the carrier and her arm had gotten twisted back as she fell.

She considered just lying there a moment while she collected her scattered wits. It felt easiest to stay still as the cats yowled in her ear and footsteps crunched on the gravel. Someone was hurrying over to her and Lydia blew some hair out of her eyes so she could see who it was.

"Lydia?" The man sounded bemused. She blinked, staring up at him. He was tall, dark-haired, with a long, high-cheekboned face that was undeniably handsome. His dark eyes were softened with concern. Perhaps she'd been knocked unconscious and was having a nice little dream. He was certainly fun to look at, even from this nearly upside-down angle.

As he bent over her, she also had the odd sensation that she knew him. *Ah, love at first sight!* she thought woozily. Wasn't that how it was in the movies? Star-crossed men and women meeting for the first time, feeling as though they'd known each other all their lives— "Lydia Taylor, what've you done to yourself?" he was asking, a faint smile stealing over his soft, full lips. With a start, she realized that she *did* know him. Of course! She'd seen this handsome face only a year ago—it was Jake's! Lydia struggled to sit up, feeling the blood rush to her head, but he was already easing her back, an arm solicitously underneath her shoulders.

"Slow down," he admonished her. "Take it easy."

What a perfectly ridiculous way to re-encounter the person who'd occupied such a special place in her memory. "Jacob Harrison," she began. "What—"

"Very good. You obviously haven't suffered amnesia," he said.

Was he making fun of her? There was nothing Lydia disliked more than having a man, even an extremely attractive one, treat her as if she were some kind of a ditzy dame. "All I did was fall on my fanny," she said. "You can let me get up now, really."

"One thing at a time," he said, not relinquishing his hold. "How's your head?"

Come to think of it, it was starting to throb in a sort of counterpoint rhythm to the throbbing of her ankle. Jake was gently probing her skull with a gentle hand. "All in one piece, I believe," she said. "Honestly, I only—"

"There's no bump," he said, ignoring her. "Okay, let's sit up now, but slowly."

"Let's stop treating us like we've had our brains knocked loose, okay?" she said dryly.

Jake Harrison smiled. He seemed to be having a good time here, kneeling at her side, his arm around her. Lydia had to admit that the experience was not entirely disagreeable. Now that she was sitting up, her face was only inches from his. As her head's throbbing began to abate, she found herself admiring the aquiline curve of his nose and the way a shock of his hair—it had a little streak of silver in it now, how distinguished!—fell over his eyes as he studied her fallen form.

"Hmm," he was saying, looking toward her feet. Lydia followed his gaze, realizing with a jolt that her long pleated skirt had parted where it was never supposed to part when a person was upright. Her splayed legs were completely bare, the left one right up to the top of her stocking, revealing an incongruously sexy glimpse of garter.

Feeling a blush rise in her cheeks, Lydia hurriedly swept down the edge of the skirt, but Jake's hand arrested hers just above the knee. "Do you mind?" she said.

"Just relax," he said mildly. She saw that he was staring, not at the run in her stocking—first time worn!—but at her ankle, where the skin was chafed and bleeding. His gentle hand was already easing her shoe off, and now he cupped her heel in his palm. Warm palm. "Can you move it?"

Lydia wiggled her toes and then slowly experimented, flexing the injured ankle. It hurt, but it moved. That was a relief. Or was it? Lydia had a small but strong hypochondriacal streak. "I don't think it's broken," she said cautiously. "I probably just gave it a good twist, that's all. Right?"

"Could be," he said. "Tell me if this hurts." He was slowly, carefully, moving her foot in a circle. She bit her lip. *Not so bad.*

"No, it's okay." Now his hand was exploring the skin above the ankle, and Lydia felt an entirely inappropriate flicker of pleasure at his practiced touch. He had, she mused, the softest hands she'd ever encountered, but it wasn't just that. There was a sureness, a gentle but completely masculine quality to the light probing of his fingertips that was, well, arousing.

"You're right," he murmured. "No bones broken. You might get out of this alive," he added, and stealing a look at his face she saw a sparkle of amusement in his dark eyes.

"I told you it wasn't serious," she said, defensive.

"So you did. Now, put your arm around me."

"Wait a second," she protested.

"Don't be silly," he said. "You're not walking on that ankle just yet. Doctor's orders."

Lydia sighed, sensing it would be useless to argue. His tone of voice was similar to his touch, like a core of steel encased in soft thick velvet. She slid her arm around his neck and let herself be lifted. Her foot hurt as she experimentally shifted weight onto it, but she was prepared to stand. "Thanks," she began. "If I lean on you, I'm sure I can—hey!"

His other arm had swooped underneath her legs and she was suddenly aloft in his arms. Lydia looked from the ground below her to the smiling face next to hers. "Comfortable?" he asked.

"Is this necessary?" Her heart was beating fast and loudly as he gently shifted her even closer to his chest. Her senses were being confused by a sudden variety of impressions—the softness of the cashmere sweater he wore, the warmth and strength of him easily enfolding her, the faint scent of some minty cologne mingled with a masculine scent that was distinctly his.

"Absolutely," he said, and started walking up the drive. Apparently her nearly six-foot frame and the—dieting currently successful—hundred and forty-five pounds of her didn't faze him in the least. "I'll come back for your luggage in a minute."

"You're too kind," she said wryly, trying to resist resting her head in the crook of his shoulder. *Come on,* her body urged her, it would fit so nicely there! But she held her head upright, though she couldn't help but smile at the picture this would've presented to a passerby. *Talk about a scene from a movie.* She'd been literally swept off her feet, and her savior, though he lacked a white horse, was acting the heroic part in every way.

Except that he was sneezing. "Bless you," she said.

Jake nodded, but immediately turned his face away from hers again. The second sneeze was louder.

"Do doctors catch colds?" she asked playfully.

"Never," he said. "It's just—" He wrinkled his nose, frowning with concentration, and successfully staved off another sneeze. She noticed that his eyes were watering.

"Maybe you're allergic to me," she said.

"I doubt that," he replied. "But I am allergic to..." He paused before the steps to the house, suddenly taking in the distant meows of Dexter and Dumpster.

"Cats," she finished for him. "Really?"

"Really," he said. "You must have a few stray hairs on you."

"I'm sure I do," she said. "Look, if you put me down, I can make it—"

"No, no," he said, wrinkling his nose with a noble effort. "Let's get you up these steps and inside."

Lydia shrugged. She relaxed back into the comfort of his steady embrace as he hurried up the front steps. "I'll get that," she said, reaching past him for the doorbell.

"Thanks," he said. They were silent a moment, looking at the front door. Then he turned to her, as casual as an acquaintance one ran into at a San Franciscan bus stop. "So, how've you been?"

Lydia laughed. "You mean, for the past fifteen years? Or since I saw you last year?"

"Has it been that long?"

"It has, yes," she said. In one of life's little coincidences, Jake Harrison had been the doctor at Grammy's deathbed. Naturally enough, he'd stopped by to visit a few days after the funeral, to see how the Taylor women were doing. Lydia hadn't been there, but Jake had asked about her. Clarissa, she remembered now, had insisted that the doctor was interested in Lydia.

Of course Clarissa had no way of knowing how well she and Jake had known each other. They'd barely acknowledged it themselves, when he stopped by again and found her at home a few nights later. He'd "just wanted to say hello" and express his condolences. Katherine had come upon them, unwittingly interrupting what Lydia had hoped might be a more meaningful reunion. But Jake had seemed anxious to leave, anyway. He'd avoided referring directly to the summer in Cape Cod, and she'd followed his lead, figuring that if the incident was that far in the past for him, it might as well be for her.

Incident? She'd thought she was in love! Not that the eighteen-year-old Lydia had really known much about love. Looking at Jake now, it was hard to believe either of them was the same person as the two who still inhabited her memory. What was he thinking? she wondered. Was this an intentional flirtation? Or was it merely a particularly chivalrous form of professional courtesy?

The door was opening. "Lydia!" Peter Bradford gaped at them. "Hey, Jake, I thought you were leaving."

"Hi, Peter. I had a little accident," Lydia said meekly.

"Come on in," he said hurriedly, stepping aside. Jake steered her through the door and headed for the stairs. "Can you manage?" Peter called, behind them.

"Sure," the doctor affirmed, and sneezed yet again.

"Bless you. You can put me down now," Lydia said. "There's a couch in the..." She stopped, staring at a wall that was where the entrance to the living room was supposed to be.

"No more couch. No more living room, remember?" Peter said. "We live upstairs now."

"Up we go," her white knight said, with what sounded like forced breeziness.

"If you drop me, I'll never forgive you."

"I'll never forgive myself," he said, panting a bit as he took another stair. Lydia clung to him, feeling a giggle bubble up inside her at the absurdity of her arrival. She was the one who'd planned to take care of her invalid sister. Now she was being treated like an invalid herself. Even more amusing was the gallant doctor, who, she suspected, had taken on more than he'd bargained for.

"Seriously, I can try to walk," she murmured at his ear.

"No," he huffed. "You can't walk. And in a minute I probably won't be able to, either. But as long as I can—"

She waited for his sneeze, holding onto the banister as both of them shook with the force of it. "Bless you," she said again, and out came the giggle.

"Glad you're enjoying yourself," he breathed.

"Do you rent out by the hour?" she asked. "I've always hated having to climb these stairs."

Peter was tromping up the stairs behind them, the meowing of her cats signaling that he'd retrieved Lydia's luggage. "I think we're putting her in the bedroom to the left," he told Jake, who nodded, and turned down the hall. He carried her through the doorway, into the room that had once been Lydia and Katherine's bedroom, and set her down gently on the bed.

Lydia sat up, her leg stretched out in front of her, feeling her entire body vibrate slightly as Jake knelt down for another look at the wounded ankle. "Thanks for the lift," she said.

"I haven't had that much fun in weeks," he replied. "Jake, got any iodine and Band-Aids?"

Now that his arms weren't around her, she was suddenly aware of what an exciting sensation it had been to be carried around like that. It was certainly the most fun *she'd* had today. "Do you need this stocking?" he asked. Lydia shook her head.

"Oh," she said then, understanding, as he fixed his gaze on her foot. She reached under her skirt and undid the top of the already ruined stocking, appreciating his gentlemanly decorum as she rolled it down.

"Thanks," he said, sliding it off her foot. "Okay, prepare to be stung," he said, taking the iodine from Peter, who'd reappeared.

"How's the patient?" she asked him.

"Asleep," he said. "She's still feverish."

Lydia winced, stifling a little gasp as Jake cleaned her out. "Is she getting any better, though?"

Peter frowned. He looked tired, she realized, not the robust and high-spirited man she remembered from the wedding. "Ask the good doctor," he said.

Lydia turned back to Jake, who was efficiently smoothing an oversize Band-Aid onto her ankle. "What's the diagnosis?"

Jake looked up at Lydia, then Peter. "Well, we've got some kind of particularly ornery bug here," he said. "Seems like a standard flu, but it's a doozy."

"Kath's having these major headaches," Peter said. "I've never seen her so completely wiped out."

"We're making some headway, though," he said, getting up. "The aspirin seems to be keeping the fever down."

"Down," Peter repeated. "But only down. She's still got 102, and it's midafternoon."

"That sounds terrible," Lydia said. "Isn't there anything else you can do?"

"Jake's doing the best he can," Peter said, rubbing a hand over his face. "We'll just have to wait it out a little, right?"

"Right," Jake said. "And as for you, I don't see any swelling. Lydia, let's see how well you can stand on it." He held his arm out for her to grasp, and Lydia got to her feet, thankful for his support. Peter turned at the sound of a phone ringing down the hall, and moved quickly from the room as she shifted her weight gingerly, leaning on Jake. She was happily surprised to feel only a dull ache from the ankle when she stood upright.

"It's really not bad at all," she said. Tentatively she took a step, and then another, wincing as she went. "I can walk, sort of," she said. "What do you think?"

"You may never be an Olympic ice skater again," Jake said, smiling. "But I think you gave your ankle a twist, period."

"Brilliant," she said, shaking her head, both relieved and annoyed at him for making such a fuss and feeding her fears. "After all that..."

Jake smiled. "Oh, it's been my pleasure," he said. "You have one of the nicest ankles I've ever treated. And we're talking about years of ankles."

He held her gaze as she looked back at him. The smile on his face was infectious. For a moment she stood merely smiling dumbly back at him, wondering why all rational thought had seemed to leave her head. Maybe it was the subtle but alluring pull those dark eyes of his had, combined with the still-vivid memory of how he'd held her in his arms, strong but tender at the same time.

"Thanks," she managed. "I don't usually get compliments on my ankles."

He nodded. "That's right. You get compliments on your hair."

He did remember some things. She pushed a strand of it back behind one ear, suddenly self-conscious. Her waist-length tresses had been a prized possession since childhood, when her long neck and ungainly limbs, combined with the characteristic long, thin Taylor nose had made her quite the ugly duckling.

When she'd met Jake, that summer when she was just out of high school, poised on the perilous brink of what had seemed like instant adulthood, she'd only just begun to realize she was turning into an attractive young woman. In fact, Jake had been a decisive factor in that realization.

Lydia reminded herself again that obviously, the brief time they'd spent together back then hadn't had the same significance for him as it had once had for her. Now was not the time for such reminiscences. "Yes, these days men occasionally ask me if I play the flute," she said, smoothing her hair back from her forehead. "Or if I'm a ballet dancer."

He nodded. "I can see why."

"Please. Those come-ons only show the average man's total ignorance of the classic arts," she said wryly. "I can't hold a tune to save my life, and I'm certainly too fat and wide-hipped to dance ballet."

"Fat?" He looked incredulous.

"I like your bit of silver," she went on, indicating the streak in his hair.

"Oh, yes, distingué," he said ruefully. "Long as it stays where it is, I can deal with it."

He was only a year older than she, she knew. He'd been a freshman in college when she was a high-school senior. And he'd aged well, though his aura of paternal understanding, that bedside manner, made him appear older. The phrase "bedside manner" made her suddenly aware that she was standing in front of a bed with one stocking off, and that he was looking at her with an appreciative glimmer in his eye.

Dexter chose that moment to start scratching vigorously at his carrier cage. Lydia bent down to quiet him. Frankly, she was enjoying Jake's obvious interest in her, but she also welcomed the distraction. "You'd probably better back up a few feet," she warned Jake. "The sneeze beasts are about to be unleashed."

"I have to get going anyway," he said, glancing at his watch. "See if you can rustle up a walking stick somewhere, all right? Even though you're not mortally wounded...."

"That's funny," she said, remembering. "It so happens I have about a dozen canes to choose from. My father collected them."

"Good," Jake said. "Use one." He moved around the bed, keeping a good distance between himself and the cat carrier. "I'll see myself out. And I'll try to see you tomorrow."

"You will?" She rose from unhooking the carrier's door, surprised.

"Well, I've got two patients to look after here now," he said.

"Make that three."

Lydia and Jake turned to the doorway. Emily Atchins was standing there, a pale child with tears streaming down his face at her side. "Doctor, can you stay another few minutes?" She indicated the girl, who was shivering and sniffling, a miniature portrait of misery. "Carrie seems to be running a high fever."

Chapter Two

"Let's look on the bright side. You're an extremely healthy young lady."

Lydia frowned at the white-haired doctor on the other side of the desk. "Considering my condition, you mean." Dr. Newcomb shrugged. "Isn't that a little like the old joke, 'Other than that, Mrs. Lincoln, how did you enjoy the show?'"

Dr. Newcomb chuckled and shook his head. "Not at all, Lydia. According to these preliminary tests, you stand a very good chance of achieving success when you try again." His intercom buzzed and he leaned over to exchange a few words with his nurse-receptionist. Lydia looked at her watch. The appointment had run a little late. Restless, she got up and paced to the window.

Dr. Newcomb's office was in a building adjacent to the new John Nathaniel Hospital in Boston. She could see the white, ultramodern building across the parking lot. The whole complex had an air of up-to-the-minute high tech, both inside and out. But technology was one thing. What had gone awry in her interior wasn't necessarily going to be fixed by the latest wizardry of modern science.

Dr. Newcomb rose from his seat. "Staying in Greensdale, are you?" She nodded. "Send my regards to Dr. Knowles, if you see him."

"Actually, Dr. Harrison's been the one treating my sister," Lydia said.

"Ah, give him my best. His late father was an old friend."

A half hour later, when Lydia emerged into the cool Cambridge sunlight, the folder from Dr. Newcomb was still clutched to her chest. The clock in a nearby church tower was tolling eleven. She'd have to walk quickly if she was going to beat Grady to the store.

She'd staved off the depression she'd felt coming on in Dr. Newcomb's office for a while. But getting up the energy to rush over to Sellars Street just now seemed exceedingly difficult. And a twinge from her still-sore ankle reminded her that moving too fast was a bad idea.

"Too many doctors," she murmured, walking down the street. She'd thought that her trip East might provide some relaxation, aside from the business she had to do. But with Katherine's illness, her minor accident and Dr. Newcomb's examination, she was feeling anything but relaxed. *Oh, yes, and let's not forget the possibility of catching the flu,* she thought ruefully.

After Jake had examined Carrie, that poor feverish little girl, he'd said, though he thought it too early to tell for sure, that she might be coming down with the same flu Katherine had. Before driving Carrie home he'd suggested Lydia double her vitamin C doses and take every precaution; Katherine wasn't contagious at this point, but if there was some kind of bug in the air...

Just what she needed. Lydia tried to keep up a brisk pace though her spirits were still sagging. Why had she let Dr. Lyndon back in Berkeley talk her into seeing Dr. Newcomb? She should've known this experience would be as debilitating as all the others had been. And sure enough, though the weather was gorgeous, not too cold or windy, the Radcliffe campus bright and clean in the sun, the entire effect was lost on her this morning.

Inside the folder she clutched was the printout of her medical chart from California and Dr. Newcomb's report. She'd go over it all later, but at the moment she had to find something, some shred of hope to hang on to, if she didn't want indulgent self-pity to cast a pall over the rest of her stay. What was the most optimistic thing Dr. Newcomb had said?

One phrase came back to her and she repeated it silently, as if it were a medical mantra as she passed the quaint little shops on Sellars Street. *Fifty percent of infertile women treated are able to achieve a pregnancy.* Fifty percent. That was fair enough odds, wasn't it?

"Even women like me?" she'd asked. "I mean, after that miscarriage? . . ."

"There's still a chance," the kindly old man had said. "Dr. Lyndon seems to have come to a different conclusion from your old doctor in San Francisco. And I can see some other possibilities that neither of them have highlighted. So you see, you're doing the right thing to keep investigating."

"But what's the conclusion?" she'd asked, impatient.

"Well, we'd have to continue testing," Dr. Newcomb said. "And it would be best if your current partner was willing to come in for testing as well."

And that had brought the conversation to a swift dead end. Because there was no—wonderful euphemism—"current partner." And to really continue with her case, Dr. Newcomb needed Lydia to be in the process of trying to conceive. Which she certainly wasn't. No, she was still recovering from having tried with James. And she was still suffering from her failure, an experience that felt as though it had happened last week instead of nearly two years ago.

So much for trying to predict the future, she mused. She didn't know anything more about what might lie ahead than she had when she left California. And what did doctors really know?

This question led her, predictably enough, to consider a certain doctor with a distingué streak of silver in his dark wavy hair. Now, there was a better subject for contemplation. There was a doctor who inspired confidence. He knew a few things, didn't he? Like how to make a woman's heartbeat increase with one or two practiced moves.

She smiled to herself, remembering the way he'd handled her yesterday. And that was the proper expression, he *had* handled her, expertly. She still couldn't figure out if he'd been purposefully flirting, which would be odd, considering his behavior so many years ago. Or did he, too, have certain lingering memories he wanted to revive? Jake's presence was, at the moment, the one intriguing bright spot in this otherwise glum beginning to her time away from work. She was looking forward to his next professional house call.

Why, though? she thought suddenly. For all she knew, the man was married, with children. Children! Lydia paused, annoyed that her mind refused to get off the subject. A pair of coeds who were all notebooks and giggles were waiting at the corner with her. Lydia sighed as they suddenly trotted across the intersection in between oncoming cars. They didn't have the kinds of worries she had, did they?

Good Lord, she thought, appalled at her own frame of mind. *You're thinking like an old lady.* Lydia glanced at her reflection in a drugstore window. That long and almost lean woman with the cascade of blond hair, in the fashionable oversize cardigan and scarf? She didn't look a day over, well, thirty, she decided. So. Looking three years under her real age wasn't bad.

And think about Katherine! Remarried at forty-three to a wonderful man like Peter. If her big sister was any example, she shouldn't be worried about such things. As long as whatever man she might be lucky enough to meet wasn't set on raising a family....

Stop it, she commanded herself. For the moment she'd have to be content with the knowledge that her body, which had betrayed her so tragically in the past, still held the potential for motherhood. Fifty percent potential, at least. Lydia shoved the folder into her shoulder bag and chin up, headed for the store.

There was no sign of Bob, but the front door was open, and two men in paint-spattered overalls were busy on ladders in front. At last, the eye-boggling fuchsia and green color scheme left by the former owners was disappearing under a more conservative, though still cheery, off-white and beige trim.

And they'd even removed the old store sign without any visible damage to the front. That in itself was enough to buoy her spirits, and Lydia sprinted the last few yards across the street, ankle and angst forgotten in her hurry to see the work inside.

"HERE, I'LL HELP YOU with that." Jake took the suitcase from the girl's hand, hurriedly ushering her inside. She'd only brought the one bag, but it weighed a ton.

"Such a nice little home!" Sophee exclaimed, looking around the living room. Jake cast a quick glance over his attempts to clean the place up. To him, the "nice little home" was more like a spartan bachelor's crash pad. Though he'd been living in the small brownstone for nearly two years, there were still cartons of books in the study he hadn't unpacked.

"Your room is at the top of these stairs," he said, swaying on the landing below as her suitcase threatened to topple him backward. His beeper chose that moment to go off, but there was nothing he could do about it.

"What is this bipping?" Sophee asked behind him.

"I have to call the hospital," he told her, lurching up the last few steps and setting down the huge suitcase just inside the door of the spare room. He reached inside his jacket pocket and shut off the infernal nuisance, glancing at his watch.

"I'll have to show you around when I get home tonight," he said. Sophee was walking around the room, nodding approval at the empty bureau, bed and closet space. The spare room had never really had anything moved into it, so preparing it for the au pair girl hadn't taken much effort. His own bedroom, however, he'd spent some time on. He wanted Max to love it a lot.

"My son'll be staying right down the hall, in the main bedroom," he told her.

"And you, Mr. Harrison?"

"Dr. Harrison," he corrected her absently. "I'll be sleeping downstairs. The couch pulls out."

The dark-haired woman nodded, taking out a pack of Gauloise cigarettes as she surveyed her surroundings. She stopped short when she felt Jake's stare. *"Oh là là!"* she muttered. "You don't like?"

"Didn't you say you were a nonsmoker?"

Sophee smiled ingenuously. "I try to quit," she announced. "Sometimes smoke, sometimes not…" She waved a hand, shoving the pack back into her pocket. "You don't like, I don't smoke."

Jake frowned. He'd gotten Sophee through the Byzantine network of au pair girls that his colleagues' wives at John Nathaniel were hooked into, and was operating more or less on blind faith. The interview had been cursory, since as usual he'd had no time. But she came well recommended, and had struck him as intelligent and friendly. "If you must, don't do it in the house, please," he said. "Or when you're with Max."

Sophee nodded vigorously. "When does he arrive, your boy?"

"Tomorrow morning," Jake said, feeling his anxiety heighten at the thought. He didn't know how he was going to swing picking Max up at the airport, bringing him back here and still going on his rounds, but he'd have to. Every little thing counted with this first trial custody. He wanted to make sure Max would have such a good time that he wouldn't want to leave.

"I cook a fabulous breakfast!" she exclaimed, smiling.

"Fine," he said. Actually, the flight was due in after breakfast hour, but these and other sundry details would have to be gone into when he came back. "Look, just make yourself at home. There's some dishes in the sink you could do—oh, and a shopping list on the refrigerator door. I left some money on the table—"

His beeper was beeping again. Jake didn't feel at all secure about leaving this nearly total stranger to fend for herself here, but then, wasn't that what Sophee was supposed to be best at?

"Don't you worry 'bout a thing," she said. "We talk when you get home."

Meager reassurance, but it would have to do. Jake hurried down the stairs, grabbing his coat from the banister post. "Call me if there's any problem," he called. "The number's on the kitchen table."

"O-kay-do-kay," she trilled, singsong. "Bye-bye!"

"If the tutor calls, give him that number," he yelled, halfway out the door.

"No problem!"

What would Max make of a French accent? he wondered, jogging over to his car. What if he returned to his mother talking like some weird polyglot? These and other questions would have to wait, he thought grimly, gunning the motor. Right now he had an entire missed forty minutes to make up, and who knew what kind of medical crises could have transpired in that short time?

"How was it?"

"It was almost right," Lydia said.

Katherine was propped up against her pillows in the big four-poster bed that had once been Grammy's. Her pale skin looked even more wan in contrast to the pink flannel nightgown she wore, and her eyes had a bloodshot cast that Lydia found hard to accept. This was not the Katherine she was used to, the strong older sister who had always seemed physically and emotionally invincible.

When she'd seen her last night Lydia had had to conceal her unease. This afternoon she was making it her business to be cheery and entertaining. As soon as she'd returned from Boston she'd whisked Katherine's tea tray out of Emily's hands and brought it up herself, along with some magazines she knew her sister would like and some throat lozenges she'd requested.

"And almost doesn't count?" Katherine asked.

"They're still renovating," Lydia explained.

Katherine managed a weak laugh. "Well, we certainly know about that routine, don't we? If you're figuring, just double every figure you've got."

"Come on, this place wasn't *that* expensive to do over."

Katherine sighed. "Don't get me started." She forced a smile. "But it was worth every penny."

"Seems so," Lydia agreed, although she hadn't actually had much of a chance to see the day-care center in action. She planned to spend some time downstairs with Emily and the others, after Jake came for his visit.

"Why do you keep looking out the window?"

"Oh, it's just . . . you're expecting Dr. Harrison, aren't you?"

Katherine coughed gently into a handkerchief. "Me? I think *we* are expecting the handsome doctor, aren't we?"

Lydia shrugged. "Well, I do want to hear if he thinks you're getting any better."

"I appreciate the sisterly concern," Katherine said. "But since you *are* my sister, Lydie, you can't fool me."

"Who's fooling?" she said, then sat down abruptly at the foot of the bed, arms folded. "All right, tell me everything you know."

"He's single," Katherine said promptly. "What else do you need to hear?"

Lydia smiled. "If life were that simple . . ." Katherine knew about Lydia's medical problem, but Lydia hadn't mentioned her visit to Dr. Newcomb, figuring she had enough to worry about. And Lydia was happy to put it out of her mind. As to her relationship with Jake in the past— could she call it that, a relationship?—Lydia had never told Katherine anything about it. She'd been married and living in Amherst with Jeffrey Cartwright by then. "Well, there must be something wrong with him," she said lightly. "How can there be an eligible bachelor just lounging around Greensdale?"

"He lives in Great Oaks," Katherine said. "Had a residency at John Nathaniel when it first opened, but he's in private practice now." Her hand transcribed a zigzag trajectory in the air. "One day a week he drives west to us, three days he stays in Great Oaks and whenever he can he apparently drives east to Nathaniel, doing research in some branch of medicine I can't pronounce or remember."

"And that's all you know?"

"If there's anything wrong with him at all, it's that he doesn't lounge, as you put it. The man keeps himself awfully busy."

"Married to his work? Well, I can respect that."

"Yes, I guess you can," Katherine said pointedly, and took a sip of her tea.

"Don't start," Lydia warned.

"I'm not starting anything," Katherine said.

"Don't continue, then," Lydia amended. Whenever Lydia called from California, Katherine invariably inquired about the men—or lack of them—in Lydia's life, and she was starting to tire of it. "You should save your mothering for Clarissa."

"Well, since Grammy's gone, I have a big maternal role to fill," Katherine said. "Can I help it if—" The end of her sentence was cut off by another fit of coughing. Lydia rose, moving to Katherine's side but feeling more helpless than useful as her sister's coughs gradually subsided.

The sound of a car pulling into the driveway was particularly welcome. "Here's Jake now," Lydia said, refilling Katherine's mug with hot tea from the silver pot.

"Oh, it's *Jake*, is it?" Katherine said, smiling weakly as she dabbed at her teary eyes with her handkerchief.

"If you must know, I've met him before," Lydia said. "We ran into each other in Cape Cod. Remember that summer I stayed there with Holly?"

"A secret past!" Katherine exclaimed. "Well, no wonder there's something going on here. You'll have to reveal all, little sister."

"Later," Lydia said with mock sternness. "I don't want to hear another cough out of you." Katherine nodded. "I'll go let him in."

"No, that's okay. Tucker'll do it."

"Who's Tucker?"

"She's a Greensdale girl we hired as a kind of general housekeeper. Comes in weekdays, when the center's open," Katherine said. "Haven't you met her?"

"I don't think so," Lydia said. "Unless you mean that sullen-looking teenager who was banging around the kitchen this morning when I came downstairs."

"Sounds like Tucker," Katherine said. "She's not big on conversation, but she's all right."

"What sort of a name is Tucker?"

Katherine shrugged. "That's what she calls herself. Her first name must be something truly horrendous. Emily and I are having a private contest to guess it. Adelaide's her current favorite, but I say Eloise."

"Why don't you just ask her?"

Katherine smiled. "You try it. Oh, hello, Dr. Harrison."

Lydia turned, realizing that some sixth sense had already alerted her to Jake's approach. Although she hadn't heard his footsteps, she had felt his presence in the hall, and when she faced him now, he was looking at her, not Katherine, with a smile of greeting.

"Afternoon, ladies."

"Hi," she said, returning the smile. His dark eyes held hers a moment longer than she'd expected. She had the odd sensation that he was studying her, briefly and intently, before he turned to Katherine.

"The one lady in the room is my sister," Katherine was saying, falling limply to one side, mouth distorted like a comical rag doll. "I myself feel more like a sick dog."

"I don't treat dogs," Jake said, as Katherine sat up again, instantly demure. Lydia knew her well enough to be able to tell that this kind of clowning was a form of nervousness.

"Well, I hope you *like* dogs," Katherine said, looking significantly towards Lydia. "You do like animals, don't you?"

Shut up, Lydia mimed behind Jake's back, then smiled prettily as he turned to look at her again. "How's my other patient?" he asked. "I don't see any cane in your hand."

"I only used one for a little while last night," she told him. "I'm healed and healthy."

"And very pretty," Katherine chimed in. "I like that color on you, Lydie."

Lydia concentrated on not allowing her face to color as Jake's gaze roamed appreciatively over her maroon print dress. If Katherine made one more provocative remark...

"I'm going downstairs while Dr. Harrison looks after you," she said. "Need anything?"

"If Emily's got any coffee on, I'll have a cup," Jake said.

"No problem." With a last glare of mock outrage at Katherine, Lydia left the room. She could use a cup of Emily's coffee herself. She was still feeling a little low-spirited from her morning at the doctor's and Emily's espressolike brew's strength was now legendary at the Taylor House.

It was still disorienting to have to reach the kitchen by going to the right at the foot of the stairs instead of to the left. The way the downstairs had been divided, going through the now nonexistent living room as she used to do was impossible. Instead, she continued down the hallway and turned at its end, where a new door with a latch lock led to the kitchen pantry.

Inside, it was sunny and noisy. Lydia remembered to re-latch the door after her to keep the exit child-proof, and stepped carefully between two children who were studiously investigating a disabled toy rocket ship. Another pair were at the kitchen table, squealing with laughter as Emily applied a soapsuds topping to what were, she saw, some expertly fashioned mud pies in tins.

"Take these back outside," she directed them, "and show Mrs. Travis. David, don't drip that! Oh, hi, Lydia."

"Hi, Em." She nodded appreciatively as David and his companion held up the mud pies for her approval. "Got any coffee on?"

"Sure. Tucker, are there any clean mugs up there?"

Lydia noticed Tucker for the first time. She'd been quietly stacking some cans in a cupboard behind her. Thin, brownish hair pinned up behind her head, clad in jeans and a sweatshirt turned inside out, she nodded silently and reached for a mug from a nearby shelf. Tucker struck Lydia as someone who was very intent on blending in with the scenery.

"Thank you," Lydia said. Tucker put the mug down on the stove by the percolator with the barest nod of acknowledgment. *All right, then.* Lydia filled the mug in silence and got milk from the fridge, careful not to get her feet run over by a now remobilized rocket.

"Outside with the Space Ranger. Roger, tie your sneaker. How's your sister doing?"

"Oh!" Lydia realized this last question had been directed at her. "Jake—Dr. Harrison is with her right now," she said, and took a gulp of coffee. "So we're waiting for a report. As a matter of fact, I kept a light under that pot for him. He'll want a cup when he comes down." Emily nodded, busily folding a pile of linen. "Is there anything I can help with?"

"No, you just drink your coffee," Emily said.

"All right if I take a look around?"

"Honey, it's your house!" Emily said, chuckling. "Here, why don't I give you a little guided tour?"

Emily led the way from the kitchen to what had been the back parlor and now was an open play area. There were piles of toys neatly stacked on shelves against the far wall, divided up, she saw, into board games, vehicles and a collection of dolls. Colorful blocks and other shapes filled an area where the wicker couch had once been, and the walls were each painted a bright primary color. The effect was clean and cheerful.

Four children were on mats in the middle of the sun-filled room as they came in, watching Barbara Wainright and miming her calisthenics exercises. She was busy counting as she led her little group but smiled a hello as the women went past. "How many children do you have now?" Lydia asked Emily.

"Nineteen this afternoon. Twenty-two is capacity so far," she said. "Still recognize the place?"

She was indicating the living room, where part of a wall had been removed, so that parlor and living room led into each other, creating a larger open area. Thick wall-to-wall carpeting covered what had once been the polished hardwood Grammy had prized. Colorful mobiles hung from the ceiling, a new television set was ensconced on some unfinished cabinets, and one whole area was clearly an "art studio," where newspaper covered the floor beneath some standing easels.

"It's...something else," Lydia said, both pleased and disoriented by the many changes.

"You remember the nursery?" Emily asked. "Look, it's full up now." She moved quietly over the carpet to the hall leading into what had been the professor's study, and eased the door open. Inside, six cribs faced each other in neat rows of two. The walls had been painted to suggest a blue sky with white fluffy clouds. A woman Lydia hadn't met before was cradling one cherubic infant in her arms while the gray-haired one she remembered as Marsha dangled a toy over another gurgling baby in the farthest crib.

Lydia felt something tug at her heart. For a moment she had what was by now becoming a recurring fantasy, the daydream that any of these infants might be her own. She was half tempted to go down the line of cribs and pick out one that struck her as the cutest, though she knew it would be a tough decision. Then the futility of the fantasy struck her with full force.

"It's really lovely," she told Emily, abruptly turning back. "I'd like to spend some time here later and meet them all."

"Sure," Emily said. "Have you seen the yard?"

"Just briefly." She was happy to leave the nursery and follow Emily down the hall that led outside.

"You might want to put your sweater on," Emily suggested, gesturing at Lydia's cardigan, which was hanging from one of the wooden pegs. Lydia took it and stepped out into the bright sunlight after Emily. The cries of children playing filled the air. Some were playing tag on the lawn, each in brightly colored coats that made them look like round munchkins with flailing hands and feet. A woman that Emily introduced as Betty was overseeing a line of kids who were climbing up the silver slide.

Lydia breathed in the air that already smelled of winter, hugging the cardigan around her. A dog that looked like some mix of golden retriever and Irish setter was nosing around the edges of Grammy's garden, followed by a little girl. Lydia smiled, taking it all in. It was a bittersweet feeling, being amid these children. But their energy and high spirits buoyed her up. She couldn't feel selfishly sad for herself with so much happiness surrounding her.

"They're a wonderful bunch of brats, aren't they?" Emily was back at her side. Lydia nodded. Emily had an expression on her face that almost mirrored Lydia's, and she remembered suddenly that Katherine had said she was moving out of Greensdale.

"I guess it'll be hard to leave them, won't it?"

Emily looked at her with a slight frown. "Your sister's told you, I see." She sighed. "Yes, it's going to be one hard adjustment to make, no joke. It's tough enough being separated from my own kids when I'm working part-time in town. But I've really gotten attached to . . . well, everybody else's here," she said with a laugh.

"You're more or less running the day-care program, aren't you?" Lydia said. "Any ideas about who's going to take over?"

Emily shook her head. "That's the problem. None of the other Alliance women have enough time to really be here as much as I've been. And we've only got a month or so to figure something out." She shrugged. "Well, we *will* work it out, I'm sure. Even if I have to do some commuting from Great Oaks to help out at first."

The screen door behind them swung open and shut. Lydia turned to see Jake Harrison, coffee mug in hand, walking toward them slowly to keep from spilling its contents over the leaf-strewn grass. Instinctively she submitted him to the same kind of inspection she'd felt him giving her earlier. She noted his conservative but casual dress, the powder-blue button-down shirt, the slightly askew dark tie. He was one of the few men she'd ever seen who could wear a corduroy jacket with leather patches on the elbows, and not look pretentious or scholarly in it.

No, there was nothing wrong with him that she could see. She liked looking at him. Somehow his presence seemed to make her mood brighten. *Careful,* she told herself, *or you'll start to develop that old crush all over again.*

"I see you've got your hands full," he said, nodding in the direction of the now screaming children.

"They keep us busy," Emily said. "How's Katherine?"

Jake took a thoughtful sip of coffee. "Status quo, I'm afraid. I'm keeping her on the aspirin and vitamins. A flu like this can't really be handled any other way."

"She still has fever?" Lydia asked.

He nodded. "Not as bad as it was, but it's hanging in there. Emily, you're still plying her with liquids?"

"I'm just cooking up another pot of chicken broth."

"Good." He took another sip of coffee and raised an eyebrow. "This has a stronger kick than pure amphetamine."

"People seemed to like it," Emily said. "You want some watered-down decaf, Doc?"

"No, no." Jake smiled. "I can use the boost."

"Roger, stop bothering Tessie with that rocket!" Emily bellowed. "Excuse me," she said calmly, and then went striding off to police the latest kiddie fracas by the swings. Jake glanced at his watch.

"Have you got a few minutes?" he asked.

"I might."

"Good. Is there some place a little more quiet? . . ."

Lydia looked at him for a moment, curious. Maybe he *had* been thinking about their past encounter. Maybe there were some things he, too, felt were unresolved, things left unsaid that he wanted to say now.

"It's about this flu," he added, in response to her questioning gaze. She immediately felt foolish. Of course, he just wanted to discuss Katherine's condition with her. "Fine," she said. "We can sit in the little parlor up front."

She strode quickly back toward the house, annoyed with herself for being disappointed. *Grow up,* she told herself. He had. Why couldn't she?

Jake followed her through the kitchen, back down the hall, and then into the little room that had once been no more than a coatroom off the front door foyer. Now, with no living room at all downstairs, Katherine had converted it into a cozy, pint-sized den, just big enough to contain a comfortable armchair, a rocker and a small antique card table.

One window overlooked the front grounds, and sunlight was streaming in as she motioned Jake into the chair, taking the rocker for herself. From the magazines lying around, she intuited that the women of the Alliance most probably used this den as a refuge in between day-care shifts, a stopgap site for the regaining of their sanity.

"Welcome to our spacious living room," she said.

Jake smiled. "How's the ankle?"

"Like I said, still a bit sore. But I'm—hey!"

He was already lifting her foot and propping it on his thigh. "We should make sure you haven't strained a muscle," he said. "Does this hurt?"

All protests died on her tongue as he eased down her woolen sock, his strong fingers gently pressing the bare flesh of her ankle. He homed right in on the sore spot there and kneaded it. "Na-umm," was the sound that escaped her lips.

"And this?" he continued innocently. His lean, muscular hands were continuing a lazily provocative caress, sending a warm tendril of pleasure seeping from ankle to knee and regions above.

"I wish you'd . . ." she began, but her tongue had lost its power of speech. His hands were gliding higher, molding the soft skin of her calf, thumbs grazing the underside of her knee. *I wish you would stop,* she finished the sentence in her mind. Why couldn't she say those simply words aloud? Because she was thinking, as he leaned forward, tantalizingly close to her, *I wish you'd...hold me again, like you did yesterday. I wish you'd...kiss me? Like you did when I was young and foolish?* Her mind was definitely going off the deep end. But if he didn't let go of her leg, her body was going to melt.

"You've got some tense muscles here," he murmured.

"Thanks," she finally managed. "But I don't think I need a masseur."

Her leg was still prisoner, his hands resting below her knee. "Sure about that?" he asked, a teasing twinkle in his eye. She wondered if he could feel her skin pulsing to vibrant life against the soft skin of his palms, if he could read the whirling, ambivalent thoughts behind her transfixed gaze.

Fantasy was taking over again. If he didn't stop touching her, looking at her like that, she could imagine herself leaning forward as he was leaning. She could picture herself tracing the curve of those sensual lips of his with her finger, or tracing the line of his jutting chin, just as she'd done once, as she'd done many times since in erotic daydreams.

Mesmerized by his dark eyes, she saw his lips part slightly, so close to hers. Her skirt was bunched above her knee. When had she last let a man seduce her in the middle of an afternoon in broad daylight? Had she ever? But then, when had a man last made her feel so breathlessly aroused, so smoothly and swiftly?

In another moment, fantasy could become reality. It was only a matter of inches between his lips and hers....

"Oh! Sorry."

Jake and Lydia drew back simultaneously. Barbara Wainwright was at the door, her cheeks flushed with more than the autumnal air. "I just needed my..." Quickly she darted past Jake to grab a small pile of knitting from under the table. "Sorry," she repeated, and backed out of the room again, closing the door.

Lydia looked at Jake, and simultaneously they both burst into laughter. It was a welcome release from the pleasur-

able tension that had undeniably been simmering between
them. "You're going to give me a bad reputation," Lydia
chided him.

"We were engaged in a perfectly innocent medical examination," Jake said, but his eyes held hers in a knowing
way that made her realize he'd been perfectly aware of where
that moment could have led. Then he looked away, checking his watch again. "I'm sorry," he said more soberly. "I
really do need to talk to you, and then be on my way."

Lydia nodded, thinking that there was no way she could
figure out Jake Harrison. Whatever tantalizing ambiguities
lingered in the air between them, he certainly wasn't in a
hurry to resolve them. Resigned to the idea that they might
remain unresolved, she sat back and looked attentive.
"What did you want to discuss?"

"Well, I'm a little concerned about your sister."

"Is she getting worse?" Lydia asked, sitting up in alarm.

"No, but she's not getting any better," he said. "If the
fever doesn't go down within the next thirty-six hours, I've
talked to Peter about possibly moving her over to John Nathaniel for some tests."

"Tests? For what?"

Jake put his hand lightly over hers as he held her gaze a
moment. "Take it easy," he said, giving her hand a gentle
pat and then removing it. "I don't *think* there's anything
truly serious for us to worry about, but I'd just like to rule
out a few things, to be on the safe side."

"Such as?" She was doing her best to keep her voice level.
The warm aura of well-being that Jake's sensuous ankle
massage had induced was already vanishing as a chill of
anxiety took hold in her stomach.

"These headaches worry me," he said. "I'd rather not
give her anything stronger, but with the aspirin they only get
contained, not truly diminished. There could be any number of things that are responsible, from pure psychological
stress to something neurological, but I don't carry around
the kind of equipment in my little black bag that can give us
the kind of information we need."

"You don't think this is just an old-fashioned flu, do you?"

Jake drummed his fingers on the table. "If it is, it's a kind I haven't encountered before," he said. "And the thing is, your sister isn't being very cooperative."

"How do you mean?"

"I mean, without Peter around during the day to act as a watchdog, she's not taking good enough care of herself. She was out of bed the last time I came by, though I told her to stay under the covers. And she's pooh-poohing my concern."

"Sounds like Kath," Lydia murmured.

"Do me a favor and get tough with her, will you?" he asked. "It's hard enough helping her when there's no miracles that the wonders of modern medicine can make happen, but a rebel patient . . ."

"I get the message," Lydia said. "I'll watch her like a hawk."

"Good," he said. "We could just have a very resilient virus here . . . which brings me to the other subject I need to broach."

"Yes?" She found it hard to conceal her anxiety.

"That little girl who got sick yesterday, Carrie Lane? I left her in the care of Dr. Knowles, since I won't be able to be in town tomorrow and he usually treats the children here, anyway. But the point is, Carrie's symptoms aren't all that dissimilar to Katherine's," he went on. "So there is a possibility we're dealing with a contagious flu. It's a little early to tell, but according to Patrick, Carrie's is the first case he's seen."

"And? So?" she prompted him.

"Well, I'm probably being a bit paranoid," he said, frowning as he smoothed back that distingué lock of hair. "But I want you to call me if any of the other children here show signs of getting sick. Even a sniffle. If we do have something contagious on our hands, I'd hate to see an in-house epidemic get started. So be on the lookout, okay?"

"All right."

He was scribbling a number on a card. "This is the research lab at Nathaniel. They can always reach me." He handed it to her and stood. "I'm sorry I have to be in such a hurry. I was hoping we could spend some time together."

"That would be nice," she said cautiously. Jake was staring at some fixed spot in space, brows furrowed in concentration. He murmured one word under his breath, and she could've sworn it was "bedtime." But that couldn't be right.

"Tomorrow night," he said abruptly. "Can you have a late dinner with me?"

"More professional consultations?" she teased.

"We've got about fifteen years to catch up on, isn't that right?" He smiled. "I'll pick you up at eight-thirty."

Chapter Three

Jake pulled into his parking space, turned the motor off and checked his watch. "Unbelievable," he muttered, smiled, and sat back for a moment, taking a deep breath and letting it out slowly. He'd done it.

He'd been there to greet Max at the shuttle, which had been right on time. Max, not the most demonstrative of nine-year-olds, had nonetheless given him a hug and actually seemed excited to see him. Jake had managed to get him back to the house in Great Oaks, introduced him to Sophee and even sat down for a little while for a glass of milk. Max seemed to like the place, took to Sophee well—*praise the Lord*—and had been in good spirits when his father left.

Jake had sprinted into his Great Oaks office, seeing three patients, then extricating himself in time to be only a perfectly respectable ten minutes late for his appointments at Nathaniel. All in all it was an amazing feat.

He got out of the car and nearly walked right into a white-haired man headed for the car in the adjacent space. "Dr. Newcomb!"

"Jake! Long time no see." They shook hands. "How goes it, Doctor? The wife well?"

Jake cleared his throat. "She's well, yes, but no longer the wife," he admitted.

"It *has* been a long time," Dr. Newcomb said. "Sorry to hear that. And your mother?"

"Just great, thanks. Pat Knowles tells me your grandson John is going into medical school. Should I congratulate you or not?"

The older man laughed. "Oh, he'll find out what he's in for, soon enough. You look well, Jake."

"Thanks, Dr. Newcomb. You're looking great yourself."

"I persevere." He smiled. "Your patients speak well of you. That Taylor woman who was in yesterday made you sound like God's gift to modern medicine."

Jake stared at him, startled. "She was here? In her condition?"

Dr. Newcomb made a face. "Oh, come, she should be all right. The girl overreacts. I told her there was no need to look into the in vitro business yet."

"Wait," Jake said, utterly confused. "Why was Katherine Taylor seeing you?"

"Katherine?" Dr. Newcomb stared back at Jake, then let out a rueful chuckle. "Oh, I see, my mistake. She's the sister you're treating, that's right. So she said."

"You saw Lydia Taylor?"

"Charming young lady," Dr. Newcomb said. "How's the sister doing? Flu or something, wasn't it?" Jake nodded, preoccupied. So Lydia had been consulting a gynecological specialist? Dr. Newcomb was holding out his hand. "Jake, I do have to be going. Stop in some time for a cup of java."

LIFE WAS TOO ODD, Lydia mused, studying her reflection in the mirror on the back of her bedroom door. In a sense, she was about to go out on a date that had been broken in 1973.

If she squinted her eyes, she could imagine herself as she must have looked back then: fresh out of high school, as innocent and naive as any girl of eighteen who thought she was already mature could be. That summer, the future had stretched before her, limitless and exciting. The world was hers and Holly's; at least, all of Cape Cod was.

Holly Pine was her best friend from school, as short and stocky as Lydia was tall and slender. They'd had to put up with their share of Quixote and Sancho jokes over time. Actually the comparison wasn't entirely unsuitable. Holly was the wilder, more irresponsible of the two girls. Whooping it up and having a good time was her first priority, whereas Lydia tended to be more introspective.

Holly's folks had rented a cottage on the Cape for the summer. Lydia's mother, though good-naturedly complaining that Lydia was about be away from home for years at a stretch, had agreed to let her stay with Holly for a few weeks at the summer's end. The two girls luxuriated in that ephemeral, on-the-brink time, full of long, soul-searching walks on the beach while they compared imaginary lives they had yet to live, and flirtatious nights in town where they could flaunt their newly legal drinking age and dance to the local bands.

Then one morning when Holly had "partied down" so hard she couldn't quite get up, Lydia had gone for a solitary walk on the beach. Over by a deserted jetty she found a sea gull fluttering about between two rocks, apparently trapped in the tide's undertow. Her heart went out to the creature, who wasn't able to get free.

Lydia had always been attracted to every kind of animal, walking, flying, small or big. She was clambering about the slippery, moss-covered rocks, trying to free the gull without falling into the water herself, when a tall, dark-haired young man in rolled-up khaki trousers and a button-down shirt, with pen clipped to pocket, both of which seemed too serious for the beach, hurried over to give her a hand.

That was Jake. Even then he'd had that solicitous, confidence-inspiring air. Rather quickly he managed to get a hand down beyond Lydia's reach, and pulled the gull loose from the rocks with only a minimal loss of wet feathers. Lydia had thanked him profusely, while the rescued bird, a bit bewildered by this human intervention, flew around them in a circle, occasionally landing on the sand below to cock its quizzical head in their direction.

They'd laughed together, then strolled up the beach. Lydia had insisted on buying him a soda for his stalwart efforts on the gull's behalf. Then they'd spent the morning strolling along the waterfront, talking. For Lydia, it hadn't exactly been love at first sight. She'd thought Jake a little bookish and unathletic. After all, Steve Arnold, the boy she'd been going out with in her senior year, had been a track champion and basketball star.

But in subsequent walks on the beach with Jake, their casual friendship began to mean more to her. At first, they "ran into each other" at the same spot as if by accident. They took an even longer walk, comparing pasts, beginning to confide in each other about their imagined futures.

Jake was already thinking about going into medicine. He was about to start his second year at Boston University and was looking into East Coast schools, planning to transfer to one that was stronger in premed. Since Lydia was toying with the idea of becoming a veterinarian, they were on common ground. She was taken with Jake's boundless enthusiasm for all things scientific. He was scholarly, but not in a dull way. He wanted to make this world, the real world, a better place to live in, and for him, all knowledge was fuel for his fiery imagination.

Soon, without ever verbally acknowledging it, they were meeting nearly every morning on the beach. She liked talking to him. His mind was his most seductive part, at first. It was Holly, joining them one morning in their routine—cappuccinos to go from a local café that opened early, then down the beach to what they'd labeled Lame Gull Jetty—who alerted Lydia to the idea that there was more going on than she'd let on, even to herself.

"He's a complete hunk!" Holly enthused after that meeting. "No wonder you're so crazy about him—and no wonder you've been keeping him to yourself."

Jake Harrison? Lydia laughed Holly off at first. Their friendship was exactly that, purely platonic. Still, the seed was sown. He was, if not her immediate ideal, a very attractive young man. She had to admit there were times when they were strolling down the beach together that it had seemed to her almost unnatural that they weren't holding hands. And when she'd worn a particularly daring bikini the other day, she hadn't failed to notice that he was more flustered than usual, his eyes seeming to dart everywhere than at her revealed anatomy.

Two things began to dawn on her simultaneously. One, Jake *was* attracted to her, but he was a little shy. Secondly, she did indeed have a sizable crush on the idealistic young doctor-to-be. Holly was already speaking of the two of them as if they were destined to be lovers. It appealed to her romantic imagination.

"It's like Romeo and Juliet or something," she enthused. "Think, in just a few days, you'll be going West and he'll be headed East. You may never see each other again! All you'll have are these brief, wonderful moments together, to cherish all your lives. What a great way to lose your virginity!"

"What are you talking about?" Lydia cried. "We haven't even kissed."

"Oh, you will," Holly assured her. "And then one thing will lead to another, and . . ."

"Stop," Lydia protested, blushing.

"You may be a virgin, but I'm sure he isn't," her friend persisted. "You say he's sensitive and caring, but he's also one sexy-looking guy. You could do a lot worse, Lydie, for a first time."

Holly, ever the more outrageous, had already experienced the infamous act with her boyfriend Chuck. Holly's experience and Lydia's lack of it had been a much-discussed topic between them this summer. But Lydia had an idealistic notion about saving herself for her first true love—whom she was undoubtedly destined to meet at Berkeley. She laughed off Holly's urgings and tried to put it all out of her mind.

Nonetheless, once she became alerted to the subtle sexual tension that was there between Jake and herself, she couldn't help wondering what might happen. Jake, too, seemed more attuned to every casual physical contact they had. He might have been shy, but he wasn't made of stone, and a few days before the end of her stay, he broke precedent by arranging to meet her at the beach at sundown the following evening.

They met at a clambake on the beach. They wandered off together to a group of dunes near their jetty, ostensibly to watch the sunset. In one way, it was like all the other times they'd spent together, but in another way it was definitely not. Jake was nervous, Lydia more so. They shared a beach towel, watching the red ball of sun go down in a perfect, technicolor vista over the sea—still not touching, still never having touched.

When he did finally turn to her, taking her hand with an adorably apprehensive—hopeful?—look in his dark eyes, she'd thought her heart would implode. Their first kiss was exquisite. In fact, so was everything about that wonderful night, even its anticlimactic finish.

Because, as she'd had plenty of time to ruminate in the intervening years, wasn't that the essence of erotic romance? Endless, fantastic foreplay, enriched with unrequited longing, ever building to an ever-withheld consummation, that was the breathtaking bliss they'd shared for hours on that blanket, hidden from view by the soft dunes, their supple young bodies caressed by cool summer night breezes, bathed in moonglow.

He was every bit as gentle and commanding as she'd hoped he would be, not at all an impatient fumbler like Steve Arnold. With Jake she felt herself truly opening up, more vulnerable, more trusting than she'd ever been, and more adventurous. That night they did everything she'd ever allowed herself to do with a man, and a little more. But at the last moment, when she was truly ready, convinced finally that indeed, it couldn't be righter than this, all her fears swept away by his passionate but patient touch, Jake put on the brakes.

Apparently he hadn't realized she was a virgin. Of course he hadn't come right out and asked her until now, and when she told him, Jake was troubled. Lydia found herself in the surprising and somewhat embarrassing position of wanting to persuade Jake to keep going, when he—unlike Steve, for example—possessed a conscience, and seemed to think it was time to stop.

After a torturous discussion, the two of them now practically wearing nothing but the moonlight, Jake had gently but firmly stalled them where they were. In fact, with that supersoft practiced touch of his, he expertly brought her to an orgasm so intense as to make her wonder if those things she'd experienced before had really *been* orgasms. She brought her own not so practiced skills into play to do as best she could for him.

And then they had kissed and cuddled together, and it had been almost as satisfying as she had imagined it might be; in one sense, even more. Rapturous in his arms, Lydia had made him promise they would meet again the next night. It had to be then, as both of them were due to leave the Cape in another two days.

She spent that next day, seemingly as long as three, in anxious anticipation. As Holly pointed out, fate had clearly decided she should find her first true love *before* college. Dazed by the heady sensation of what could only be love, she looked forward to a second night that was bound to top their almost-consummation. She was at Lame Gull Jetty early, dressed, coiffed and even perfumed in readiness. Jake's conscience was sure to give way before the powerful force of true love, and it would be a historic night of romance to remember.

Two hours later she was sitting in the dunes, her makeup in ruins, weeping. Jake Harrison had not shown up.

It was, even when she thought about it now, one of the great tragedies of her early life, only the deaths in her family preceding it in order of woe. The next morning a friend of Jake's found her back at the jetty, once again wandering disconsolately across the sand, and gave her a note. In it, Jake apologized for having stood her up, claiming he'd had to return to Boston sooner than he'd planned, begging her forgiveness and enclosing his address at school, wanting her to write. Devastated, she'd torn the note in two.

She had never written, but the taped-together note from Jake was still buried in some carton of memorabilia back in California. Lydia lost her virginity to a Berkeley sophomore who wasn't half the Mr. Right that Jake had been. And although she had thought she was in love, the experience had none of the romance she'd once come so achingly close to experiencing with him. Which was why, now and then over the years, her mind had returned to that magical night on the beach. The perfection of it somehow still exceeded, in memory, the erotic realities of the perfectly rewarding love life she'd shared with her former fiancé.

And now, she realized, coming back to this evening's reality as she stared at herself in the mirror, that lost second evening loomed before her. She wondered what he thought about it all.

In the years since that fateful summer, she'd occasionally analyzed his actions. At eighteen, she'd perceived Jake's sudden disappearance as an out-and-out rejection. Clearly he hadn't enjoyed being with her the way she had with him. Certainly their time together hadn't meant as much to the older, more experienced college student.

But in retrospect, she often gave Jake the benefit of the doubt. Possibly, just possibly, he'd been afraid of the responsibility that initiating young Lydia Taylor into the mysteries of sex could have engendered. Maybe he *had* cared about her, so much that he didn't want to begin a relationship that he would never have been able to maintain.

In either case, he had broken her young heart in two. But his motives had been the stuff of idle speculation for too long. It was a fascinating quirk of fate that she might know the truth at last. If Jake hadn't taken the initiative and invited her out, she might have thought the whole thing was in the past for good, and best left there. But since he had...

Lydia had showered, shampooed her hair, put on the nicest lingerie she'd brought with her and the most fetching dress, a one-piece black cashmere number with a provocatively plunging neckline. She'd applied her makeup with extra care, and was even going to wear the heels that pinched her left foot slightly, just for the added inches and effect.

She was dressed to kill for this date, she mused. Satisfied with her reflection in the mirror, she smiled. She wanted Jake Harrison to want her badly tonight. Because if he had the slightest desire, the barest thought of attempting a seduction, of finishing what he'd started so many years ago, he was in for a surprise.

Although Lydia had never been prone to manipulative game-playing with men, she was actually contemplating a revenge that could be much more rewarding. She hoped he'd try to seduce her. Because there was no way in hell she was going to let Jake sleep with her. She owed him, and herself, that much satisfaction.

THE FOUR CORNERS INN was one of the oldest establishments in Greensdale, the sort of place high-school seniors went to on prom dates and where married couples celebrated anniversaries. Although not ritzy by cosmopolitan standards, it was the one restaurant in town with a genuine maître d', namely, Bob Clemmons, a white-haired, red-nosed gourmet who was a staple of the Inn. His specialty was the wine list. Though he was often vague on the evening's specials, he prided himself on having tasted every vintage in the Inn's small cellar, and no one disbelieved him.

One of the nice things about the Four Corners was its wood-burning fireplace with real wood. Jake had gotten them a table not far from its smoky warmth, in a little booth in the corner that overlooked the Inn's backyard. The red wine Bob Clemmons had recommended was warming her up on the inside as she sat across from Jake, and all in all, she reflected, this was an excellent place to be on a chilly November evening.

"Only the chef's salad?" he asked, as she pushed the plate back, comfortably satiated. "Don't tell me you're dieting." He seemed genuinely dismayed.

"Well, yes, if the truth be known," she said. "Which is why I'll be skipping dessert."

"But you're so thin," he said.

"In parts," she said wryly.

His gaze flickered briefly over her head and shoulders with an appreciative glimmer. "Things seem to be in proportion," he said. She reached for her wine, covering a smile. Jake was making little effort to hide the fact that he appreciated her even more as a full-grown woman than he had when she was a love-starved teenager. And she was enjoying every minute of it.

In the short drive over here, they'd only chatted about differences between Greensdale and the larger Great Oaks, and the early part of dinner had been spent discussing how the latter town was experiencing a minor boom with the opening of the ConCo plant on its outskirts. The corporation had been able to build quickly by converting what had formerly been an old metal parts factory into a new facility.

Lydia told Jake the story of their battle with the town board over letting ConCo build in Greensdale. He knew of the situation but hadn't realized how much Katherine and she had been involved. Then the conversation turned back to Katherine, who was much the same, with a small drop in temperature that day. So far, no one else at the center had been taken ill. Fingers were crossed.

Lydia had kept her sister company for most of the afternoon, in between phone calls to San Francisco to make sure Pet Sanctuary West was still standing. Albert seemed to be managing things decently, but Lydia couldn't help worrying about particular animals that needed special attention. Her two favorite rabbits had a touch of some kind of virus, ironically, and not being able to diagnose and treat them in person made her uneasy.

Then there were a number of lengthy calls to and from her accountant in Boston, who was overseeing the budgeting of her renovations. Talk of all this made the meal pass pleasantly. Their more personal past had been avoided, at least until now. Lydia decided to ease their way into it. "So, I guess you've actually done what you set out to do," she said.

Jake raised an eyebrow. "How do you mean?"

"You're a doctor with a private practice and you're still involved in research. Isn't that exactly what you had in mind for yourself, when we had those long talks in Cape Cod?"

"You mean at Lame Gull Jetty?" Lydia smiled. Maybe his memories were as vivid as hers. "I don't remember having bacteriology in mind, specifically, but yes, I guess you could say things have worked out close enough."

"You seem happy," she ventured.

Jake shrugged. "I'm busy," he said. "And you?"

"Also busy. I didn't become a veterinarian, after all, but I do spend all my time with animals."

"Have you started filling the new store with them yet?"

There they were, back in the present again. She wondered if he was purposely avoiding talking about that summer. It wouldn't surprise her. She let him draw her out about the pet shop and her plans as they continued eating. The wine was softening whatever edge she'd come in here with, and revenge was seeming a little silly by the time the dessert cart rolled around. Maybe the past *was* best avoided.

Still, she couldn't help remembering how he'd held her the other day, and flirted with her just the previous afternoon. And she was conscious of the solicitous way he watched her, and occasionally touched her. It wasn't just her imagination. He was interested in her. How much? His gaze had strayed to her left hand, so his next question didn't come as a complete surprise.

"Do you always make trips like this alone?"

Lydia smiled. "No, I'm not married," she said. "And neither are you, I hear. Why is that?"

His smile vanished. "I was, once," he said. "It didn't work out."

She hadn't meant to touch what appeared to be a still raw nerve. "I'm sorry," she said. "I didn't know."

"That's all right," he said.

She could see that it wasn't, though. It was almost as if an invisible wall had come down around him at the mere mention of his marriage. She made a mental note to steer clear of the topic...at least for the time being. Lydia was too naturally inquisitive to let it lie for long.

"But then, I don't know much about what you've done with your life," she went on, trying to keep things on a lighter note, "outside of making what looks like a successful career."

"I'm afraid that's all there is to it, really," he said. "I've been working in medicine ever since college. It's the kind of work that's never done. If anything, the research work load only increases as time goes by. The more you find out, the more you need to find out. One answer leads to a new question...."

He paused, shaking his head. "Don't get me started; I'll talk shop all night. You're more interesting," he said, his eyes once more making an intent and affectionate perusal of her features. "What about your...marital history?"

"I never got married," she told him. "I was engaged for a while, a few years ago, but—" She stopped. She didn't feel like going into the details of that disappointing relationship, and he certainly had skirted any description of his. "Like you said, it didn't work out."

Jake nodded, fingering his wineglass. He seemed to be considering a question, then thinking better of it. "Coffee?"

"No, thanks, I've had enough of Emily's lately to keep me up for a week," she said. "The wine's fine."

"Yes, we might as well finish it off," he said, pouring the last of the bottle into her glass and then his own. A little splashed on Lydia's sleeve. "Hell, I'm sorry," he said.

"It's just a tiny stain," she said. "I need to go to the ladies' room, anyway." She rose from her seat. "I'll get some club soda for it on the way."

JAKE MADE IT to the phone in the lobby and back in record time. According to Sophee, Max was still asleep though how he could sleep well through the rock music he heard in the background, Jake wasn't sure. He asked her to turn it down. He wasn't sure about Sophee, either, but Max said he liked her okay. And at the moment, the French girl was his only support system.

Now, back in the booth awaiting Lydia's return, he wondered if he was being foolishly overprotective. He probably should've been willing to tell her more about what was going on with him. But those kinds of confidences didn't come easily to Jake.

Wasn't that one of the things Judith had been so critical of? Telling him she'd married him, hoping to get to know him better, but knowing him less and less as time went on? Jake felt his defensiveness mounting even as he reviewed the old arguments, and reached for his glass of wine.

No, now wasn't a good time to go into all of that. If he did see Lydia again, and he knew he wanted to, there'd be time to talk about their respective inner lives. If there was any time at all, he thought ruefully, looking at his watch. These days even sleep got short shrift, let alone things like dates with an old acquaintance.

Funny, but she didn't really fit that description. Seeing Lydia again was almost like meeting a new and very attractive woman who was magically imbued with the qualities of a long-lost friend. Maybe having been out of the swing of things was a factor, but simply being out with her like this was exciting him in a way he couldn't remember having been excited before.

But what was he thinking of? His life was complicated enough as it was, and his main priority had to be his son. Jake had a point to prove, to Max, to Judith, and to Judith's attorney. If he could show that Max could live with his dad, get his schoolwork done—having Max come a few weeks before the official start of Thanksgiving vacation had obligated him to hire two tutors—and be happy, maybe Jake would stand a better chance of getting him for longer stretches of time in the future. That was what this first trial custody was all about.

Lydia was on her way back to the table. As Jake watched her walk down the aisle, he wondered how she might react to hearing that he had a child—one he usually only saw once a month or less, true, but still his child. As he was mulling over the option of telling her, after all, both he and Lydia saw the little girl in the high chair at the same time.

She was seated with her folks at a table farther down the aisle, happily waving her fork around as the adults smiled and her mom cut up some food for her. Jake studied Lydia as she slowed, her eyes fixed on the girl in the cute little frock. And the look in her gaze brought him up short, reminding him of his encounter with Dr. Newcomb.

There was pain in her eyes, and he hated to see it. Jake had been able to put two and two together from the older doctor's remarks that morning. Clearly, Lydia had suffered some kind of gynecological trauma. If she was consulting a specialist on this coast, and even considering in vitro fertilization, it was possible that childbearing might be a serious risk for her.

But then Newcomb had seemed to make light of it. Jake frowned, watching Lydia move on, her expression as she passed the little girl a mixture of affection and sadness. Obviously this issue of children was a sensitive one, as sensitive as the subject of Jake's failed marriage was to him.

Jake had dealt with enough patients with like difficulties to know what approach was the best. There was no need to confront Lydia with his good fortune, mixed though it might be. And Max would be gone in a little while, anyway. He resolved there and then to avoid any mention of his son.

"SORRY TO TAKE SO LONG," Lydia said, taking her seat.

"That's okay."

"So, what were we saying?"

Jake shrugged, smiling. "Nothing of any earth-shattering importance."

Lydia nodded. Before this interruption, she'd had the feeling he was editing himself, choosing what he had to say with a good deal of caution. Even now he seemed carefully composed, but he was smiling, and his gaze was appreciative.

"You've grown into a truly beautiful woman," he said. "Or did I tell you that already?"

"Never hurts to be flattered twice," she said.

"It's not flattery," he said. "I'm just stating the facts. We men of science tend to be big on facts, you know."

"I see." She sipped her wine, wondering where this was leading. She couldn't help but be titillated by the way he seemed to drink in her features as he looked at her.

"But it's funny—" he shifted in his seat "—I can still see the younger you there, too. I mean, here you are, a sophisticated and successful entrepreneur—"

"*That's* flattery," she said, smiling. "I run a pet shop."

"Same thing. The point is, you're a grown-up businesswoman, but I can't help remembering you as, well, a high-school senior."

"Maybe I haven't changed that much."

"I think you have," he said, nodding his thanks as their waiter brought him the check.

"In what ways?"

"You seem a lot more self-assured," he said. Lydia said nothing, thinking that she hadn't exhibited much self-assurance when he'd had to carry her into the house the other day. "You've also lost a bit of your New England accent."

She smiled. "Do I sound Californian now?"

"I haven't heard you lapsing into surfer jargon, no," he said. He paused to scribble on the credit card slip. "Do you like it better back there?"

"The weather's glorious," she said, downing the last sip of wine as she watched some red leaves dance past the windowpane. So they were back to the present, talking about things as safe as the weather. Still, she had to admit she was enjoying herself. Even if the date didn't lead to any moment of consequence, Jake Harrison was good company. "But I do miss seeing the leaves turn, the way they just did here."

Jake rose from his seat, moving to hers as she put her napkin down. "Maybe we should take a little walk, then.

We can stretch our legs and you can breathe in the authentic New England air."

"All right." He was holding her sweater for her, ever the gentleman.

"There's a bright moon," he added, smoothing her collar for her, his fingers brushing the edge of her neck. She felt a little shiver shoot down her spine. *Walks. Moonlight.* There was a lot of resonance in those simple words. Was he aware of it?

He followed her out of the restaurant into the crisp evening air. There was, as promised, a nearly full yellow moon in the sky. Jake fell into step beside her as her heels clicked on the sidewalk. *Not barefoot, no sand,* she noted. It seemed both perfectly natural and exceedingly odd to have him at her side like this again.

"Thanks for the dinner," she said, as he was silent. "It was really a wonderful meal."

"It's the least I could do," he said. She caught the rueful tone in his voice and slowed, turning to look at him. Ahead, the edge of the village green shone beneath the street lamps, but here there was only moonlight to illuminate his face and highlight the glimmer in his dark eyes.

"How do you mean?" she asked.

Jake sighed. "All right," he said. "I've been putting this off and putting this off, but since it's been on my mind ever since you came back to town . . . ever since it happened, actually . . ." He slowed to a halt, facing her beneath the rustling maples that lined Grove Street. "To tell you the truth, I've been surprised you've been this friendly," he said. "After what happened."

"It was a long time ago," she said carefully.

"So you've forgiven me, then?"

She gazed back at him, surprised to see how vulnerable he looked. "Well, yes and no," she admitted with a nervous smile. "I'm not sure we both remember it the same way."

"I'll tell you what I remember," he said. "I remember getting close to this really fantastic girl I met . . . and then letting her down," he murmured, frowning.

"It was just a harmless little summer flirtation, though," she said lightly. "Wasn't it?"

"No." He held her gaze, the moonlight molding the lines of his face in sharp relief. "If you want to know the truth..." *Yes!* she thought, her heartbeat beginning to pound with renewed intensity. "I was pretty infatuated with you," he said quietly. "But I suppose you knew that."

"Not really, no," she said, and cleared her throat, aware that her voice was sounding tremulous. "In fact, from the way you acted, I pretty much thought you didn't care for me."

Jake's eyes narrowed. "Didn't care...? Lydia, if I hadn't cared, if I hadn't been concerned for your feelings and my own, I never would've left the next day. I'd have shown up the next night and been with you."

She stared at him, still disbelieving. These were the words she would've died to have heard, so many years ago. And somewhere within her that teenage girl was responding, an old unrequited need was reawakening. "But...didn't you know how I *would* feel?" she said.

"Call it choosing the lesser of two evils," he said wryly. "Lydia, there was no way I could have made love to you, knowing it was your first time, knowing how important the whole thing was to you...and then just gallivanted on out of your life for good. It wouldn't have been fair to you—or to me."

"To you?"

"I was falling in love with you." He said the words almost bitterly. "And since I knew there wasn't any future possible for us, I guess I didn't want to fall any harder."

Lydia shook her head. "I can't believe I'm hearing this."

"You don't believe me?" The look of genuine outrage on his face was almost comic. Lydia gave a nervous laugh.

"No, I do!" she assured him. "It's just... Jake, I won't pretend I haven't thought about you, over the years. And I always wondered..."

"You never wrote," he said, with a trace of sadness. "Not that I blame you. I felt so guilty about the way I'd handled it that although I started about a dozen letters to you, when I was back at school, eventually it seemed the best thing to do was just let the whole thing go.''

She nodded slowly, a little dazed by these late but still welcome revelations. ''How you handled it,'' she repeated. ''Yes, it would've been better if you'd said no to me in person.''

''I know,'' he said softly. ''Well, call me a coward, but I was afraid if I *did* see you, I'd lose the courage of my convictions.''

She smiled ruefully. ''Maybe that wouldn't have been the worst thing,'' she told him. ''Maybe I would've been able to handle one night of love, after all.''

''Oh?'' He smiled, and his hand stole out to gently cup her chin. ''That's right, you were a big girl even then,'' he said, his eyes aglow with amused affection. ''So how much do you think you could handle now?''

And then, before she could even think to reply, Jake kissed her. His mouth was like warm silk as it brushed hers, the softly tingling touch too exciting to resist. His lips plundered the tender fullness of her own, and a sense of delicious warmth overcame her as she moved forward, instinctively fitting her body to his. Her eyelids fluttered shut. She leaned into the deepening kiss, delighting in the moist feel of his tongue gliding to meet hers.

An inner voice registered each intimate detail with unabashed enjoyment. Perfect lips, so soft but commanding, so familiar and so new at the same time. Soft, fine dark hair that had been—was now—so ideal for running her fingers through. Fantastic skin, so warm to the touch. And, yes, there was that fine, huggable torso....

It seemed so easy to move into his arms like this. It was as if fifteen years had been crossed in that movement. They were gone in the intensity of his embrace, and she'd never experienced this particular intensity before. It was a memory and a fantasy and a reality converging into one blissful, overpowering sensation, and all she could do was give herself over to it.

She was awash in a liquid pool of voluptuous sensation as his tongue slowly circled hers, teasing and then thrusting to meet it with even more fervent force. His hands were encircling her back, roving eagerly over every plane and curve in a hypnotic, sensual massage. She heard a tiny groan of passion come from deep inside Jake's throat and an equally ardent moan answer him from hers.

Slowly he eased her lips away, breathless as he gazed at her, his fingers lost in her hair. "You didn't mind that, did you?" he whispered, his voice a hoarse rasp.

"No," she admitted. "I even liked it." Liked it? She hadn't felt such a sweetly painful surge of desire since... then, she realized dimly. But this wasn't what she'd wanted to happen. Wasn't she supposed to be teasing him, distant and remote, preparing to pull away?

The very thought seemed ludicrous right now, as his lips gently captured hers again and her heart pounded all the harder. Little shooting stars that weren't in the November sky were firing off in the velvet darkness behind her tightly closed eyes. She could almost imagine the pounding of the waves close by as he covered her neck with kisses, molding her pliant form to him in the moonlight.

"Lydia," he murmured, voice husky. "We probably shouldn't be doing this, but..."

Shouldn't? Why was that? Her only answer was an inarticulate moan as he fitted his mouth slowly over hers again. She tried to think about what she was doing, but thought was impossible—

A loud insistent beep broke the spell. Startled, she drew back, eyes opening as Jake withdrew. As he muttered a soft curse and reached under his jacket to quiet the beeper, she stood there, blood pounding and body weak.

"I don't believe this," he said. "But I have to get to a phone." *He* didn't believe it? Lydia could only stare at him, her senses still reeling. Jake was already stepping away, his other arm sliding from around her back. "They wouldn't page me at this hour if it wasn't important," he said, apologetic.

She found her voice at last. "They?"

"The hospital. Look, I'd better go back to the restaurant. It's just down the block. Don't—don't go away." With a sheepish smile, he brushed her forehead with his lips. Then Lydia watched Jake Harrison sprint away into the darkness.

For one crazy moment she wasn't sure if what she'd thought had happened had really taken place. *But no,* every inch of skin he'd touched seemed to be vibrating as she demurely smoothed her skirt down. She didn't know whether to laugh or cry. Instead, she merely walked, a bit unsteady on her feet, in the direction of the restaurant.

By the time she reached the path to the inn's front steps, Jake was already hurrying down them with a preoccupied air. "Looks like I'm going to have to cut this shorter than I'd planned," he said grimly. "I have to get back there."

"Boston?"

"One of my patients in sudden remission," he said. "Lydia, I'm really sorry. There was no way of knowing—"

"It's okay," she interrupted him, forcing a smile. "I understand."

"I'll drop you at the house."

She understood what his priorities had to be, certainly. It was only her own emotions that were confusing her. What had happened to her plan of sweet revenge? And how had fate conspired to deprive her both of it and an unexpectedly sweet consummation?

"History repeating itself," he said wryly, as he hurried them back to his car. "But this time, I'm only leaving your side temporarily. We'll have to make a rain date."

Seated in the car again, she'd regained a little of her lost equilibrium. "Perhaps," she said, affecting nonchalance.

"Perhaps?!" he echoed, and she could see she'd scored a direct hit on his male pride. "Somehow, some way, I'm going to have to make the time to see you again," he said. "Don't you want to see me?"

She had some idea of how busy Jake was, so the fervor in his voice impressed her, but she still kept up a noncommittal front. "Oh, I'll have to think about it," she said.

He shot her a shocked look as he reached for his ignition key. "Really?"

"Well, I *hope* I'll still be in town tomorrow," she said, unable to resist this opportunity. "But you know how it is...."

"Lydia Taylor," he said, chuckling as he gunned the motor. "If *you* skip out on *me* this time, you won't get away with it."

The teenage Lydia was inwardly beaming at such a response. The adult did her best to remain cool, calm and collected. She smiled. "I guess we'll have to see what happens," she said.

Chapter Four

"Hey, Harrison, what's your hurry? Got a hot date waiting for you on Ptomaine Row?"

En route down the hospital corridor Jake stopped in midstride. Dr. Laurence—Larry—Baxter was leaning out of the Radiology Lab, his bushy eyebrows wiggling with Groucho Marx-like suggestiveness. Jake sighed, doubling back.

"I am going to the cafeteria, yes," he told his friend. "But the only hot date waiting for me there is a bowl of chowder."

"Well, then cool your jets for a second and I'll do you the honor of accompanying you," Larry said, darting back into the room. Jake hovered in the doorway, watching the short, prematurely balding and hyperactive doctor whiz around the dimly lit lab, flicking off banks of illuminated X rays on the wall.

"You know, Lar, you ought to run some tests on your own blood composition," Jake said.

"Why's that?" It was a little dizzying to watch Larry zip around the small space, but Jake was used to it by now. When they'd roomed together during medical school, Larry had actually worn a groove in the carpet with his obsessive pacing.

"Because your system is probably running on some chemical compound far more powerful than caffeine," Jake said, as Larry joined him in the hall, locking the door behind him. "If you could synthesize the formula for the open market..."

"Then other people might be able to function at my speed. Sure, it's occurred to me," Larry said. "But who has the time to waste on that kind of research?"

He grinned as Jake shot him a dirty look. Larry knew full well that whatever time Jake had free, in between rounds at the hospital, hours in the clinic at Great Oaks and the time he put in once a week in Greensdale, Jake spent with his colleagues in Nathaniel's biological research lab, poring over bacterial specimens until fatigue finally drove him homeward.

"Yes, you're right," Jake said dryly. "Research is pointless. It's only responsible for every technique you use every day, like radioactive substance injections, the whole of interventional radiology—"

"Okay, okay." Larry threw up his hands as they both nodded hellos to Dr. Howell and Dr. Naidich, who were leading a phalanx of bright-eyed interns along the corridor. "But why don't you and your buddies in the basement come up with something *really* useful, like an anti-spousal-equivalent-argument agent? You know, something simple and nontoxic, that I could slip in her morning coffee...."

"Troubles with Teresa?"

"That's a, whaddyacallit, redundancy. Teresa thrives on trouble. It gives meaning to her life."

"Lar, I'm going to be straight with you," Jake said, putting a friendly arm over the shorter man's shoulder as they entered the elevator. "You've been saying pretty much the same thing about every woman you've gone out with ever since I've known you. Has it ever occurred to you that, well, there might be some constant factor here you're overlooking?"

"You're right." Larry nodded vigorously, moving restlessly in a little circle, the only man Jake had ever seen try to pace in a twelve-by-twelve elevator. "It's not Teresa. The problem is, *all* women are trouble. Why can't I ever accept that?"

"I give up." Jake chuckled, following Larry as he cata-
pulted through the just-opening elevator doors. The cafeteria wasn't too crowded at this time of the afternoon. Jake
rarely made it in here at a normal lunchtime, his schedule
being too overloaded and idiosyncratic for such regulari-
ties. Even now, he mused, glancing at his watch as he joined
Larry by the main hot food counter, he had barely a half
hour to spare before his next battery of patients.

"Couple of clam chowders," Larry ordered. "We'll take
some of those hard rolls, extra crackers . . . What else, Harrison?"

"That'll do me," he said. "You want coffee?"

"Does an antibody eat antigens?"

Jake groaned and went for the coffees. He found a table
not far from the windows that overlooked the grounds behind the hospital, where the late-afternoon sunlight
streaming in would have to serve for his one reminder, this
particularly busy day, that there was indeed a world out
there.

"Here we go." Larry bustled over and set down the tray.
"So, now that we've talked about me, and what you think
about me, I guess we'll have to talk about you," he said, and
sipped his soup. "That is, before we talk about me in depth.
How's life?"

"I think Max likes it here so far. I'm not so sure about
Sophee, though."

"You're not supposed to make the au pair girl happy,"
Larry said. "She's supposed to make *you* happy."

"I might have to get someone else," Jake mused. "She
smokes in the house and plays loud rock 'n' roll."

"How old is she? Sounds like someone I'd like."

"Very funny." Jake stretched, yawning.

"Ah-ha! The telltale yawn. Come on, out with it—your
hot date keep you up all night? Tell Uncle Larry."

"There's not much to talk about," Jake said.

"You mean, you didn't see her?"

Jake shrugged. The last time they'd hung out a little, he'd
mentioned to Larry that he'd seen Lydia for the first time in

years and that it was likely he'd try to see her again. "Yes, I had my date," he said, not sure he wanted to talk about the rather complex emotions the experience had left him with.

"And she shot you down, huh."

"No, not exactly."

"Then why aren't you looking ecstatic? This woman sounded like a real contender."

"That's the problem." Jake drummed his fingers on the tabletop. "Larry, let me ask you something."

"Fire away."

Jake wasn't prone to disclosing his feelings, but Larry was one of the few people he felt he could open up to. Under his friend's wisecracking exterior was a kindred spirit, and each had helped the other get through many a personal and professional crisis over the years. "Okay," Jake began. "If you felt a connection with a woman, a real . . . spark of something, and you were attracted to her, and you could sense she was attracted to you—"

"You give the au pair girl a tip and tell her not to wait up. Then you book a room at a nice hotel somewhere here in town—"

"Would you come off it? I'm trying to bare my soul to you, dingbat."

"Sorry, sorry. Go ahead and bare, I'm almost done with my soup."

Jake sipped his own, then cleared his throat. "Okay, so, we go out, we have a good time, one thing leads to another, there's a kiss . . . and kaboom."

"Kaboom?"

"The thunderclap, the bolt from above, the whatever-you-want-to-call-it, but I *know* I am seriously falling for this woman all over again, the way I did when I was just a moony college student. Only now I'm a moony adult with a lot of doctorates, but it feels the same, maybe even more intense."

"That's great."

"Is it?" Jake scowled at his soup bowl. "Boy, my life's way too complicated as it is. And the thing is, if I see her again, I'm going to want to pursue this."

"Still great."

"The point is, Lydia's the only woman I've met in a long time who I could see wanting to get serious about."

"So what's the problem?"

"I can't *get* serious about a woman, Larry, you know that."

Larry frowned. "I do? Refresh my memory on this particular data, will you?"

"After what happened with Judith?"

"But that was, what, at least three years ago, right? You learned a lesson, okay, you found out something about yourself, and now—"

"Yeah, and what I found out is, I'm incapable of living the kind of life I lead, being a doctor, and being involved in a serious, committed relationship."

Larry sat back in his chair, eyes narrowing as he gave Jake the once-over. "Let me refresh *your* memory," he said. "Judith was a very demanding woman. She had some unrealistic expectations about you and the kind of a life you two would have together. The word 'compromise' wasn't in her vocabulary, and she lacked even a modicum of patience."

"She was patient for years."

"Not really," Larry said. "She never really accepted you on your terms. And you worked overtime to try and make it work, meaning figuratively and literally. I remember you, man, the Zombie of the Day Shift."

"Still, the accident . . ."

"Wasn't your fault," Larry said sharply. "After all this time, you're still kicking yourself over that? Come on, Jake."

Jake gazed out the window. Certain memories never diminished in clarity, no matter how much time went by. He could still see the strange look of the apartment when he'd come home late that night, the odd stillness in the air that was actually palpable. He remembered his blaze of anger when he'd found the note, and realized she'd packed, left Max temporarily with her folks, and disappeared.

He remembered pouring himself a rare drink, pacing and brooding; remembered the ring of the phone and how he purposefully let it ring three times before picking up, affecting a detached coldness in his tone, as he was certain Judith would be on the other end, still unable to let their never-ending argument alone, even after her melodramatic gesture of walking out.

Then there had been the shock of the nurse's voice, the quick consultation, the frenzied dash back to the very hospital he'd left only an hour before, after a grueling fourteen-hour intern's shift. And his helplessness while other doctors more skillful than he had attended to Judith, leaving him to roam the corridors like a crazy person until learning, finally, that the worst was over. Judith would live, and considering that the front end of the car had been totaled, it was practically a miracle she was in as good a condition as she was....

"Jake." Larry's hand was on his arm. Jake looked away from the bare trees he hadn't really been seeing, and met his friend's concerned gaze.

"Sorry," he mumbled, attacking what was left of his soup with renewed intensity.

"How long is she in town?" Larry asked, after a tactful pause.

"Maybe a month."

"How often does she visit?"

"I'm not sure," he admitted. "Although she's opened a store in Cambridge."

"Well, then, you really don't have to worry about rushing into a committed relationship," Larry mused. "What's wrong with having a little healthy fun, for once? Where's the harm in you and this old friend Lydia going out a few times, while she's in town? You're a couple of grown-ups of consenting age. Live for the moment!"

"Sure," Jake said. "But the funny thing is, given our own little history—" he smiled ruefully "—maybe we're fated to pass like the proverbial ships in the night."

"Doesn't have to be that way."

"I have to be there for Max," Jake said. "This is crucial."

"So is your mental health," Larry said. "Don't get me wrong," he continued. "I've never been an advocate of the casual but friendly one-night stand—"

"Please!" Jake groaned.

"But if she's interested, and you're interested, and neither of you has all the time in the world—"

The insistent sound of a beeper interrupted the philosophical discourse of Dr. Laurence Baxter. Both men reached instinctively for their coat pockets, but it was Jake's call. He hurried to the phones outside the cafeteria doors and upon checking in, found out it was Lydia who'd had him paged. Noting the oddness of the coincidence, he dialed the number of Taylor House.

Emily Atchins put him through, and with the first syllables he could detect the upset in Lydia's voice. "Jake, something is definitely going on here," she said. "The twins are really sick."

"Twins? Sick how?"

"It's the Carter kids, a boy and girl, nearly five years old. They both complained about sore throats yesterday and today Melissa had terrible stomach cramps. She got sick and so did Michael. Now they're running a fever and they've got headaches, and Tammy Carter's got them over at Dr. Knowles's. He wants you to call him when you can."

"All right. How about the other children?"

"As far as we can tell, no one else is sick. But Roger Bartlett has a sore throat, if we can believe him."

"What do you mean?"

"Oh, Roger's just a troublemaker. He tells lies the way other kids breathe, I'm told. So Emily's convinced he's only saying that to scare us."

Jake could tell that Lydia *was* scared. He put on his best I'm-your-doctor-and-everything's-fine voice. "Well, it sounds like your typical early winter flu, all right," he said. "But there's no reason to get alarmed." *Yet,* he added mentally.

"Normally I wouldn't be," Lydia said. "But you did tell me to call if anyone else—"

"No, I'm glad you did," he assured her quickly. "I'll talk to Dr. Knowles as soon as I can."

"Have you seen Carrie Lane? I understand she was checked into Nathaniel this morning."

"Was she? Good. I'll take a look at her," he went on, checking his watch, "when I make my rounds. How's your sister?"

"Well, that's the good news," Lydia said. "Her temperature's down to something reasonable. Just under 100."

"Glad to hear it," Jake said. "And how are you?"

"99.6, I think," she answered.

Jake smiled. "I mean, beyond your temperature, how are you?"

"Frazzled," Lydia said. "But I'm sure you're very busy and I don't want to keep you. I feel guilty enough bothering you at the hospital."

A very Lydia-like thing to say, he noted, as opposed to Judith-like. But why was he even making the comparison? "Don't feel guilty," he said. "Give your sister my best. I'll try to stop by and see both of you this evening. And in the meantime..."

He paused, deliberating. Having Lydia send all of the children home at this point might create an unnecessary panic, and until he could get some test results from Carrie Lane's doctor it was too soon to determine what they were dealing with. There were only the smallest of danger signs that they were looking at anything other than a particularly virulent flu.

"In the meantime, business as usual," he continued. "Okay?"

"We'll try," Lydia said. "Jake, you don't have to stop by if you're too busy. Katherine's really feeling better."

"That's okay, I may have to see Bob Knowles in person anyway," he said, though even as the words came out of his mouth he couldn't imagine how he'd find the time. But the truth was, he wanted to see her. Not that he'd admit it: years of caution about revealing his true feelings made those particular words stick on his tongue.

"Well, when should we expect you?" she asked. "I could wait dinner—"

"No, no," he protested, touched by her friendliness. "The soonest I could be there would be after nine or so."

"All right, then." He could hear her hesitation. "Jake, if this whole thing is too much of an imposition—"

"Not at all. Keep popping those vitamin Cs, dress everybody warmly, and send anybody who even has a sniffle home immediately. And keep those cats out of my way when I get there, that's all I ask. Okay?"

Lydia laughed, a warm, welcome sound. "Yes, Doctor," she said. "Take care."

When he hung up the receiver, that warmth stayed with him, the sound of her voice lingering in his ear. Through the cafeteria doors he could see Larry Baxter dumping their trays, en route to meet him. Larry was right about one thing: it didn't have to be a ship passing in the night scenario. But what it was, exactly, still eluded him. All he knew was that Lydia and Taylor House were fast becoming a major preoccupation.

"TOO MUCH LIGHT IN HERE?"

Carrie Lane shook her head. Her face was nearly as pale as the pillowcase underneath her golden curls. Jeff Wood, the pediatrics intern on this ward, had already had the blinds drawn, as the child's eyes were reddened and sensitive. He silently handed Jake Carrie's chart on a clipboard.

"Head still hurt?" he asked her quietly. Carrie nodded. "All over, or one side . . . ?"

"All over," Carrie whispered, and a little tear slid from the corner of one eye.

"You're being a very brave girl," Jake told her, and gently squeezed her hand before leaving the bedside, clipboard in hand. Jeff joined him outside the door as he perused the chart.

"Fever's constant, some edema, drowsiness, stiff neck ... we're ready to run central nervous system tests and maybe one on cerebrospinal fluid."

"Any indication of jaundice? Hepatitis?"

"Not from the initial exam," Dr. Wood said.

"Let me get a look at the test results as soon as they're available," Jake said. "I know, it's not my case or even my ward," he said, in answer to the intern's raised eyebrows. "But we may have more of these kids coming in from Greensdale, and I want us to know what we're dealing with here."

He was glad the younger doctor hadn't asked him what it was they *were* dealing with, he reflected as he hurried down the corridor toward the elevator, trying to make up for lost time. But if Pat Knowles was concerned enough to have sent Carrie over here this quickly... He shook his head, remembering that jumping to conclusions was usually a bad idea. He'd wait until he heard what the pediatrician had to say.

"HOW MANY GERBILS IS THAT?" Lydia yelled. Bob Grady, his longish blond hair dusted with sawdust, mimed incomprehension over the roar of the carpenter's sanding machine. "How many gerbils?" she repeated.

"Because they shipped early!" he yelled back.

"I know the gerbils are early!" she called, exasperated. "I wanted to know how many we had!"

The carpenter turned the sander off midway through her reply and in the sudden silence her voice was a shrill incongruous shriek. The carpenter, his assistant, Bob, the new guy whose name she couldn't remember and the delivery man who'd brought the gerbils in all looked at her as if she'd gone mad.

"Two dozen," Bob said quietly, poker-faced.

"Thank you," said Lydia, ears ringing and face burning. In a way, it *was* a little like going mad, trying to get a store ready for opening. Chaos was the norm, what with the painting, the building of extra shelf space, the delivery of equipment and now the unexpected arrival of their first animals happening simultaneously. The interior of Pet Sanctuary East looked more like a by-product of a World War II air raid than a newborn place of commerce.

She was taking it all in stride, though. Bob was a godsend, unflappable when the realization dawned that they were still missing an entire wall's worth of shelves, efficient when the back office turned out to have been painted a hideous dark brown by mistake. And the new guy—what was his name?—was being very good about overseeing the phone installation and other such vital details.

Lydia stepped over the carpenter's tools, pointedly ignoring the work in progress that was already destroying the careful cleaning she and Bob had overseen on the store's main floor, and moved to the cages near the front windows to check on the gerbils. They were puttering about there, obviously disoriented after their long trip. She felt bad for them.

"Early gerbils," she addressed the two dozen. "I welcome you to your new home, which is not yet a home." They ignored her, climbing over each other, sniffing at the cage's edges. "I know this may be a traumatic experience for you, as it is for me," she added under her breath, "since neither you nor I are fully prepared to cohabit here. Nonetheless!" She paused, wondering what peppy words of cheer she could offer them.

"How much are they?" said a voice at her elbow.

"We're not open yet," she said automatically. "Nonetheless," she began again, then stopped, turning. A dark-haired boy wearing a V-necked sweater, brown corduroys and a baseball cap turned backward on his head was stand-

ing next to her. His eyes were large and brown and currently wide in fascination as he stared at the scurrying
gerbils.

"We're not open," she repeated, more gently.

"When *do* you open?" he said, gaze still fixed on the cage
before him.

"Not for nearly a week," she said. "How did you get in
here?"

The boy's eyes flickered briefly in her direction. "How do
you think?" he said.

Momentarily startled by his arrogantly bland tone, Lydia
stared at him, then past him. The store's door was wide
open. Lydia nodded. "Yes, that was a stupid question," she
murmured. "Now, maybe you'd like to go out the way you
came in."

"Nuh-uh," he said. "I want one of these guys."

"Sorry," she said. "They're not for sale yet. In fact,
they're not supposed to be here yet. Like you," she added
pointedly.

"Oh. Is that why they're called early gerbils?"

"Well, yes, but they're not really called that." The boy
nodded vaguely, poking his finger at the cage. "Careful,"
she said. "If they're hungry, they might bite."

He turned to face her for the first time, looking up with
his nose wrinkled in incredulity. "I'm supposed to be scared
of a gerbil?" he asked. "What, are you?"

Lydia tried not to smile, but it was hard. "Don't you have
some place to be?" she asked. "Where's your mom?"

"Seattle," he said promptly. "If they're early, why don't
you let me take one off your hands?"

Lydia shook her head. "You're shopping by yourself?"
she asked. "How old are you?"

"Nine. How old are you?"

Lydia stared at the boy, who stared back soberly, merely
curious. She was trying to figure out what to say when a
voice came from the doorway. "Max! There you are!"

The girl was dark-haired too, but had an accent. Lydia
couldn't see any familial resemblance, but the kid dutifully

moved away from the cages as she leaned into the store, smiling apologetically.

"I thought you said your mom was in Seattle," Lydia said.

"She is," said Max. "That's just somebody I go out with."

Lydia laughed. "Oh, I see."

"Max, come on. The lady, she's busy."

"Come back next week," Lydia suggested. "I'll be happy to do business then."

"I'll come back, all right," Max said, and smiled suddenly. It was the kind of smile that transformed his face for an instant into something quite innocent and beautiful. "This place is neat."

Then he ran out the door, the French woman shrugging and smiling as she followed him past the store window. Lydia watched them go, amused by the precocious Max. Then she turned back to her new wards. "Early gerbils," she informed them. "You've apparently just met our first early customer."

"ANYBODY'S GUESS." Pat Knowles leaned back in the chair behind his desk in the old, oak-paneled inner sanctum of his father's Greensdale office. "You know how it is," he added. "Most diseases are easy to nail, but now and then you get something that won't stick to the textbook. You get symptoms that could point you in a dozen directions, a little of this, a little of that..." He raised his hands, palms up. "That's why I sent Carrie your way. Although a four-and-a-half-year-old running 104 fever for more than one night is reason enough for hospitalization."

"They've given her some acetaminophen and she's down one point three degrees," Jake told him. "Test results in the morning."

"That's what I want to see," Knowles said, straightening up in his chair. "Jake, I'll level with you." He paused, the soft light from the green-shaded lamp on the desk making his thick wire-rimmed glasses gleam. "I've treated plenty of kids with flu, winter colds, strep throat, you name it. But the only time I've encountered something that looked this mean...it was encephalitis.''

Jake looked back at the pediatrician. "You think that's what we've got here?"

"Could be. Could be meningitis. Or maybe we'll be lucky and it's some strain of hepatitis I'm not familiar with.''

Jake was suddenly very weary. He rose from his seat because he feared he could easily sink right into it and not move for quite some time. "But Katherine Taylor's not a preschooler," he mused aloud.

"Adults can get encephalopathies as a late consequence of a viral infection," Knowles said. "Especially if we've got some biological vector in the environment... Anyway, we're still talking in the dark until we get those test results.''

They chatted for a few more minutes before Knowles closed up his office for the night and Jake got behind the wheel of his little blue Mazda. Driving through town toward Taylor House, he considered what Knowles had said, or rather, what the doctor had left out. He appreciated his ironic remark that a diagnosis of hepatitis would be "lucky." Because if they were looking at a central nervous system disease like encephalitis...they might be looking at an epidemic.

Again he felt a wave of fatigue wash over him. It was a familiar sensation, this time of night. Jake was used to the state of almost perpetual motion that being a doctor with more than one practice and a research project created. It was these moments when you slowed down that you felt the weight of it; as long as you kept moving and didn't think about it, the energy was there.

Tonight in particular, there had been the added excitement of rushing home for dinner with Max. That made all the grueling efforts of the day worthwhile, seeing him at the dinner table when he came in. The kid was tough, too, as defensive and wary as he'd always been with his father. But Jake could see through it. He knew Max was happy to be taking this adventurous vacation.

He'd barely had time to put the boy to bed and give So-phee a little lecture on housecleaning before racing west to Greensdale. Sophee's days might be numbered. Though the prospect of replacing her was daunting, she wasn't what he'd had in mind. Jake yawned. He'd been tempted to slip right under the covers with Max. But as he approached the turnoff to the Taylors' driveway, he felt as keyed-up as ever, and he knew why.

He'd been secretly looking forward to this moment all day long, using the prospect of seeing Lydia again as a magical carrot at the end of a long day's work. The mere thought of her smiling face brought a smile to his lips, but that smile immediately twisted downward again as he parked and cut the motor.

What was the point? He was foolish to let himself get swept up in these feelings. She'd be gone before he knew it, and he already suspected that her absence might leave a gap in his life. Her presence here was tapping into a part of him he'd managed to shut down for the longest time. Maybe that was a good thing.

But then what was he going to do when Max was gone, when he'd be alone again as usual—when he didn't have Lydia Taylor to look forward to at the end of a day?

Shaking his head, Jake trudged up the steps to the porch. He listened to the old-fashioned chimes ring after he pressed the doorbell, gazing around at the comfortable wooden porch with its inviting rocker at one end. He liked every-thing about the house, and could readily understand why the two sisters had been so hell-bent on keeping it alive and well.

He hadn't heard her approach, so when the door opened suddenly, filling the porch with warm light, he stepped back, startled. Lydia was framed in the doorway, looking as lovely as some image from a dream. Her long blond hair was piled on her head, soft coils kept in place by an Oriental-looking beret, a few damp curls falling over her forehead and fram-ing her flushed cheeks. Her light caramel-colored skin seemed dark beneath the thick white terry cloth robe she wore.

He drank in every detail; the feet encased in some incongruously childish slippers, the hands playing nervously with the belt of her robe, and the inviting warmth of her smile as she stepped back to let him in. For a moment he luxuriated in the fantasy that it *was* a dream, that this vision of loveliness was his to cherish. He found himself smiling dumbly back, and it was only when he saw her shiver slightly from the cold night air that he came to his senses and hurried inside.

"I was just in the shower," she said, pulling the collar of her robe closer. "You look tired, Jake. Are you hungry? We've got some great potato-leek soup on the stove."

He was trying to stop smiling, enjoying every bit of this, her self-consciousness that had no coquettishness about it, her homey air of concern for him. But the smile wouldn't fade. "Come to think of it, I only had a quick bite for dinner," he said.

"Oh, so the dedicated doctor doesn't eat?" She frowned. "If *you* get sick, I'll never forgive you," she said, shaking a finger at him in mock admonishment. "Come on, this way to the kitchen."

He paused, gazing up the staircase. "I should check on Katherine first," he said. "Before it gets too late."

"You're right," Lydia said. "Peter's with her now. You go on up and I'll have your soup ready for you when you're done." She favored him with another dazzling little smile and then turned, heading for the kitchen. Jake couldn't resist watching her receding form. A couple of things occurred to him. One, that terry cloth robes had obviously been invented for figures like hers, and two, that the reason her hair had an Oriental look about it was that she was keeping it up with a pair of chopsticks.

As Lydia turned the corner she glanced back over her shoulder. In the split second of eye contact she seemed to acknowledge that she'd known he was watching her and that she was pleased he was. Jake lifted one hand in an awkward half wave. Then she was gone and he started up the stairs, feeling as though he was back in college again—or was it high school?

His thoughts of doom and gloom in the car had evaporated in a kind of light-headed giddiness that was only partially due to overwork. What was it Larry had said about living for the present moment? He had a point. Smiling to himself now, Jake walked down the hall to Katherine's bedroom, surprised and relieved to hear laughter from within. He knocked on the half-open door.

"Come in!" Peter Bradford rose from the bed as Jake entered. He was wearing a flannel shirt and the kind of jeans Jake recognized as any man's favorite, full of holes and rips and really not fit to wear, but absolutely irreplaceable. With his unkempt hair and easy smile, he didn't resemble any of the attorneys you saw on TV, but Jake understood he was a formidable man when he was on the job.

"Doctor, I hate to disappoint you, but I'm feeling nearly human again," Katherine said, smiling, as Peter and Jake shook hands. In a brightly colored calico nightgown she was propped up against her pillows in the big four-poster, and Jake could see that there was a lot more color in her cheeks.

"Yeah, and now I've got a runny nose," Peter said ruefully. "I knew this would happen."

"Temperature?" Jake asked him.

"Just a clogged head," Peter answered.

"Couldn't keep away from her, eh?" Jake joked. "Well, that's what you get for being a dutiful husband."

"That's not all I get," he said, smiling at Katherine, who lifted a pillow to throw at him, then relented.

"I've been complaining to him," she told Jake.

"Still got the headaches?"

"No, actually, I've got a different kind of headache. What do you prescribe for a wayward daughter?"

"She's not wayward," Peter said with a sigh. "I've just been reminding my wife that when she was Clarissa's age, she'd already gotten into more than her share of trouble."

"Let's spare the good doctor the sordid details of our domestic life, shall we?" Katherine said sweetly. "Maybe you'd like to see if the nine-hundredth pot of tea might be brewed below. Jacob wants to examine me."

"Take a good look at her head," Peter said. "If you figure out how it works, draw me a diagram, all right?"

"Out!" Katherine commanded. Peter winked at Jake and went to the door. "If Clarissa calls again, don't you talk to her, you'll say all the wrong things. *I'll* talk to her."

"Yes, your mother-ness." Peter closed the door behind him.

Jake set down his bag at the foot of the bed. "Well, I don't need a stethoscope to tell you're feeling a lot better," he said.

"I'm on the road to recovery," Katherine announced. "Oh, don't be so formal. Sit." She patted the bed next to her, and began undoing the top of her nightgown. "What's the story on Carrie Lane?"

"She's stable," Jake told her, taking out the tools of his trade. "We still don't know exactly what she's got...or even if it's the same thing you've had," he admitted. "The symptoms are a little different."

"What is going on here?" Katherine shook her head. "Can you believe this?" She was staring over his shoulder as if addressing some unseen personage. She met his questioning gaze and laughed. "Just talking to my mother," she said. "It's her house, and I'm sure she's as upset as we are."

Hallucinations had not been one of the symptoms that he could remember, but Jake just let this pass, gently feeling the sides of Katherine's throat. "Well, we'll know more tomorrow," he said. "Look up," he added, shining a light in her left eye.

"Lydia had a wonderful time the other night," Katherine said. The abruptness of this non sequitur threw him momentarily, but he held the light steady and kept his voice noncommittal.

"I'm glad."

"I didn't realize you two knew each other," Katherine continued. "Small world, huh?"

"It is."

"Going to see more of each other?"

Jake straightened up. "You're looking healthier," he said. "When did you take your temperature last?"

"An hour or so ago. 99.8. You didn't answer my question."

"Say 'ah.'" Katherine narrowed her eyes at him and then stuck out her tongue. Jake smiled, applying his compressor. "Not bad." He removed it.

"I take it you think I'm being nosey," Katherine said.

"No, not really."

"Call it an older sibling's prerogative. I've just noticed that she likes having you around, that's all."

Jake met Katherine's level gaze. "I'm glad," he said honestly. "I like Lydia."

"I worry about her," Katherine said. "She doesn't have enough fun in her life, I don't think." Jake didn't know what to say. He closed his bag, nodding absently. "And you know what? I'd hazard a guess the same goes for you, Dr. Harrison."

Jake looked up. "Why do you say that?"

"Your brow's furrowed," she said. "You're going to get one of those permanent creases in it if you're not careful. Jacob, you're too young to have worry lines in your forehead."

Jake cleared his throat. "I appreciate your concern," he said, and smiled. "Now, are you done with your examination?"

Katherine laughed. "I guess. And my prescription is, you ought to take my sister out to dinner again—if the idea appeals to you, of course. It does, doesn't it?"

"It does," he said quietly, and stood up. "As for you, it's the same stuff you've been doing—the liquids and the bed rest. Just because your fever's down and your throat's in better shape, don't go running around the house. Understand?"

"Yes, sir." Katherine demurely tied the top of her nightgown. "When's my term of imprisonment up?"

"When you've had a normal temperature for forty-eight hours," Jake said. "We're not taking any chances. Okay?"

"Okay," Katherine echoed. "Do you think you could take a look at my husband when you go downstairs? It might just be a common cold, but . . . I wouldn't want him going through what I've been through." Jake nodded. "Thanks a lot."

"Get some more rest," he said, at the door.

"Get some more fun," she said.

Jake smiled and left the room. As he headed slowly down the stairs he found himself feeling his own forehead. Was he really frowning that much? Katherine might've been just teasing, playing matchmaker. But she wasn't far wrong, he knew. He'd been so immersed in work for the past three years that "fun" had ceased to be a focus.

He followed the sound of Peter and Lydia's voices when he reached the end of the downstairs hall and turned left, moving through the pantry area and into the kitchen. He glimpsed the white of Lydia's robe through the kitchen doorway and continued on into what was clearly the main playroom of the Taylor House Day-care Center.

Peter was on his knees in the fireplace, his upper torso obscured by the brick. Lydia turned to greet Jake as he walked in, stepping carefully past a mound of toy robots and some inflated globe balls that rolled away from his feet.

"This is useless," Peter called, his voice muffled from within the hearth. "It won't give."

"I had this bright idea to make the first fire of the season," Lydia explained. "But we can't get the flue open. Here, have a seat."

She indicated a chair by a child-sized desk, where a bowl of soup, spoon and cloth napkin had been set out for him. "Thanks," Jake said. He sat, inhaled the delicious aroma from the simmering soup, which was thick with potatoes and leeks, and dug in, suddenly aware that he was famished. He'd spent most of his dinner hour talking with his son, not eating. When he looked up a few gulps later he saw that Lydia was watching with an air of expectation.

"You like?"

"Fantastic," he said, mouth still full.

She smiled. "One of Grammy's recipes," she said, adding with a trace of pride, "my first attempt."

Peter was scrambling out of the hearth, wincing as he held his head. "Little tight in there," he muttered.

"You're smudged," Lydia said, wiping at his forehead with her thumb.

"I'm dizzy," he said, sitting on a stool and holding his head for a moment. Lydia looked over at Jake, concerned. Jake managed to wolf down another spoonful of what tasted like the most excellent soup he could remember eating before he rose, dabbing at his mouth with a napkin.

"Got a fever, Peter?"

Peter shook his head. "No, like I said, just your garden variety head cold." He sneezed, as if to demonstrate. Lydia handed him a Kleenex. "Thanks."

Jake took a good look at him and felt his neck and forehead. "You don't feel warm. But look, considering the circumstances, why don't you hit the sack early tonight? Take a couple of aspirin with some juice."

"And some of my vitamin Cs," Lydia offered.

"You guys," Peter said, shaking his head. "I don't get sick."

"Neither does your wife, usually," Jake reminded him.

"A little coddling wouldn't hurt you," Lydia chimed in. "Come on, I'm going to fix you a cup of tea and get you into bed."

"I'm a married man," Peter said, then chuckled as Lydia took a swat at him. "Okay, okay, I'm going."

"And you finish your soup," Lydia instructed Jake.

"They're bossy, these Taylor women," Peter told Jake, as he let Lydia push him along the thick carpet. "See you later."

"Call me if you get a temperature," Jake said. He watched Lydia march her brother-in-law out of the room, then returned to his soup, which was now the right temperature for rapid eating without scalding his tongue. The house suddenly seemed quiet except for the ticking of a grandfather clock in the far corner and the rustle of trees in the wind scraping the shutters outside.

Temporarily sated, Jake eyed the fireplace and the pile of firewood stacked at its side, newspaper and kindling readied. Lydia was right, a fire would be just the thing for a night like this. He got up, determined to work that flue open.

Crouched inside the hearth, he could see why Peter had had a hard time. There wasn't much room to maneuver, and the flue catch was stubborn. Using a piece of kindling wood he jabbed at the rusted metal edge of the thing, aware that he was getting himself a head full of soot but too caught up in the challenge to care.

It took a good amount of patience and brute force, but at last, with one final push, he got the catch to give, losing his balance in the process. His head hit brick, his elbow, too. He heard a rip of cloth and felt his ears ring as he sprawled across the hearth, the wind now whistling loudly overhead.

"Good grief, Jake!" Lydia was hurrying over to the fireplace, reaching out to help him up. When she saw his face she burst into a peal of laughter. "Oh, dear...you look like a coal miner."

"Great," he muttered, dusting his hands on his pants and stopping in mid-dust as he saw the grimy imprint he was leaving.

"It's all over your...everything," she said, unable to keep another helpless giggle from bubbling out.

"Well, at least you'll get your fire," he said grimly, gathering up some newspaper.

"No, let me, you go wash up."

"That's all right." He waved her off, determined to build a good working fire in the way he knew best. Lydia hovered around as he put the balled-up wads of newspaper beneath the old iron grillwork, topping it with kindling.

"Oh, Jake..." Lydia clucked her tongue. "You've really done a number on yourself. You can't go around in those clothes.... Look, why don't you take a quick shower? I'll get a clean shirt of Peter's for you to wear, okay?"

Jake shrugged, intent on placing the first logs just right. Actually, a shower sounded good, especially as his forearms were streaked with grime and his hair was full of soot. Wood in place, he backed away from the hearth, satisfied with his handiwork.

"Matches?"

Lydia handed him the box of blue-tips. Jake struck one on the brick, and lit the kindling in the back corners, then the front. In moments, the fireplace was ablaze. Jake slapped the wood chip dust from his hands. "There you go," he announced.

When he turned to look at Lydia, her eyes were dancing in the firelight. She was smiling, her face glowing as a child's might for a moment with the purest pleasure. He was struck by how beautiful she looked, and in that moment, she caught his eye, catching him in the act of watching her with undisguised delight.

Impulsively, Lydia darted forward to brush his lips with hers, so lightly and swiftly that for a moment he thought he might have imagined it. But from the tingle on his lips and the warmth that seemed to surge through him, he knew it had been real.

"Come on, Dr. Chimney Sweep," she said. "We'll run you a shower." She turned quickly, motioning him to follow. Jake didn't even think to protest. At this particular moment he would have followed her anywhere.

Chapter Five

It was a hot cocoa kind of night, with the fire in the fireplace and the intimation of snow in the air, and if she'd been planning to spend the rest of the evening settling in with a good book, cocoa would've been just the thing. But Jake Harrison was bound to be more stimulating than a book. The situation called for something a little more sophisticated.

So while he was upstairs showering, Lydia searched the many cupboards of Grammy's kitchen for that bottle of brandy she could've sworn she'd seen on her last visit. She found it in the back of the bottom shelves below the counters that had served years ago as Father's liquor cabinet.

Lydia broke the seal, certain this was just the right occasion for putting the brandy to good use, and took out the two snifters still remaining from the great Taylor House yard sale. She and Katherine had seen to it that two of every set of kitchen items remained, Noah's ark style, in the family.

Back in the main room, which was formerly the living room, she set down the brandy and snifters on the hearthstone, and picked out a couple of the brightly colored pillows from the pile in one corner. Seated comfortably by the crackling blaze, she took a sip of brandy and awaited Jake's return. A warm surge of creature comfort flowed through her, laced with a tingle of anticipation.

It occurred to her suddenly that she was feeling very happy. For this particular moment, at least, basking in the fire's heat as she looked forward to Jake joining her there, all seemed right with the world. She felt as if the whole day, with its alarming trauma of the twins getting sick and the absolute chaos that had reigned in the store on Sellars Street, had been a trial she'd willingly gone through to arrive precisely here.

What was it about this evening here that was so satisfying? She listened to the sounds from upstairs, able to surmise that Jake was out of his shower and most probably trying on Peter's green corduroy shirt. She hoped it fitted. Lydia smiled at herself, both amused and a little disturbed by her behavior thus far. What she liked about this evening was the role she'd fallen into playing, that was it; she was being, for want of a better word, domestic.

Her feeling of enjoyment at having "a man in the house" and of pleasure in taking care of him, was silly, she knew, and entirely reactionary. But she lived the role of independent career woman well and long enough to be able to appreciate the attractions of more traditional roles. Every now and then it was fun to feel a little, well ... wifely.

Lydia put down the brandy snifter, shaking her head. Where had *that* thought come from? She certainly didn't have any vision of a cozy domestic life with Jake Harrison. *No,* it was just an idle moment's fantasy on a cold November night. What she was being was friendly, that was all.

She could hear Jake's footsteps on the stairs. Lydia was conscious of her heartbeat quickening as she listened to him approach. Friendship, that was the idea, she reminded herself. Jake was still toweling off his hair as his bare feet moved across the carpet. Peter's corduroy shirt fitted him just fine, she saw, though he was wearing it untucked and with the sleeves rolled up. He'd neglected to button it all the way, too, revealing a manly thatch of curly dark hair on his chest that still glistened slightly with drops of water.

Lydia did her best to affect nonchalance as he smiled at her, towel draped around his shoulders, then sat down on the pillow next to her. Much as she wanted to ignore the sensation, she could feel her whole body tremble slightly at the nearness of him. Maybe this friendship concept was a bit naive.

"Lydia, you've read my mind." He was indicating the brandy bottle. "I'm not much of a drinker, usually, but after the long day I've had, this is perfect." He accepted the snifter she offered him with a nod of thanks, and raised it. "To working fireplaces," he said, and their glasses clinked.

"To men with the necessary brawn and bravery," she added, smiling. "Feeling clean and refreshed?"

"Exactly," he said, smoothing down his unkempt damp hair. "You know, Peter did all the hard work. I just gave the flue one more good whack, that's all."

"You built a good fire," she said, turning to gaze into it again. "Boy Scout training?"

Jake chuckled. "No, but we had a fireplace in our house, where we grew up."

Lydia remembered vaguely from their long-ago talks that Jake had a number of stepbrothers from his mother's remarriage after he'd left home. The fact that both he and Lydia had lost their fathers at a fairly early age had been something they'd had in common, and had bred a sympathetic understanding. "Is your family still in Great Oaks?"

He nodded, taking another sip of brandy. "Sure, my mom runs a little bookstore there, and my youngest brother teaches at the public school. I guess I've never strayed all that far from my roots. Unlike some," he added pointedly.

"Well, I'm still in touch with mine, as you can see," she said. "But I've just gotten so used to the West Coast lifestyle, especially the weather, that being here for more than a visit seems strange to me by now."

There, she was doing admirably, considering how she still felt an unnerving excitement tingling through her system as his hand brushed her arm, reaching past her for a piece of kindling. Here they were, chatting about the weather, and if she kept it up, she'd probably be able to forget about the pleasure his embrace had given her the other night, and the kind of longings his kisses had awakened in her. She'd stick to her original plan to keep the man at bay. That way she could get out of this little interlude with her emotional stability intact.

Jake poked at the bottom log with his stick, seemingly quite at ease. "Weather isn't everything," he said. "Besides, isn't it always the same out there? Sunshine for days on end would bore me silly. I like these cold New England winters."

"The Bay Area has seasons!" Lydia exclaimed, immediately defensive. "We get everything, hot, cold, rain and shine. You're thinking of Southern California. That's where it's mostly the same dry heat." Speaking of which, her hair was definitely dry by now. She undid the twists in it, removing the sticks, and shook the long tresses loose.

When she swept the hair back out of her face, she saw Jake watching her with an expression on his face that she couldn't quite decipher. "What?" she asked.

"Nothing," he said, glancing away again. "So, how are things at the Pet Sanctuary East?"

"It's far from being a sanctuary," she said dryly. "This job may take a lot longer than I'd anticipated."

"I'm glad," he said. "I mean," he added, looking slightly sheepish as she stared at him, surprised, "I'm glad you're not running right back to the Coast. After all, we've barely filled in the gaps here. I want to hear more details about the woman you've turned into, Lydie."

"Oh, there's not that much to tell," she said, taking her hairbrush out of her robe pocket. "I'm sure your life's been more interesting than mine."

"Hardly," he scoffed. "We're talking about years of study followed by years of study. And then work that pretty much consumes all my waking hours. Does that sound exciting to you?"

"It must be," she mused, running the brush through her hair, "if you're that dedicated. Tell me again about which area of research . . . ?"

"Bacteriology," he said. "I'm working with a team of infectious-disease specialists who are in the process of, well, to put it plainly, finding more effective ways of combating the current crop of illnesses."

"Sounds heroic," she said.

He laughed. "Not really. It's a lot of endless sifting of data, analyzing test results—if I described any of the specifics it would put you to sleep."

"Running a pet shop isn't the most scintillating way to pass the time," she said wryly. "But I guess while you're trying to better humanity, I'm doing my bit for the animal kingdom. What else is there to say about it?"

"Actually, the kind of details I'm interested in don't really have to do with your livelihood," he said quietly, turning to watch her brush her hair, his eyes following each stroke.

"What, then?"

"I was wondering why you hadn't married."

Lydia's hand stopped in midstroke. "Ah," she said. "I thought we'd deftly avoided that whole topic the other night, for whatever personal reasons."

"I hope I didn't seem rude."

"No, more like mysterious."

Jake shrugged, gently rocking the brandy snifter in his hand. She sensed him editing again, weighing carefully what he had to say. "I didn't mean to be. I just had a bad experience, that's all. Since I was in the middle of having a good time with you, I didn't feel like going into it." He smiled. "Doesn't mean I can't still be curious about you."

Once again he was being evasive, but she let it pass. "Well, all right, I don't have any big mysteries," she said. "I'll give you the bare bones. About four years ago, I got involved with a man named James, who ran a sporting goods store in Berkeley. We lived together for a long time before we found out we didn't really want the same things." Now it was her turn to edit. She'd really left out the important things: James's initial reluctance to have children, how her unplanned pregnancy had upset him . . . how her tragic miscarriage had set them apart. "We split up, and I've kept busy since."

"That's bare bones indeed," he said. "Mind if I ask a question?"

"Sure, I can handle one," she said breezily.

"What was it you wanted?"

This one required some thought. Lydia traded her hairbrush for her brandy glass. "I guess I wanted the best of both lives," she said carefully. "I wanted a committed relationship with a real intimacy at its core...and I also wanted to be able to go off and run my business. I wanted us to live together—and have my own space."

"And he?"

"He made all the right gestures toward a kind of interindependence," she said. "But ultimately what he wanted was a stay-at-home wife. And family," she added, more to herself, and steeled herself against the inner chill she always felt when she thought about that particular issue. "But that wasn't in the cards," she said, hoping he wouldn't be too inquisitive.

"I see," he said, and she breathed a quiet sigh of relief. Thinking about it now, the irony struck her anew. To have hemmed and hawed, agonized and debated over whether or not she was ready to take on having a baby—and then, when she'd begun to embrace the idea and started to get truly excited about it, to have that choice snatched away from her...

Lydia took another sip of brandy, and let the velvet warmth slowly soothe her system, eyes half closed. *Tell him? Hear more words of sympathy, or worse, see a change in his expression that she didn't want to see?* She'd seen it before, a kind of tiny door closing in the eyes of interested men. She wasn't up for a repetition of that, not now, not with Jake.

"I couldn't do it at that point," she said. There, that was simple and ambiguous enough. End of story. "But don't get me wrong," she went on. "Given the right circumstances..." She thought of Dr. Newcomb's cheery optimism, and clung to that image. "I'd like to have a child someday."

"You want to 'have it all,' as it's called."

She smiled ruefully. *Certainly,* given a medical miracle and the sudden appearance of a shining-armored knight who wouldn't walk away as James had. "Given the right circumstances, as you say, I guess I'd want it all—the career and the family."

"A real eighties' woman," he said.

"I suppose. But who knows? My career, such as it is, is in fine shape now. It doesn't need as much attention as it used to. I might even sacrifice a little independence, if I could have a child," she said. *Careful.* Perhaps it was time to change the subject.

"So that is what you'd ultimately want," he persisted. "Someone to have a family with."

"Ultimately," she said uneasily. "I suppose so." Why was Jake so curious, anyway? He was looking at her with a peculiar expression, as if he'd been both pleased and disappointed by what she'd told him. "What about you?" she asked.

"You mean, children?" She nodded. Jake rose to lift a log from the pile. "I don't think I'm an ideal dad," he said soberly.

"No? Why?"

Jake frowned, carefully dropping the log into place and then stepping back as some sparks flew. "I haven't figured out how to be there for someone, really be there," he said, and she was struck by the seriousness in his tone. When he turned to look at her, his expression was deeply troubled. She'd touched that nerve again. Lydia immediately felt guilty about pursuing subjects that were obviously painful for them both.

"That's hard to do," she said quietly. "And you must give a lot of yourself to so many people. Your patients..."

"Who's more important?" he asked, then shook his head. Jake brushed his hands off against his thighs. "The woman I was married to didn't like having a husband who wasn't there. Can't blame her," he said, more to himself, and then his eyes met Lydia's.

She saw the sorrow there, a look she'd glimpsed that first night. She recognized it and wondered about the specifics of what he'd suffered through, the details he chose not to dwell on as she chose not to dwell on hers.

But then the look was gone, and he was smiling, holding up the bottle of brandy. "That was then, and this is now," he said. "Refill?"

"Just a touch."

Jake poured, the amber liquid seeming to blaze with the firelight dancing behind it. "I should probably be on my way," he said. "But I'm much too comfortable to move."

"No one's rushing you out into the cold," she said.

"I'm glad." He smiled at her again, and she smiled back, feeling more than the warmth of brandy and fire inside her. As his eyes held hers, she was aware of the house's silence, and the rustling of wind-tossed branches against the roof made her feel all the more warmed and secure. It was as if they were the only ones awake for miles around, safe and sound here, surrounded by darkness.

The way he looked at her—it gave her an unusual feeling that was at the same time oddly natural, as if she was re-learning something she'd known a long time ago. As Jake's hand stole out to smooth a long curl of hair from her cheek, she knew what that feeling was. It was the experience of being womanly, feeling admired and sexy, not as an object or casual plaything, but as herself. He was somehow admiring her inner self, the self she rarely showed.

She realized then that they'd been silent for some time. There was an invitation in the smoky depths of his eyes that was unmistakable. This time she didn't force herself to turn away. "What are you thinking?" he asked softly.

"I'm thinking...I don't know quite what we're doing, you and I," she said truthfully.

"That makes two of us," he said. "Is that a bad thing?"

She shook her head, their gazes still locked. Another log gave a sudden pop and crackle. Only as a spark shot from the hearth, landing too near her robe's hem, did he look down, his hand brushing the material just below her knee.

Lydia shivered slightly at the casual contact. Jake sat back again slowly, staring into her eyes once more.

"I'm having a little trouble not looking at you," he confessed with an apologetic air. "You mind?"

"I can handle it so far," she said. His hand reached out again to gently stroke her cheek, fingers tenderly playing with a wisp of hair around her ear. Lydia could feel the simmering pleasure that had been subtly exciting her all evening deepen at his touch. Instinctively she wet her lips with her tongue, the warmth from his fingers' caress fanning the flame that seemed to flicker within her until it burned as brightly as the fire beside them.

The feeling swelling up in her was impossible to ignore any longer. As he watched her, he seemed to be waiting for a sign or a signal. Did he know she wanted him and was tired of denying it? All of her playful plans for keeping Jake at arm's length looked like so much childishness just now.

His fingertips were feather-light, tracing the line of her chin, and the incandescent glow of his watchful eyes held her still, even as she thought to move away. Her hand stole out to arrest his, as the delicate touch of his fingers on the soft skin of her neck provoked another shiver. But instead of pushing his hand away, she found herself, mesmerized, slowly pulling the palm downward, so that his fingers traced the line of her neck and paused finally at the pulse near its base.

His eyes still held a question as he faced her expectantly in the firelight. Her eyes must have given him the answer, or maybe it was her pulse beating so strongly beneath his fingertips, because without another word his lips dipped to meet hers.

For a moment she was aware of nothing but the wonderful feel of his warm lips against hers as she yielded, unquestioning, to their exquisite touch. Then, as the heady soft pressure increased, her senses took in more of the moment.

The scent and taste of him were intoxicating as his tongue sought hers with the gentlest of caresses. The smoky air, the silence that seemed to throb around them, the feel of his

corduroy sleeve against her skin, all was wonderfully vivid
as she gave herself over to their deepening kiss. His hands
cradling her face were amazingly soft. Their tongues
touched, tentatively at first, then slowly tangling in a playful, languid dance.

His arms were around her now, and as he gathered her to
him the sudden surge of desire was bewildering. But through
the haze of shimmering pleasure she realized that it had been
there all day, ever since the other night, really, when one kiss
had seemed to melt so many years away. It was so familiar,
so comforting, yet so new—and even a little dangerous.

His lips left hers as he hugged her to him, her head sliding naturally into the crook of his shoulder as his arms en-
circled her. She was grateful for the breather, staring at the
blurred fire until it sharpened into focus and she caught her
breath.

"This is almost too good to be true," he said, his voice
husky. "Being able to hold you again like this."

She murmured an inarticulate sound of agreement, shifting her body so that she could lean back against him, cradled half in his lap, legs stretched out toward the fire, her
head nestled against his neck. His arms covered her arms,
his hands slowly caressing hers as they both gazed at the fire
in silence.

If she could freeze this moment, not having to concern
herself with either past or present, it would probably approach perfection, Lydia thought. None of their lives' various complications would exist if one could stop time.

"I could sit like this forever," he said.

"Me, too," she murmured.

"But I'd probably fall asleep."

She turned toward him, indignant. "Really? Bored already?"

"Hardly," he said, smiling, one hand stealing up to cap-
ture her chin again. "But you have to understand, I've been
on my feet since seven-thirty this morning."

She looked up into his eyes, hesitating. She wondered if
this expression of fatigue was calculated. Even if it wasn't,

it seemed perfectly natural to extend an invitation. Why couldn't he stay the night? Didn't she want him to?

"Well, if you're truly exhausted . . ." she began.

"Another kiss would revive me," he interrupted gently. He'd misunderstood, and she wanted to complete her sentence. But she couldn't, not while he was touching her, not while his eyes loomed before her so brightly and his lips seemed so sinfully inviting. So instead, she let him guide her forward into another taste of heaven.

Her eyes closed as his lips found hers and a glowing deep red light filled the darkness. It was the fire, she knew, its warmth caressing her upturned face. But the heat that swelled and coursed through her veins was brought on by these strong arms enfolding her, these bewitching lips that coaxed her own into parting.

It felt as if she'd always needed this, the exquisite pleasure she felt when their tongues touched, when the soft curves of her body molded to his. The firm strength of his body beneath hers felt like a natural fit. She luxuriated in the feel of him, stretching with feline grace against him.

She returned the kiss with a breathless fervor, one of her arms gliding up to encircle his neck, fingers restlessly playing with his soft, thick hair. Jake's lips left hers to kiss a soft moist trail down the arch of her neck as he leaned back, and a soft moan of pleasure escaped her.

She was aware more than ever of her nudity beneath the robe. Only the merest slips of clothing lay between them and it would take only moments to have no barriers at all. Even now his arm was beneath her breasts, nudging the folds of her robe up and open slightly as his lips softly nuzzled the sensitive spot between neck and shoulder.

His hand shifted, ever so lightly grazing the swell of one breast under the terry cloth. She could feel its tip already swelling with the anticipation of those supple fingertips' stroke. If he parted the robe and slipped his hand beneath, she knew he'd touch her there with the surest, most satisfyingly knowing of caresses, a caress she ached to feel.

The depth of her longing was a little scary. And no sooner did she give in to the uneasiness than her demons appeared as if on cue.

Lydia had fallen into the habit of actually visualizing Fear and Anxiety. The former was a thin, pasty-faced wide-eyed gremlin with horns and the latter a fatter, grubby one, its lips chapped from perennial biting. Fear was seated at Jake's feet, trembling as it stared up at her, ready to bolt.

What are you, nuts? said Fear. *The guy just got finished telling you about how he can't Be There for anyone! Why do you want to get any closer to him?*

Anxiety was perched on the mantelpiece, nibbling at its nails. *It'll be worse than last time,* it hissed. *You'll get all wrought up over him and then you'll have to go back home and your heart won't ever recover!*

Lydia closed her eyes and bade the demons depart. But their messages were in her now, and she involuntarily stiffened, moving away from Jake. Pride, not a demon but still an operative force, was reminding her that she was *supposed* to push Jake away. What had happened to her plan about getting even, anyway?

Jake's hand slipped to a more chaste position above her waist as she freed herself from his embrace, shifting her weight, sliding away so that she could turn and face him.

"Something wrong?" he asked.

"Well, it really is getting late," she said, sitting up.

He was trying to read her, she felt, as his eyes explored hers. "Too much, too soon?" he asked quietly.

Lydia nodded. "Maybe so," she said. "Jake..."

But before she could even formulate an apology, he was sitting up as well, forehead creasing in a frown. "No, it's okay. You're absolutely right," he said. "I should be on my way." He ran a hand through his hair, his eyes now looking everywhere but into hers.

Lydia gathered the collar of her robe, frustrated by her own emotions. But he was backing off without much protest, so maybe she'd made the right decision.

"I have to be up at the crack of dawn again," he said. "And I've got some driving to do before I sleep."

She could sense she was only hearing half the truth. She'd felt his desire for her only moments ago. She'd known that he wanted her the way she wanted him; it was something you could tell intuitively. Was he really just so burned out from overwork that even this kind of heady arousal couldn't keep him here?

"I understand," she told him quickly, both relieved and oddly upset that he was letting her off the hook.

Jake was getting to his feet. "I've got some shoes and socks around here somewhere...."

"Upstairs," she reminded him. Jake nodded. "I'll be right back."

Lydia watched him go, still unable to believe that once again, she and Jake Harrison had come so tantalizingly close to the fulfillment of physical intimacy, only to end up apart. Fate was playing a cruel game.

Or was she herself? She didn't think of herself as a tease. Still, some perverse imp within her had first let things get out of hand, then made her pull back at the crucial moment. No, it wasn't a game, she decided, it was self-preservation. She was afraid of giving in to him, of being that vulnerable again.

And maybe it was for the best, better for him, too, she rationalized. Maybe the man would be better off with a good night's sleep. He certainly did work hard enough. And she hadn't offered him a bed for the night, had she? She'd thought about it, but then, she'd thought she might end up sharing that bed with him....

JAKE STARED AT HIS SHOES, suddenly too confused to do something as simple as put one on. Why was he leaving? But then, how could he stay?

He thought about Max, and knew he had no choice. Then he thought, as he had so many times tonight, about explaining the whole situation to Lydia. Well, he'd have to, immediately, the next time they saw each other. He was already too uncomfortable with what was beginning to be a deception by omission.

But on the other hand, he selfishly just hadn't been able to bring himself to spoil what had been a nearly perfect evening. Talking about Max meant talking about losing the custody suit and why, and what had happened with Judith and the whole depressing mess. And being with Lydia, being so happy to do even the simplest of things with her, had effectively wiped away all those bad memories and the bad feelings that went with them, had wiped them clean out of his mind for the first time in a long, long while.

With Lydia tonight, he mused, finally putting his left shoe on and lacing it, he'd gotten back a bit of his old self-confidence. He'd started to feel like the Jake he'd been before, before the failure of his marriage. He'd been enjoying a clean-slate, new-beginning feeling. *Why chance ruining it by dredging up the past?* He'd tell her next time. He *wanted* to tell her, which in itself surprised him. It had been a long time since he'd opened himself up to a woman, but Lydia made him feel like opening up.

Yawning, he laced the other shoe. Thinking about the grueling day ahead made his spirits sag. *Harrison, you're crazy,* he thought, anxiety returning. *Why even involve Lydia in your complicated chaos of a life? How do you know the same thing won't happen again?*

Right now, Max, the child that had been taken away from him because of his "neglect," was asleep at home. Wouldn't he be doing the same thing all over again, if he let himself get involved with Lydia at this crucial point? It wouldn't be fair to her or to his son.

Jake rubbed his eyes. Sleep was what he needed, he thought grimly. He couldn't think straight, and there was much too much to think about. But one thing was certain: he was doing the right thing by leaving now. Only time—and hopefully a more clearheaded perspective in the morning—would tell if he should leave her alone for good.

JAKE WAS BACK, shirt still unbuttoned but socks and shoes on. Lydia downed the last of her brandy and stood, back to the fire, watching him finish dressing. She considered extending her invitation, after all, but some vestigial uneasiness kept her quiet. If the man was so intent on leaving, *then let him leave*.

He stood and crossed over to her. Lydia took a step back, but he reached for her hand before she could move away. "Listen," he said, his eyes troubled as they searched hers. "I'm sorry if I got . . . carried away. I didn't mean to upset you."

Here in the stronger light she could actually see how tired he did look, and how . . . unhappy. That was the only word that came to mind. Curious and at once concerned, she brought her other hand to hold his as he stood there.

"That's okay," she said. "You look completely beat. It's really all right."

"No, it's not all right," he said gruffly. "I shouldn't have let things . . ." He sighed, his frown deepening. "Lydia, I don't want to do what I did the first time, back when we were kids. I don't want to lead you on."

"We're both adults now, Jake," she said warily. "It's not quite the same situation."

"No, but some things are," he said. "I'm finding out that I care about you a lot. And I won't pretend that I'm not more attracted to you than ever. Which is why—" he shook his head "—it's probably best that you put a stop to things when you did."

He looked so disgruntled and upset that a thought suddenly occurred to her, one she hadn't contemplated before. "Is there someone else . . . that you're seeing now?"

He looked so absolutely startled that she nearly laughed. "Someone else? Only about three dozen patients and a whole lot of slide specimens, and . . ." He paused. "No, Lydia, but that is a point. I don't know how much I'll be able to see you while you're here."

"I wasn't expecting that you would be," she said, though even as the words were out of her mouth she realized that in fact, she'd begun to hope for exactly that. "I'm going to be incredibly caught up with the store and everything, as it is."

"So I guess we're both being...responsible," he said, with such a rueful tone that she had to smile.

"Terrible word, that," she said, nodding. As he smiled back at her, her feelings were still in total conflict. One part of her was appreciative of his gentlemanly self-control. Another part was bridling at his assumption that she was the one whose feelings might get hurt if their involvement were to be short-lived. *What about his feelings?* How removed was he?

His lips brushed her forehead and then his hand slipped from hers. He was already moving away, picking up his jacket from the chair nearby. Lydia was in danger of merely standing there, transfixed, all those conflicting feelings churning around in turmoil, so she moved to the pillows, gathering them, picking up the brandy glasses. Wordlessly she moved past him into the kitchen.

She heard Jake behind her, lingering at the doorway as she put the dishes into the sink. "I guess I can let myself out," he said. "Are you all right?"

"Sure," she said lightly, turning back to look at him. "Just a little confused. I guess it's like what you said before—what are we doing here?"

"I think we like each other's company," he said quietly.

"Well, then, maybe we're better off leaving it at that," she said, hoping she sounded convincing. She herself certainly wasn't convinced of the idea.

He looked at her, his expression indicating that he might have a lot more to say, and crossed the room to join her at the sink. She turned her attention to the glasses, running the tap water, but he turned off the faucet, his hand gently but firmly taking hold of her shoulder, forcing her to look at him again.

"You're a good woman," he said softly. "Someone's going to love you right and give you everything you deserve to get—which is more than a weekend's fling."

What made him so positive he could never be that some-one? she wondered. "You've got a disposition that borders on saintly," he went on. "You also make the best potato leek soup I've ever tasted in my life. If I had any sense I'd drop everything and follow you back to San Francisco."

Lydia couldn't help smiling. "You mean, this is a case of soup versus slide samples?"

"Something like that," he said. "Thanks for the brandy, Lydia."

"Thanks for the fire," she returned, and his smile indi-cated he'd read a double meaning into her words.

"Took two to get it going," he murmured, and bestowed the lightest of kisses on her upturned cheek. "Call me with all and any news reports. I'll give you a ring from the hos-pital when we've had a chance to see what's going on with Carrie Lane."

"No problem," Lydia told him.

NO PROBLEM?

She spent the following morning wandering about Tay-lor House in a fog, having spent most of the night tossing and turning until she'd practically fallen out of bed. She didn't know how many hours of sleep she'd managed to get, but it wasn't only being deprived of rapid-eye-movement dream cycles that was wreaking havoc with her emotional stability.

Try as she might, as she helped Emily supervise the morning's day-care activities, she couldn't keep from re-playing every significant moment of last night's encounter in her mind. Finally being the one to put on the brakes, to say no and back off—that was supposed to have given her great satisfaction. Instead, she was alternately irritated and touched by Jake's apparent acceptance of what she'd done.

The question, What sort of a woman did he think she was? formed a double-edged metaphysical sword. If he re-spected her too much to sleep with her "casually," that was flattering in one way, also sensitive and perceptive. In truth, she never had been able to "casually" sleep with anyone; in

Lydia's moral vocabulary, the two words just didn't go together. She had to know someone and really care about him before she'd consider venturing further, and in her experience, that had always taken a lot of knowing and caring.

On the other hand, it would've been more flattering, more satisfying, if he hadn't wanted to take her no for an answer. The idea of Jake Harrison being so beside himself with desire for her that he wanted to possess her, *morals be damned,* was pretty attractive in its own way. *Never satisfied,* she mused.

"This is the, ah, fuselage holder. Lydia? See?"

Lydia looked down at the brightly colored plastic form George was thrusting under her nose. She was watching four of the children build an elaborate structure out of interlocking plastic sticks in the smaller playroom. According to George, whose thick glasses gave him the appearance of a mini mad scientist, they were creating a launching pad for the first Taylor House rocket to the moon.

"Very nice," she said absently.

"Lydia? Phone call." Tucker was in the doorway, just long enough for Lydia to acknowledge that she'd heard her over the general din of the children at play.

"Sadie, I'm stepping out for a moment," she called, and the other woman nodded from where she sat, surrounded by children fastidiously creating junior masterpieces at easels in the other corner of the room. Lydia stepped carefully around the rocket launch pad under construction and strode to the kitchen, where Tucker had left the phone receiver on the counter for her.

It was Albert, long-distance from the Pet Sanctuary, returning the call she'd put in earlier. Tucker was at the kitchen table, efficiently polishing a batch of Grammy's copper pots at a fast clip, as Lydia brought Albert up to date on the progress, or slowing of it, at the new store. "Think you can hold the fort for a while longer?"

"We're surviving," he said. "But the mood in Rabbit Row is definitely doom and gloom."

"Are they eating okay now?"

"Honey, they're voracious. Business is a little slow, so I sent Margaret home early yesterday...."

He rattled on, giving her enough detail to set her mind at ease about the state of Pet Sanctuary West. Lulled by the young woman's whirling hands, she watched Tucker scour an entire set of copper utensils in record time, and was suddenly surprised to hear Jake's name in her ear. "What do you mean, what happened?"

"You said you were going on a date with a handsome doctor," Albert reminded her.

"Oh. Well, there's not much to report."

"Come on, Lydie! Give us the dirt."

"There is no dirt," she said, turning away, conscious that Tucker could easily eavesdrop. "And it's just as well," she added.

"How can that be?"

"Albert." She sighed. "Trust me on this. You know me, right?"

"That's the problem," he said. "You're so wary of involvement, you could be turning down some wickedly wonderful opportunities."

Lydia had to laugh. Sometimes she wondered if God had decided that since she now lacked a real mother, she should be provided with Albert and Katherine to double up in the role for her. "You could be right," she admitted. "But, look, let's discuss my fear of commitment at a less expensive rate, okay? Like when I'm back home."

"Why not live dangerously for once?" he grumbled. "You're on vacation."

"Yes, Albert. Give my best to everyone there."

When she hung up, Tucker was still vigorously scrubbing away. Lydia lingered a moment by the phone, curious about this taciturn member of the household. But before she could think of a way to initiate a conversation, the phone rang again.

"I'll get it," she said, and picked it up once more.

"Lydia? Jake."

By the no-nonsense tone in his voice she sensed instantly that there was bad news on the way. "Hi. What's up?"

"What time does your morning session at Taylor House usually end?" he asked.

"Noon, I think. Why?"

"Now, this is just a precaution, so don't get alarmed. But I want you to send all the kids home then. Is that possible?"

Lydia looked at the kitchen clock. "That gives us only forty minutes to get hold of everybody," she said, thinking out loud. "But I guess we could give it a try. But why, Jake, what's going on?"

"I think we may have a contagious viral infection on our hands that could actually be originating from the house itself," he said. "From the initial test results, we're concerned about an outbreak of acute meningitis."

"Good Lord," she said weakly. "What do we—"

"Have Peter get on the line, will you? It might be best for all of you to move out of there temporarily, until we can be sure of what's going on."

"All right, I'll get him," she said. Her heart beating furiously, she cupped the receiver. "Tucker, could you ask Mr. Bradford to pick up the phone?"

Tucker nodded, rising from the table. "Any of the other kids feeling ill?" Jake asked.

"Not that we know of."

"And how are you?"

"Me?" Flustered, she shook her head. "I'm fine."

"Good," he said. "I'll be over there as soon as I can."

Chapter Six

"We need some extra chairs," Katherine said, as the door-bell rang again. "That should be Sadie." Dressed in pants and sweater, a robe over her shoulders, she'd been helping Lydia prepare the kitchen for their impromptu summit meeting.

"No, don't you go, I'll get some from the other room," Lydia said. "You really shouldn't be out of bed. When Jake gets here, he's going to—"

"Hush," Katherine said. "I've been 98.6 since I woke up and I've got about six layers of clothes on."

They both turned to the kitchen windows as Marsha Grimes walked by, with Sarah Fine, Tessie O'Byrne and two other children at her side, little puffs of breath showing in the air. A light snowfall having begun that morning, they were all buttoned up against the cold. Marsha waved, moving toward the driveway amid the flutter of snowflakes. She'd volunteered the use of her station wagon and herself as driver for the number of children who had to be dropped off with parents and other relatives in town.

"Have we gotten in touch with everybody?" Lydia asked.

"Nearly." Emily bustled in from the playroom, Barbara Wainright and Sadie in tow, the last two shaking snow from their hair. "Keith and David are getting picked up by David's aunt, Caroline and Joey go out in the last station wagon run, and that just leaves . . ."

"Tucker's," Katherine said, and the other women nodded.

"Tucker's what?" Lydia asked.

"Her baby," Emily said, turning off the light under the pot she had brewing on the stove, which was filling the kitchen with a piquant odor of strong coffee. "Didn't you know?" she added, in answer to Lydia's startled look. "That six-month-old fella in the last crib on the left in the nursery belongs to Tucker."

"Bart McCullum," Katherine said. "The dad's Rob McCullum, a local boy who's been commuting into Great Oaks to work at the new ConCo place."

"Oh, I see," Lydia said. Her mind was still adjusting to the idea that Tucker, whom she'd perceived as a sullen, asexual teenager, could already have mothered a child. But she didn't have time to dwell on this revelation.

"How many coffees, how many teas?" Katherine asked, as all the women assembled themselves at the kitchen table—Lydia, Katherine, Emily, Sadie and Barbara, with one prominent empty chair awaiting the arrival of Dr. Jacob Harrison. With everyone sipping their coffee or tea, nibbling at the batch of homemade oatmeal raisin cookies Lydia had prepared in an idle moment earlier in her stay, the gathering in the cozy kitchen would have seemed festive if it hadn't been for the concerned and preoccupied expressions of all in attendance.

"Jacob's late." Katherine cast an anxious glance at the clock.

"Dr. Harrison? Oh, he'll be along soon enough, I'd think," Sadie Travis. "Though not in the best of moods?"

"What do you mean?" asked Emily Atchins. "Sadie Travis, I know that tone of voice. What is it?"

"What's what?" Sadie said, all innocence.

"Whatever piece of gossip you're dying to tell us," Barbara said wryly, and the women laughed. Lydia didn't join in, looking curiously at Sadie. *Gossip?*

"Well, I was at the hospital, visiting the twins with Tammy Carter," Sadie said. "And I happened to catch sight of Dr. Harrison with a very pretty young lady. A little *too* young for a man his age, if you ask me," she added.

"Oh, Sadie," Barbara Wainright said.

"Anyway, it seemed to me like they were at the end of some very serious fight," she went on. "This poor young thing was in tears when she stormed out of that office, and by the looks of things I don't think she was planning to come back."

There were many raised eyebrows around the table. Lydia was transfixed, staring at Sadie, wondering if she could believe her ears. "Dr. Harrison didn't try to go after her, you see," Sadie was saying. "He just looked like a portrait of anger and frustration. A handsome portrait," she concluded, and there were chuckles from the other women. "But don't expect him to be jolly when he rolls in here, girls."

"Maybe you'd like a crack at him, Sadie," Barbara said.

Sadie took a mock swipe at her. The peals of laughter in the room dissipated the tension, except around Lydia. She and Jake hadn't really discussed much of each other's personal lives, and it was none of her business. But that didn't stop her feeling a jolt of searing jealousy at the thought of him involved with another woman.

Or was he? He'd said he wasn't seeing anyone. Was he telling the truth? Or had he just broken up with someone...and was that why he'd been so reticent to pursue her?

The laughter around her ended abruptly as a sneeze announced the arrival of Peter, a tall stool under his arm.

"Bless you," said Katherine, taking the stool from him.

"You should be in bed," he said, and rather gingerly applied a tissue to his reddened nose.

"You mean, you should," Katherine said.

Peter waved a hand at her and looked at Emily. "Did you make those phone calls?"

Emily nodded, turning to the others. "Now, of course I wasn't able to speak to members of every household in Greensdale," she said. "But the general consensus is as follows: we got your common colds, we got your standard first-flus-of-the-winter—which are mainly adults, by the way, and a couple of teenagers. But to the best of my limited knowledge, the only children who are seriously sick—"

"Define that," Peter interjected.

"Temperatures above 102, mean headaches that don't quit, some throwing up and the whole thing having come on kind of sudden, after a sore throat. The only kids who've got those symptoms are kids we know," she said, looking gravely around the table.

"You mean, children from Taylor House," Katherine said.

Sadie nodded. "Carrie Lane, the Carter twins, Roger Bartlett, Cynthia Maxwell. Oh, and maybe Kenny Todd."

"Kenny? He was fine this morning," Barbara protested, looking alarmed.

"Sore throat," Sadie said. "We thought Roger was faking, didn't we? Well, Kenny wasn't feeling too hot when his mom picked him up just now, so I told her to take him straight to see Dr. Wilbur. Can't take any chances, I don't think."

A silence descended on those seated around the table. Lydia looked at Jake's chair, wishing he was already in it and could be setting their minds at ease somehow. "That's five children sick," she mused aloud. "And possibly six."

"Plus my wife . . . and maybe myself," Peter said quietly.

The women turned to look at him. "But honey, yours didn't start with a sore throat," Katherine reminded him.

"True," Peter said. "And I'm running a real low-grade fever. Barely a point's worth."

"Headache?" Sadie asked.

"Bearable," he said. "But to tell you the truth, I think it's because my sinuses are completely stuffed."

"And Katherine's recovered," Lydia said cautiously. "You know, Jake—Dr. Harrison—said he wasn't sure that Katherine's illness and Carrie's were related."

"Any of the parents sick?" Barbara asked Sadie.

She shook her head. "Not the Lanes, not Tammy Carter or her husband, Zack Bartlett and Judith are fine...." Sadie shrugged. "You figure it."

"We'll have to let Jake figure it," Peter said.

Once again Lydia instinctively looked at the empty chair, drawn to her more personal predicament. What exactly was going on with that man? Did she really know anything about him at all? A past he wouldn't talk about...a fear of commitment... What if Jake routinely got involved in short-term flings and then broke them off because there wasn't room in his life for a serious relationship?

One thing was certain. If he'd turned into some kind of two-timing womanizer over the years, she wasn't going to have anything to do with him at all.

"I DON'T HAVE TIME to meet more than one or two," Jake said, rubbing his face fretfully, the phone at his ear. "And this Jacqueline sounds good. She's got to be better than Sophee."

"What was the problem?" Andrea Knowles asked. Patrick Knowles was signaling that he needed his consultation room back, and Jake mimed that he'd be off the phone in a moment.

It was Andrea who had originally put Jake in touch with the au pair network, and a friend of hers who'd recommended Sophee. Now that he'd fired the girl, he was turning to Andrea again, this time in desperation. He needed a new au pair by the end of the day.

"The problem is, I don't like coming home at night and finding the woman in charge of my household locked in her bedroom with a boyfriend," Jake said.

"Yikes," said Andrea. "She never did anything like that when she was working for Sarah Miller."

"The girl's unstable," Jake said. "She made such a scene at the hospital today, after I paid her for an extra week, too." He shuddered at the memory. He hated it when women cried, and especially hated it when his personal life spilled over into the workplace. He'd felt horribly guilty about the whole thing, even though he knew she was the one who should've felt guilty.

"Well, Jacqueline worked for one of my best friends for a year," Andrea was saying. "And you can trust her implicitly."

"She's not French, is she?"

"British. And the only reason she's available is that the Martins are on vacation till after Thanksgiving."

At least he wouldn't have to worry about mangled language. "Nonsmoker?"

"A health nut," Andrea said.

"That's perfect," Jake said. "I only need her through the holiday, anyway, so it should work out fine." He looked at his watch, stifling a yawn. He was late for the meeting at Taylor House, but this had to be attended to. How? He'd figure it out, fit it in somewhere, though his schedule was already so overloaded that he was starting to wonder if he'd ever see a bed again.

"Okay," he told Andrea abruptly. "I'll grab Jacqueline. When can I meet her?"

WHEN THE DOORBELL RANG, Lydia was tempted to answer it, but she forced herself to sit where she was. This meeting was about more important things than whatever was going on between Jake and herself. Somehow she'd have to put the whole thing out of her mind.

And ask questions later.

"Any more coffee?" Barbara asked, as Peter shuffled down the hall to get the door.

"I'll get it," Lydia said, and rose. She saw that Tucker was seated by the pantry doorway behind them, her child in a sling at her chest. She'd come in so quietly Lydia hadn't noticed. "Would you like some coffee?" she asked.

The younger woman shook her head, as opaque and closemouthed as ever. The baby was silent, too, possibly asleep. Lydia gave the two of them a friendly smile that felt as though it came out crooked, and busied herself with pouring coffee refills.

She heard Jake's familiar voice coming down the hall and noted a slight tremble in her pouring arm. Lydia returned the pot to the stove, doing her best to ignore the tremor she felt inside as Jake strode into the room, Dr. Knowles behind him. But she couldn't help looking at him, smiling as he smiled at her, their gazes holding a beat longer than she'd planned as Katherine introduced him to the group.

He looked positively haggard. Was this a man who was still in the throes of some romance gone awry? Looking at him now, it was hard to believe he could be duplicitous.

In fact, absurd as it was at a time like this, when she watched Jake take his seat, she was only thinking about the softness of his hair, which needed some combing after a bout with the snow and the November wind. And when she should've been listening to his words, she was looking at his hands, remembering how they'd felt holding hers.

Lydia forced herself to focus, putting aside those bittersweet feelings. What good did they do her, anyway? Hadn't they made it clear to each other that they were both better off keeping at a distance? Once again she'd lost the train of what he was saying. She took a bracing sip of coffee, fixing her gaze at some abstract point on the wall to the left of Jake, and listened.

"...which I mentioned to Lydia on the phone," he was saying, glancing her way. "But I don't want to cause any kind of a panic. A number of disorders resemble bacterial meningitis. We're still not a hundred percent sure that's what we're dealing with."

"Has Carrie gotten any worse?"

"Do we need to get inoculations?"

"What *is* meningitis?"

Jake raised his hands, warding off the barrage of questions from the group around the table. "Dr. Knowles is more of the expert here," he said. "He's dealt with these sorts of diseases in children before, and successfully, I should add. Why don't we let him tell us what his theories are and then if you have more questions..."

Pat Knowles adjusted his thick glasses, pursed his lips, and began his explanations. There were two main kinds of central nervous system infections they'd narrowed it down to, according to preliminary test results from the hospital, either a bacterial meningitis or a viral encephalitis. The fever made accurate diagnosis a little tricky, and they hadn't completed all the possible tests as yet. Both could be dangerous if they weren't caught early, but Carrie and the other children were already under hospital supervision, so he hoped whatever it was might be contained.

"The thing that's worrying both me and the doctors at Nathaniel," he went on, "is that many forms of such diseases have important public health implications, depending on the etiology."

"On the what," Sadie said.

"The cause," Jake said. "You see, we're talking about an infectious disease. If half a dozen children already have it, it's possible we're going to see a lot more."

"You mean, like an epidemic?" Barbara Wainright's voice was a bit unsteady.

"That's what we want to avoid, of course," Dr. Knowles said. "If possible. If the children who are already ill can be successfully isolated, and the specific disease pinned down, with antibiotics prescribed if it *is* a bacteriological infection...we might be able to lick this without any major consequences."

"That's a lot of ifs," said Emily.

"True. But we're still in the dark, and every conceivable precaution has to be taken. Which is why..." Dr. Knowles paused and looked at Jake.

"Dr. Knowles has already notified the National Institutes of Health," Jake said. "If whatever's given rise to this disease is present somehow here in Taylor House, specifically, we should have a public health department official give the place a once-over."

"And what does that mean, exactly?" Katherine asked.

Jake cleared his throat. "We're going to have to shut the place down for a little while, Katherine. Not officially, but just out of plain common sense."

A new kind of silence fell over the room. Lydia could almost palpably feel all the women around her holding back exclamations of dismay and protest. In her short time back here at Taylor House, she'd come to realize how much this close-knit community depended on it. Suddenly removing the place as a daily haven for their children and their friends' children was going to traumatize everyone.

Katherine's voice was calm and steady as she broke the silence. "Jacob, maybe I'm being a little dense, but you're going to have to spell it out for me. You think that the cause of this disease is . . . the house itself?"

"Something in the house or on the grounds could be the prime factor, Katherine, yes."

"But, why all of a sudden?" Lydia asked, intuiting her sister's next logical question. "I mean, we've all been in and out of this place for years, for generations. None of us ever got sick before, not like this."

"The renovations." Peter spoke quietly, leaning forward. "Jake, is this something like that Legionnaires' disease? Some kind of bacteria in the air ducts, was that it?"

Jake nodded, looking from Lydia to Katherine. "You did all kinds of extensive work on this house last year to create the day-care facilities. It doesn't usually happen, but there've been many cases where a disease was bred by a combination of organic and chemical elements in a newly created environment. There could be any number of factors that could spur a phenomenon like this, some new material in the walls, or the plumbing, or the electrical system. To begin with, we can't rule anything out."

"Great," Katherine said dryly, as a murmur rose from the other women around the table. "I knew things were going along too smoothly here."

"You mean some guy from the public health department's going to come over and start chipping away at the walls?" Emily asked.

Sadie sighed. "And what are we supposed to do in the meantime?"

"Should we even be here?" Barbara asked. "Is it safe?"

"Like I said, let's not panic," Dr. Knowles said. "Everything Dr. Harrison and I are discussing with you this afternoon is half conjecture. We don't even have the disease defined yet."

"But what we're suggesting is a temporary quarantine on Taylor House," Jake said. "We don't have the power to shut down your day-care center. We're merely asking you all to cooperate, for the safety of the kids."

"Until we're absolutely certain about what's going on here, there's no reason to risk anybody else's health," Dr. Knowles added. "We've got six sick children with only one thing in common, causally speaking: this house."

"Six?" Barbara asked.

"I just examined Kenny Todd," Dr. Knowles said. "Looks like more of the same, I'm afraid."

"It's what I was telling them before," Sadie said ruefully. "I hate to throw in the towel so quick, but Dr. Knowles is making sense. Carrie's older brother Mark, over in Mrs. Mullen's second grade class? He's fine. None of the other brothers or sisters of these kids have gotten sick. It's only the ones we've been taking care of."

"How awful," Lydia murmured, feeling a queasy sensation in the pit of her stomach. She looked across the table at Katherine, who had a stricken expression on her face, and knew just what she was thinking. They'd set out to do something for Greensdale and all the women who had fast become their friends here—and now the whole thing was threatening to blow up in their faces, in the most insidious, frightening way.

"But *we* haven't gotten sick," Emily said suddenly. "And we've been with the children every day. I was teaching Carrie Lane how to use modeling clay the morning she was ill. But I'm as fit as a fiddle."

"So far," Dr. Knowles said quietly. "Ms. Atchins, it could be that the children are more susceptible to whatever element is present, and their systems aren't developed enough to withstand it. But if the biological vector—the organism—is in this environment, we adults could very well succumb to it eventually.''

"On the other hand," Jake interjected, "if the etiology of the thing is bacterial, like a certain strain of influenza, for example, an adult system might be entirely immune to it.''

"Just thinking about all of this is making my head hurt," Sadie said. "All right, Doc, so what can we do? What's the first order of business here?''

"We've already taken the first necessary precaution," Dr. Knowles said. "All the children have gone home?''

Katherine nodded. "We've told people that we had to close for the afternoon. I suppose we can get the word out that we won't be opening for... what? Another few days?''

Dr. Knowles and Jake exchanged a glance. "Katherine," Jake said gently. "There's absolutely no way of predicting when—and if—Taylor House can be open to the public again.''

"WHO ARE YOU?" asked Max.

"Max, meet Jacqueline," Jake said.

Jacqueline Becker held out her hand. "Hullo," she said, with a cheery smile. Max looked up at her, keeping his hands in his pockets. The British blonde wearing denim overalls didn't bat an eyelash. Instead, she put her own hands back into her pockets and locked sober gazes with the boy. "Not feeling sociable, eh?" she asked.

"He's... you know, a little shy," Jake said nervously.

"No, he's not," Jacqueline said, still staring at Max. "He's a bit pissed off, is all. Am I right?''

Jake cleared his throat, wondering if he'd made a terrible mistake. But Max was suddenly smiling broadly. "Yeah," he said. "That's what I am.''

"And who can blame him?" Jacqueline asked, turning to Jake. "Missing a mum, strangers barging in and out of here...tsk, tsk," she clucked. "It's a rotten life, eh, kiddo?''

Max giggled. "She's okay, Dad," he announced, and turned back to Jacqueline. "You like gerbils?"

"Not particularly," she said, making a face. "I don't fancy mice, either. But I don't mind a rabbit."

For some reason, this answer seemed to satisfy the boy. Max nodded, turned, and went sauntering down the hall to the kitchen. "I'm making peanut butter and jelly sandwiches," he called over his shoulder. "You can have one."

"Thanks," Jacqueline answered, then looked to Jake. "Well, then. We're off to a good start."

Jake nodded. "Just be careful with the language, okay?" he said. "Max picks up everything."

Jacqueline laughed. She had a nice laugh, very musical. "I'll be careful," she assured him. "Going to show me the laundry bin?"

"IT'S A NIGHTMARE," Lydia said.

"Exactly," Katherine said, putting another sweater in her overnight valise. "But we're wide-awake. Hey, did we do something truly awful in a former life, or something?"

"I know what you mean," Lydia said wryly. "I thought we already paid our hard-luck dues."

"There." Katherine zipped up the zipper. "That ought to do us for tonight, at least. Are you packed?"

"I never entirely unpacked," Lydia said. "Are you sure this is going to work out? I could try to get a room at that inn in town—"

"Let's not start wasting your money immediately," Katherine said. "Peter's place is big enough for the three of us in theory, at least. Let's see what happens."

Peter Bradford had never given up his bachelor quarters over the tackle shop in town, one room of which he'd converted into an adjunct office to store legal papers and a computer he kept threatening to put to good use. It had been decided to move Katherine and Peter in there for the moment, at least until the doctors had a better handle on the nature of the "Taylor House bug," as they'd taken to calling it. Lydia was slated for the couch in Peter's little living room.

"I'll meet you downstairs," Lydia told her sister, and went to get her bag. The other women had vacated the premises as suggested. Lydia imagined there would be a great many phone wires buzzing in Greensdale tonight—if the lines stayed up. The snowfall had thickened, and there was already a sheen of white powder on the ground outside, swirling around as the wind rose.

The house was quiet but for the sound of voices in the kitchen below. Peter was down there with someone, and she thought she recognized the voice as Jake's. That was odd. He'd left hours ago.

Lydia hurried downstairs, bag in hand, her stomach grumbling as she went. With all the excitement, she hadn't had much of a lunch. Jake was standing in the kitchen, his coat on. "Hi," she said uncertainly.

"He left his little black bag on a kitchen chair," Peter said. "Katherine ready?"

"Should be down in a minute," she said. "What are you doing?"

"Stockpiling," Peter said, his body half obscured by the open refrigerator door. He was transferring items into a brown paper bag as Jake looked on. "The only things there are to eat at my pad are potato chips, peanuts and beer."

"Exceedingly healthy," Jake said.

If she didn't know the man better, she'd wonder if he was running himself ragged. But then she didn't know him, did she? What if he was always like this, commuting from Boston to Greensdale and back to Great Oaks, with stops for his pretty-but-too-young-for-him girlfriends along the way—

Stop it, she told herself. She was going to give the man the benefit of the doubt. And it didn't matter anyway, she told herself for the umpteenth time. They weren't getting any more involved than they already, well, weren't.

"I'm grabbing anything that Lydia made, which is about half a bakery's worth of pies and cookies," Peter muttered. "And all available soups."

"Stop," Lydia said. "You're making my stomach talk again."

"Hungry?" Jake looked up. "Actually, I was thinking of inviting the Taylor House refugees out to dinner."

"Speaking for myself," Peter said, closing the refrigerator and gathering up the bag of food, "thanks, but no thanks. All I'm interested in doing is parking my stuffed-up carcass under the covers with a cup of hot something, period."

"Ditto," said Katherine, coming into the kitchen. "That sounds like a delightful way to spend our first evening in exodus. Life-styles of the Sick and Homeless."

Jake looked expectantly at Lydia. "How about you?" he asked. "Ready to curl up on your brother-in-law's couch at—" he checked his watch "—six-thirty in the evening?"

"Not exactly," she admitted. "But if we do have enough food over there, there's no need—"

"Nonsense," Katherine said. "You go have a nice meal out with the gracious Dr. Harrison. We wouldn't be good company, anyway."

Lydia could see that her sister was still on her matchmaker's track. There wasn't any way she could signal her to drop it, as this particular match was being tacitly unmade. "But you might need help over there," she said.

"We're not invalids," Peter replied. "Really, you two go on out. It's going to be a night with the cramped and cranky over at my place."

Lydia looked at Jake, wondering how he felt about this. After their disquieting time together just the night before, would he really feel like wining and dining her alone?

"They're letting us off the hook," he said, smiling. "Come on, then. Let's get a bite somewhere."

Apparently he didn't have a problem with it. Maybe whatever woman Sadie had seen him with hadn't been a girlfriend, after all. Lydia shrugged, her growling stomach urging her onward. "Okay," she said. "I'll get my coat."

LYDIA FOLLOWED Jake's lights into the snow-filled parking lot, pulling up right behind him. She peered out her car windows at what was beginning to look like a veritable blizzard as Jake hopped out of his car and hurried back to her side. She rolled her window down a crack.

"You'll see, it's worth the trip, this place," he said. "Ready for the great outdoors?"

The Four Corners had been closed when they'd pulled into its driveway a half hour ago, Wednesday apparently its night off. Jake hadn't wanted to settle for anything less than a good meal with a fine wine, and had suggested they drive over to Great Oaks. The White Raven, he'd said, was an inn very similar to the Four Corners, which he thought she'd like.

Lydia wiped her gloved hand on the window to get a better look. From the outside, the place looked fairy-tale charming, an old-fashioned, barnlike building with eaves covered with fresh snow, its windows lighted cheerily from within. It was an inviting sight, so she opened the door, stepped out and nearly fell back as the wind hit her full force. "Whoa!" she cried, laughing, leaning against Jake for balance. "We sure picked a great night for this."

"Come on," he said, his arm around her as he led them into the spray of spiraling snowflakes. "If we move fast we won't have time to get cold."

They sprinted together across the fresh snow of the lot to the White Raven's entrance and barreled on inside, stomping and gasping. The inn's interior was all natural wood, high-ceilinged, toasty warm with delicious smells of food and smoky firewood filling the air. Lydia was instantly grateful for Jake's perseverance. A place like this was just what she needed after such a difficult day.

They were early enough to get one of the nicest tables, a cozy booth near a fireplace in the back, the beveled windows glimmering with frost and the sprigs of holly and other dried flowers hung from the walls giving it a festive air of imminent holidays. Soon they were sipping a soothing red wine as they leisurely perused the menu.

"Everything looks good," she observed.

"*You* look good," he said. "The red nose is especially endearing."

Lydia smiled, rubbing at the tip of her nose. "Bad circulation, I guess," she said. "Nose, toes and hands are the last to warm up."

"Let me help," he said, taking her hands in his and gently rubbing them. She didn't have time to protest, and as his soft skin heated hers she wondered at the physical contact. Was he only being friendly? At this point, she'd almost given up trying to figure out where things stood between the two of them. The best thing to do, she decided, was let the man help warm her hands, and enjoy the sensuous sensation while it lasted.

"How's that?" he asked, slowing his ministrations.

"Warm," she announced, and withdrew the hands, her skin tingling, an all too familiar feeling of pleasurable warmth seeping through her system from fingertips to toes. A waitress was approaching the table. Thankful for the distraction, she turned her attention back to the menu.

They ordered, sipped their wine, chatted. A number of times she thought of asking him about the mysterious woman in tears at the hospital, but there didn't seem to be a way. When she asked him how his day had been, he didn't mention such an incident. But then, would he?

"More stressful than usual?" she asked.

Jake considered. "Why, do I look that overstressed?"

Lydia shrugged. "You do look tired," she told him.

"Tired's too ordinary a word," he said, giving a little sigh. "Yeah, today had more than its share."

She waited, curious, watching his face. He did seem to be thinking of something, and even looked as if he might broach whatever topic it was. Then he shook his head. "You just never know about people," was what he finally said.

"How do you mean?"

"It's just hard to judge people sometimes." He frowned. "I had to fire someone today. A woman who worked for me."

. . . be tempted!

See inside for special
4 FREE BOOKS offer

Discover deliciously different romance with 4 Free Novels from

Harlequin American Romance ®

Sit back and enjoy four exciting romances—yours **FREE** from Harlequin Reader Service! But wait...there's *even more* to this great offer!

A Useful, Practical Digital Clock/Calendar—FREE

As a free gift simply to thank you for accepting four free books we'll send you a stylish digital quartz clock/ calendar—a handsome addition to any decor! The changeable, month-at-a-glance calendar pops out, and may be replaced with a favorite photograph.

PLUS A FREE MYSTERY GIFT—a surprise bonus that will delight you!

All this just for trying our Reader Service!

MONEY-SAVING HOME DELIVERY

Once you receive 4 FREE books and gifts, you'll be able to preview more great romance reading in the convenience of your own home at less than retail prices. Every month we'll deliver 4 brand-new Harlequin American Romance novels right to your door months before they appear in stores. If you decide to keep them, they'll be yours for only $2.49 each! That's 26¢ less per book than the retail price—with no additional charges for home delivery. And you may cancel at any time, for any reason, and still keep your free books and gifts, just by dropping us a line!

SPECIAL EXTRAS—FREE

You'll also get our newsletter with each shipment, packed with news of your favorite authors and upcoming books— FREE! And as a valued reader, we'll be sending you additional free gifts from time to time—as a token of our appreciation.

BE TEMPTED! COMPLETE, DETACH AND MAIL YOUR POSTPAID ORDER CARD TODAY AND RECEIVE 4 FREE BOOKS, A DIGITAL CLOCK/CALENDAR AND MYSTERY GIFT—PLUS LOTS MORE!

A FREE
Digital Clock/Calendar
and Mystery Gift *await you, too!*

◈ *Harlequin American Romance*®

Harlequin Reader Service®
901 Fuhrmann Blvd., P.O. Box 1867, Buffalo, NY14240-9952

☐ **YES!** Please rush me my four Harlequin American Romance novels with my FREE Digital Clock/Calendar and Mystery Gift. As explained on the opposite page, I understand that I am under no obligation to purchase any books. The free books and gifts remain mine to keep.

154 CIH NBA8

NAME _____
(please print)

ADDRESS _____ APT. _____

CITY _____ STATE _____ ZIP CODE _____

Offer limited to one per household and not valid to current American Romance subscribers. Prices subject to change.

The relief she felt when she heard these words bordered on idiotic. So that was it! So much for Sadie Travis and her gossip. She smiled encouragingly, waiting for him to fill in the details, but the arrival of their entrées seemed to lay the subject to rest.

Instead, while they ate, Jake talked about other people at the hospital. He still evaded any topic that dealt with his personal life, and she wondered if his work as a doctor had made that a habit. Had inuring himself to pain and suffering in others made him repress his own deeper emotions? But she also sensed he was smoothly steering the conversation away from the problems at Taylor House, feeling that what she needed was a respite from worry.

And he was right. With unjustified jealousy set aside, anxiety over the children would've taken over. Grammy had always had a theory that as soon as you confronted one problem in your life and dealt with it, the next was standing in line, waiting for attention. Experience had shown this theory to be true.

So she was happy to let Jake take her away from it all. Soon they were swapping tales of their respective pasts, Jake telling anecdotes of the more eccentric professors he'd encountered in his studies, and patients he'd dealt with in his practice. Lydia told him about some of the more colorful characters who were Pet Sanctuary customers in San Francisco.

The food was delicious, prepared with simplicity and elegance, her stuffed veal the perfect antidote to a ravenous appetite. Outside their window the snow kept falling, dusting the panes, the eaves above them creaking quietly as the wind rose. Once again Lydia was content to let the simple pleasures of good food and wine, and Jake's company, lull her into a feeling of well-being.

Maybe it was all right, after all. Maybe it was perfectly fine to be friends with her onetime romantic fantasy, and leave it at that. She hadn't planned this trip back East with anything else in mind, had she? If you looked at it that way, a night like this was an unexpected dividend, a peaceful oasis of calm in what had turned out to be a nerve-racking succession of anxieties ever since she'd returned to Greensdale.

Even so, her mind kept nudging at the dark worries over the day-care center, which Jake had done his best to leave alone. Like a tongue unable to keep from exploring a new tooth cavity, her mind kept returning to the things he and Dr. Knowles had said earlier. "What *are* they going to do to the house?" she asked him ultimately, when they'd picked out desserts from the passing cart.

"If we pinpoint the disease, which I hope we can do within the next forty-eight hours, and the public health people agree that the culprit we're looking for is at the day-care center, they're going to go over the place with a fine-tooth comb," he said. "They'll need samples of every bit of material, from rug fiber to roofing...."

He paused, seeing the look of dismay in her eyes. "You mean they'll rip the place apart?" she asked.

"Lydie, it hasn't come to that yet. For the moment, as long as the kids are out of the house and the sick ones under medical care, that's good enough for me and Dr. Knowles."

She nodded, then sat back in the booth, her eyes closing for a moment. The stress of the day's events was finally catching up with her.

"Are you okay?"

"I'm fine," she said, meeting his concerned gaze. "Just a little tired, that's all." She yawned, then smiled, self-conscious. "Make that exhausted."

"I know what you mean," he said, glancing out at the darkness.

"Really," she said, straightening up again. "I should talk, right? You're the one who's been on his feet working since the crack of dawn."

"Business as usual," he said, then yawned in his turn. "Your fault," he said, as she laughed. "Yawns are infectious." He glanced at his watch. "Excuse me a moment."

She watched Jake stride off, wondering what extra responsibility the man was attending to now. How did the man do it? she wondered. Even though she knew what it was like to be devoted to one's work—hadn't she spent countless fifteen-hour days putting the original Sanctuary together?—still, his kind of energy amazed her.

Actually there was a lot to admire in him, she mused. Above and beyond his dedication, there were that handsome profile, the infinitely mussable hair, those soft lips.... She smiled at the way her mind inevitably returned to the physical. Once a fantasy, always a fantasy, she supposed.

Her fantasy-in-the-flesh was now striding back down the aisle with a preoccupied look on his face. Lydia wondered if he had another hospital emergency to deal with and hoped fervently that wasn't the case. She was so comfortable here, and she'd been eyeing the pastry-and-cake-laden dessert cart with great anticipation. "Sorry," he murmured, sliding back into the booth.

"Anything wrong?" she asked.

Jake shook his head, rubbing his cheek with an absent look. "Nothing Jacqueline can't take care of," he muttered, more to himself.

"Jacqueline?" Her relief at being able to try one of those scrumptious-looking chocolate éclairs—the waiter was fast approaching with cart and coffee—gave way to confusion. "Who's Jacqueline?"

Jake looked startled, then chagrined. "She's living with us at the moment."

Lydia stared at him, her apprehension mounting. "Us?"

Jake sighed. "Well, I guess this is as good a time as any," he said. "I owe you an explanation, Lydia. I've been meaning to tell you, ever since the other night—"

"About what?"

"About my son."

Chapter Seven

"Dessert?" The waiter was at her side, the gleaming confections of chocolate and sugar at Lydia's eye level. She nodded dully, her mind whirling, and pointed at not one but two éclairs. She felt a need for fortification. "And you, sir?"

Jake shook his head, his eyes still intent on Lydia. "Just coffee, thanks." They both waited, the air between them suddenly thick with tension, as the waiter served the dessert. Then, as soon as the wheels of the cart squeaked their way down the aisle again, Jake spoke again.

"Jacqueline is an au pair girl," he explained, shifting uncomfortably in his seat. "I've hired her to live in and look after my son while he's here."

Lydia found her voice. "I didn't know you *had* a son, Jake."

"Well, I haven't had one—with me," he added quickly as her eyes widened again. "He's only just arrived. Look, I'd better start at the beginning."

"Please," she said, pouring cream into her coffee with a slightly shaky hand. A terrible thought had occurred to her. "But—you're divorced...aren't you?"

"Yes," he said. "That's the thing. I lost custody in the divorce, and he's only here on a brief trial basis."

Lydia nodded slowly. "I see. But why didn't you tell me?"

"I didn't mean to make a secret of it," he said. "I was going to tell you about it that first night, but I . . . I guess I was being overprotective."

"I don't understand."

Jake stared at his coffee cup for a moment, then, seeming to reach some inner decision, he looked up and met her eyes. "The whole subject touches a lot of raw nerves for me," he said. "To tell you the truth, I've been enjoying having a kind of clean slate with you, not having to deal with the past."

"But I'm interested in your past," she said. "And if your son's with you now, he's very much a part of your present, isn't he?"

"Yes, and I'm glad about that," he said. "You can't imagine how much it means to me, to try and make up for what happened."

"Maybe I can," she said cautiously. "Jake, it can't have been as bad as you're making it sound . . . can it?"

"Well, in terms of how it's all made me feel about myself," he said ruefully. "Look, I'm sorry to suddenly spring this on you now. I mean, we've been enjoying getting reacquainted. I guess I've liked having you think only the best of me."

"I would have thought it anyway, Jake," she said softly. "We're not exactly strangers, after all."

"Yes, but we weren't exactly baring our souls to each other on that first date, were we?"

"No," she allowed.

"And we haven't exactly had all the time in the world to talk about these things since then, have we?"

"No, but . . ."

"You know how it's been for us, Lydie. I never planned on you and I getting involved with each other. I honestly didn't know where things were leading, and to tell you the truth—" he exhaled "—I'm not used to sharing my private life with people."

"I can understand that," she said. "But what confuses me is how you make it sound as if your having a child is something to hide."

"No. *Not* having him. That's what I don't feel good about," he said quietly. "I'm not too proud of the fact that I'm considered unfit to take care of my own son."

Lydia paused in the act of biting into the first éclair. "Unfit?" She looked up at him. "How do you mean?"

"That's what the court decided," he said. "Judith got custody on the grounds of neglect, basically. That's what the whole divorce hinged on."

She could see how difficult it was for him to come out with this information. That sad look she'd glimpsed before had taken over his face like a dark shadow. "Jake, I don't mean to make you bring up this stuff—"

"No," he said. "Even though it's not something I like talking about, you ought to know what sort of a man you're dealing with."

He made it sound so ominous. But she couldn't believe Jake had really done anything awful. "What sort of a man is that?" she asked cautiously. "I have a lot of respect for the one I've gotten to know so far."

Jake smiled wanly. "Thanks," he said. "But what you don't know is what a mess I made of my marriage. I wasn't a good husband, Lydia. I was married to my work, first and foremost, and for much too much of the time I wasn't there for Judith, or for our child."

"She must've known what she was in for, though," Lydia said. "Marrying a doctor."

Jake shrugged. "Yes, and I know it takes two to make a marriage work. If she hadn't gone outside the marriage, maybe it could've been salvaged."

"She had an affair?"

He nodded. "But it was basically my fault. At least, I felt responsible. I *was* neglecting her, after all."

Lydia sipped her coffee. "I'm sorry, but there's more than one way a woman can deal with neglect. And a lot of them are much more direct and constructive than having an affair. Jake, why are you taking so much of this on yourself?''

"Guilt's a potent thing," he said. "It's not rational. But if you want to know the truth, it's the accident, I guess." He met her stare with a level gaze. "Judith got in a car accident the night things finally fell apart for the two of us. She was sideswiped by another driver, not her fault, but I've always felt it was my fault she was out on the road that night, anyway. And if my son had been with her..."

He shook his head, grimacing. "Luckily she wasn't badly hurt. But when Judith sued for custody, the court sided with her."

Lydia put a hand on his. "Jake, that sounds more like the work of a good lawyer. Even with the adultery—"

"I didn't bring that into it," Jake admitted. "I didn't want to drag my kid through the whole mess. The point is, I felt that I'd failed him and her. I'd started a family without really being able to keep up my end. And the truth is, living my life the way I do, I'm not a good candidate for raising a son on my own."

"You thought he'd be better off with your wife?"

Jake nodded. "Yes, only I was fooling myself when I thought that would be okay with me." He smiled ruefully. "I never realized how much I'd miss the little guy. Visiting him on a monthly basis hasn't been enough. So I got a new lawyer on the case."

"And?"

"Judith's remarried and not bearing as much of a grudge. That's why, for the first time in two years, he's come to live with me for a few weeks, on a trial basis. We're going to see if we can work out a way to share custody in the future."

"But that's great!" she said. "And obviously, you're not the irresponsible ogre you make yourself out to be, if that's what's going on."

"You're not completely alienated, hearing all this?"

"No," she said. If anything, she was feeling closer to him than she had in a long time. "You're too hard on yourself. Jake, everything you've told me is understandable."

"Really?"

"I'm happy for you!" she told him. "But I would've been happy for you if you'd told me everything when we first got back together," she said. "Honestly."

Jake sighed. "I was only trying to do things right," he said. "Lydia, from the first time I saw you again at Taylor House, I had a feeling about you. About us. I got a glimmer of something, this sense that here was somebody I'd be able to..." He paused. She wondered what word he was carefully avoiding. "...really relate to," he said. "I mean, open up to. Be myself with."

The look in his eyes as he gazed at her was enough to make her heart melt. "Jake," she began, touched. "You don't have to—"

"No, let me finish. I wanted a second chance. And I wanted things to be...right. I didn't want to be coming at you with all of this emotional baggage I've been carrying around. I thought we could ease into things." He smiled. "Not that 'eased' has been an operative word for us."

"No," she agreed, smiling.

"Anyway, I'd hate for you to hold it against me, making things more complicated than they had to be," he said.

"Jake, if anything, I feel even better about you...and me," she said quietly. "Knowing more about what's going on with you, I mean."

Her hand was still on his and he clasped it now, giving it a gentle little squeeze. "Good," he said, and then let her hand go. "That's a load off my mind."

Lydia smiled as they both sat back, but she was feeling dazed and a little saddened inside. It was painfully ironic. Jake was obviously feeling relieved at being this honest with her, but his honesty was only deepening her own unsettling ambivalence.

How could she tell Jake that knowing he already had a child with another woman made her feel even more like an outsider in his life? She considered another round of True Confessions: *Well, Jake, now that you've told me about the child you have, I'd like to tell you about the one I'll probably never have....*

No. What was the point? She'd said she was happy for him, and she was. Her own problems shouldn't enter into this. After all, he hadn't pledged his undying love for her, or anything like that. He was confiding in her as he would in a friend. She should take it in that spirit and keep her own complicated feelings of jealousy and unrequited longing to herself.

"I'd like to meet him," she said. "Your son. If that's okay," she added.

"I'd love you to," he said. "He's quite a character."

She liked the way he smiled when he talked about his son. Lydia smiled back, and closed her eyes for a moment. If only time would stand still and the rest of the world would disappear, she mused, she could just enjoy being with him like this. Wouldn't it be wonderful to have all of their respective complications evaporate, if only for one night? To hold Jake in her arms again and feel his lips on hers, regardless of the consequences?

"You look like you could sleep right there." Lydia opened her eyes. Jake was standing by the table, the soft lips she'd been contemplating smiling faintly as he looked down at her.

"You're right," she said, unable to suppress another yawn. "I guess this coffee's useless, in my case."

"Come," he said, holding a hand out. "Let's put you into bed."

Lydia stretched, casting a wary look at the relentless snow outside. The prospect of trudging out into the cold again wasn't remotely welcome. Neither, come to think of it, was a couch at Peter's apartment. Nevertheless, she took Jake's hand and followed him down the aisle of the restaurant.

It was only when he guided them left toward a staircase, instead of right to the coatroom, that she halted, confused. "Where are we going?" she asked.

"Like I said, we're going to put you to bed." Lydia stared at him, uncomprehending. "I've booked you a room for the night," he said. "Now don't get the wrong idea," he hurried on, as her eyes widened. "It's *your* room. I've got a place of my own that's only a ten-minute drive from here."

"But, Jake, wait, this is—no, you didn't have to—"

"Stop," he said. "It's not an entirely altruistic impulse. I don't particularly like the idea of chauffeuring you to Greensdale and then driving back here to Great Oaks in that," he said, gesturing at the wind and snow outside. "So you'd be doing both of us a favor if you accepted my hospitality."

"I couldn't let you pay for it," she protested.

"We can tussle over that tomorrow," he said. "But right now, you're exhausted, I am, too, and there's a lovely little room with a comfortable big bed in it upstairs, already reserved and paid for, and it's waiting for you." He held up a key.

Lydia hesitated. When he put it like that, she could hardly deny it was an inviting prospect. "I wasn't exactly looking forward to Peter's couch," she admitted.

"This way, sleepyhead," he said. "I'll walk you to your door."

"You've twisted my arm," she said wryly, then paused. "Oh, I'd better call Katherine, then."

"Good idea."

Her sister was half asleep when she phoned, though she was awake enough to make some playfully salacious accusations when she heard Lydia wasn't coming home. "I'm not staying at *Jake's*," she informed Katherine, a little wistful as she said so. No, she wouldn't be staying with Jake and son and au pair girl, and the whole very much filled-in life he was leading, she thought, as she hung up the phone. It was just as well that a chaste friendship seemed to be what he had in mind, and she could understand why.

Then she rejoined Jake. They walked up the stairs and down a softly lit hall, its floral wallpaper in keeping with the inn's colonial flavor. At the end, Jake paused, handing her the key. "In you go," he said.

She unlocked the door. "Don't you want to see what it's like? Take a quick peek," she said, stepping inside.

He nodded, following her into the small but beautifully appointed room, with an old-fashioned four-poster in one corner, a nice little table, window seat and small divan. The room was filled with an unearthly white light that came from the snow and a lone lamppost beyond the window.

"It's beautiful here!" she exclaimed, moving to the window. "Jake, this was really a sweet idea."

"Glad you like it," he said, joining her by the window. "But it was your yawn that suggested the thought."

She turned back to look at him, smiling, and impulsively brushed his cheek with her lips. "Thanks," she murmured. That had been chaste enough, hadn't it? But Jake was looking at her with a strangely serious expression, his hand stealing out, cupping her chin between thumb and forefinger.

"I'd better kiss you good-night and get out of here," he said, his voice sounding a little husky.

"Yes, I guess you'd better," she said softly, unable to stop staring into the velvet darkness of his eyes. His fingers lingered over her hair, brushing back a lock from her cheek. For a moment, time seemed suspended. The white glow was behind his dark figure as she held his gaze, glimmering at the edges of her vision.

"I don't know if you should be allowed to look this beautiful," he murmured. "It could be bad for a man's heart, your looking like that."

Had she been entirely wrong? These were not the remarks of a purely friend-desiring man. She felt a quiver of awakening desire course through her as his forefinger gently traced the line of her cheek. "I don't know if you should be allowed to say things like that," she teased, her breath a little unsteady as she tried to keep things light.

"All right, then," he said. "I won't say another word."

Then he hesitated for the barest moment, but she could see the desire in his eyes. Her tongue stole out to wet her parted lips. Her blood seem to sing in her veins beneath the gentle exploration of his fingertips. As his hand lightly grazed the curve of her neck, descending ever so slowly to her shoulder, it seemed only natural that this should be happening, not that she had planned it, even hoped for it, but...

He kissed her softly, but with an underlying urgency that set her heart beating in double time. He savored her lips with the softest of gentle explorations, then drew back, a questioning look in his eyes. "We could call that a good-night kiss," he said.

"We could."

"So what happens now is I just walk out that door."

"I see."

"Since we know already that this can't really be leading anywhere...as we discussed..."

"Of course." Her voice was a breathless whisper.

"So I'm on my way," he said, not moving an inch.

"Right," she agreed.

"I head down the stairs, getting my coat, going out into the cold, and getting into that freezing automobile..."

"Yes, I can picture it all."

"...driving home..."

"Uh-huh."

"...thinking, Jacob Harrison, you are an idiot." He paused, his hand still resting lightly on her shoulder.

Lydia nodded. "That makes two of us," she said.

"So then," he went on, his other hand still playing with a wisp of her hair. "I turn the car around, I drive back to the White Raven, I dash up the stairs, I knock on your door..."

"Yes?"

"I'm back," he said.

Maybe time *could* stop, if only for one night. Maybe she should just be selfish and do what she wanted, regardless of what it might mean tomorrow. Emboldened by the quickening of her pulse, a sudden shifting deep inside her, she covered his hand with hers. Still holding his luminous gaze, she slowly guided his hand lower, to close it gently over her breast beneath the cashmere sweater, so that he could feel the beating of her heart.

"And I'm glad you're back," she whispered.

Jake let out a deep, shuddery breath. "Hello again," he murmured, his eyes glowing brighter as he registered the invitation in her gesture, the unspoken surrender. His lips brushed hers with a feathery tenderness as his other arm stole around her. She felt herself arch back in his embrace as his lips found the tender hollow of her neck.

Snowflakes seemed to dance on her half-closed eyelashes. She luxuriated in the pleasure of his mouth on her soft skin, letting herself go limp in his arms. She realized she was tired of fighting off these feelings, of trying to convince herself there was something wrong with loving him like this. She knew their desire was strong and stubborn, and really, it was useless trying to pretend it wasn't there.

Opening her eyes, she realized one more thing. "Jake," she murmured. "You know, you were in such a hurry, rushing to get back here..."

"Umm?"

"...that you forgot to shut the door."

He was back at her side in a moment, and in the darkness, gathering her in his arms, guiding her slowly toward the bed. She moved as if in a happy trance, drinking in each of the little kisses he showered on her lips, cheeks, chin and neck.

It was such blessed relief, really, to give in to the pleasure of him. Exquisite warmth rose from deep inside her, spiraling still higher as his lips descended to the cleft between her breasts. She lay back, holding him tightly against her, feeling wonderfully aroused and exhausted at the same time. It felt so good to just have him to hug.

And Jake, seeming to read her every thought, wasn't urgently fumbling at her clothing. He seemed content to lie in her arms, slowly, dreamily caressing her shoulders and hair. "This is nice," she murmured.

"This?" he asked, his fingers tracing the line of her collarbone.

"I mean, lying here like this, just holding you," she said.

"Mmm-hmm," he murmured. "Heavenly."

They were quiet again, eyes closed, nestled in a warm, blissful hug. His fingers had been playing with the top button of her sweater, but they stopped now, resting lightly above her breast. Again, he was being remarkably in tune with her unspoken thoughts. Even though it would have been more exciting to feel him against her without the barriers of their clothing, the effort of disrobing seemed a bit much just now.

She could hear his breath coming slowly and regularly, matching hers. She could hear the gentle snowfall on the windowpane, and...

His snore.

Lydia's eyes flicked open. "Jake," she whispered. "Jake?"

Another gentle snore was the response. She felt one brief stab of incredulous outrage, but it abated immediately and she found herself smiling in the darkness, trying to hold back a full-bodied laugh. It was too funny, and somehow only fitting.

She stroked his hair, closing her own eyes. She'd wake him, so he could get properly embarrassed at such unromantic behavior, but for the moment she was content to lie here and hold him, enjoying the warmth and the feel of his body against hers. She couldn't blame the man, really, with everything that was going on in his overloaded life.

Lydia stifled a yawn, playing with Jake's hair and listening lazily to the wind outside. Even if this was as far as things ever went, she couldn't entirely complain. After all, she hadn't heard such a sweet, quiet little snore in her bed in years....

JAKE BOLTED UPRIGHT, bleary-eyed, and for a moment didn't have the slightest idea where he was. All he knew was that he'd been feeling more happy and comfortable than he had in as long as he could remember. Then he focused on the woman who'd been the source of all this pleasure and realized what had happened.

Her eyes had just blinked open, staring up at him with a befuddled expression that probably matched his own. "Lydia! I'm sorry, I just—"

But she was smiling. "It's okay," she said. "You are one exhausted fella. And I guess I followed suit."

"No joke." He rubbed at his eyes, reality flooding back into his befuddled brain. There were already glimmers of dawn outside and suddenly he was very wide-awake. "Damn," he muttered.

"What's wrong?"

"Nothing. But I have to..." Jake stopped, looking from watch to window. Max would be getting up in an hour. But this had been his first night with Jacqueline, and it wouldn't do if he were to wake up in the morning and find his father gone. With rising panic, Jake eased himself away from the wonderfully warm body that had been enfolding him.

"Yikes!" Lydia exclaimed, looking blearily at the windows. "We must've slept for hours."

Even just woken up, in rumpled clothes with her hair all over the place, she was an extraordinarily beautiful woman. "What a missed opportunity," he muttered.

Lydia smiled. "You went out like a light," she said. "I was going to wake you, but..."

Jake winced as he tested his arm, stiff from having lain beneath her for so long. "Unbelievable as it may seem," he said ruefully, "I guess our bodies actually needed sleep more than..."

"Anything," she supplied.

"Right," he said, and with a last lingering kiss on her lips, he rose regretfully from the bed. "But that's the last time, Lydia Taylor," he said sternly. "The next time you and I end up alone in a room together..."

"Bring a pot of coffee?" she suggested playfully.

"Funny," he growled. "You know, you look so sexy, lying there, you're making it difficult for me to leave."

"Sorry, but I can't move," she said. "Every muscle's locked where it is."

"I'd stay if I could," he said, taking Lydia's hand. "But I have to be up in—" He checked his watch again. "Less than twenty minutes. And in addition to showing up for my son's morning cereal, there's things I need back at the house, including a shower and shave I haven't had in almost two days."

She looked dubious. "Jake, are you okay?"

"No. Yes," he said. "The point is, I'm dead on my feet, as you just saw," he said sheepishly. "And I'm still kicking myself for having blown what could've been a night to remember."

Lydia nodded. "I know what you mean," she said softly. "But if we've waited this long, I suppose we can wait a little longer."

The look in her eyes when she said that made something inside him—his heart, possibly?—melt. "Yes," he said, feeling a surge of . . . something—love, probably?—for her that was overwhelming. "That's exactly how I feel."

Lydia nodded, and rose slowly from the bed to face him, groaning a little as she stretched her arms. "Jake Harrison, you're one in a million," she muttered, and kissed his cheek. "Now get out of here before I decide I've been insulted."

"We'll talk," he said, and kissed her. He savored the feel of her lips on his, the taste of her, her scent mingled with his own. And then, with a last fervent embrace, he was on his way.

It was past eight when she woke again, having dozed for an hour or so after Jake left. The moment the door had shut behind him she'd felt her spirits sag, and a little more sleep had been the only antidote to his absence.

Now she walked listlessly across the room to the window, gazing out at the picture-perfect scene below. One thing San Francisco lacked was this kind of snow. Though it had stopped falling hours ago, the streets and neighboring houses had the appearance of the toy village inside one of those globes you shook, to make fake flakes swirl through the water.

When she realized she was transfixed at the window, waiting to see Jake's car materialize in the parking lot, she moved away. The intensity of her feelings for this man she barely knew was starting to overwhelm her. Into the shower she marched.

For Lydia, the morning shower was an active meditation time. When she was coming into full consciousness there, the water extra hot, she liked to plan out the day and get her energy in gear. Lydia let the water cascade over her, standing almost motionless as she tried to make sense of this situation.

It was unnatural, that was what it was. How could two people who obviously enjoyed each other so much, who'd made such a perfect physical fit, who had the potential to share so much beyond a "weekend fling," cheerily go their separate ways? After a night like that? It didn't make sense.

What didn't make sense, she reminded herself ruefully, soaping up, was her having thought she could handle this ongoing flirtation without any consequences. Of course, it shouldn't have seemed like such a loaded situation, but...

But Lydia hadn't been intimate with a man in, well, she'd stopped counting the months. It was over a year, she knew that. After a while she'd sort of gotten used to it, at least she thought she had. The problem was, the more you didn't do it, the more importance you actually attached to it when the moment finally arrived. And since Lydia wasn't a woman who'd ever been able to detach her emotions from her sexuality, it was only natural that they would be in turmoil now.

She wanted to make love with him. He wanted it, too. Somehow, at some point soon, it would happen. It seemed inevitable. At least on the surface she should've been aglow with a happy anticipation. Instead she felt nervous apprehension.

Lydia knew she had a lot to give, as well as a lot of needs to be fulfilled. And though it might be unfair to suddenly open herself up to Jake, after sleeping with him at last, what

if she did? She could already feel the burden of a year's
worth of unfulfilled wants and needs, and needing to give,
threatening to burst out and spill all over the unsuspecting
guy.

It was all his fault, she thought wryly, as she shampooed
her hair. If he wasn't such a tender, giving kind of man
himself, he wouldn't have touched off these things in her.
Maybe it would be better for them both if he turned out to
be a disappointment in bed.

Fat chance, she reflected, rinsing off. First of all she
couldn't imagine Jake as an inept lover, but even if he was,
this wasn't really about sex. It was about that way he made
her feel, appreciated, admired...loved. And the way she
loved him.

It wasn't merely the cool air that slowed her down as she
stepped from the shower, but the audacity of her subconscious. *Love?* Who'd said anything about love here? Neither of them had proclaimed their undying adoration and
commitment to each other. How could they have? They
barely knew each other.

Another lie. As she got dressed, Lydia thought over the
time she and Jake had spent together, both years ago and
now. Wasn't it true that the very quality, the initial spark
between the two of them had been a sense that they somehow did know each other intuitively? She'd felt that the first
time they'd ever exchanged a few words on Lame Gull Jetty,
and it was that kind of feeling that had made it so easy to
pick up things virtually where they'd once left off.

So, great, Lydie, she told her reflection in the mirror as
she brushed her hair. *You've found a perfectly simpatico
mate in theory, with the minor problem that he lives nearly
three thousand miles away and isn't available for most hours
of a given day even if he was in the same city. Plus he has a
son from a prior marriage and a lot of guilt he hasn't quite
gotten over. Let alone your own feelings about the whole
issue of children....*

Good work, kid.

She dressed quickly, remembering all the things she had to do today. She had to call Grady. They were due to finish the cage installations that afternoon and she figured she should check to make sure the inclement weather hadn't changed his plans. But first, she did have to touch base with Katherine.

Lydia checked to make sure she hadn't left any personal belongings about the room, took a last, sentimental look at that wonderful four-poster, and then locked the door behind her. The inn was full of quiet but cheery sounds, a maid bustling down the corridor giving her a friendly smile as she walked to the stairs.

Lydia cleared her throat to say "Good morning," but her throat felt oddly scratchy. In fact she felt parched, and the prospect of some fresh orange juice assumed first priority. After leaving the key with the front desk, she went into the restaurant.

At this early hour there weren't that many people in there. She took a booth and ordered breakfast. As soon as her juice arrived, she downed it, and then went to the little alcove off the restaurant's entrance where there was a public phone.

Katherine picked up on the second ring. "Good morning, wayward sister," she said.

"How did you know it was me?"

"Who else would it be at eight-thirty in the morning?" Katherine said. "Was it wonderful or what?"

Lydia sighed. "I *slept* wonderfully, yes," she said pointedly.

"Save the disclaimers, sweetheart. Are you coming by to tell me the entire exciting tale?"

"As soon as I get a bite to eat. I'm suddenly starved, and I—" she paused to sneeze "—excuse me. I'm going to have a little breakfast first and then drive back."

"Bless you," Katherine said. "Hey, don't tell me you're catching a cold."

"I don't think so," Lydia said. "Do you need anything from the outside world?"

"No, my foolish husband insisted on making a run to the market this morning, bundled up in enough clothing to make him look like some moon walker from NASA. Just come ahead."

Lydia got off the phone and headed back to her booth, pausing to sneeze again. She made a detour to the ladies' room for some tissues, and once inside, regarded her reflection in the mirror. Was she coming down with something? True, she still felt a bit dazed and woozy from lack of sleep, but her face didn't betray many signs of exhaustion. If anything, her color was unusually rosy.

Or did she have fever? she wondered uneasily, as she felt her forehead and cheeks and found them warm. Clearing her throat, she discovered that parched feeling was still there. Worried now, she went back into the restaurant, glad to see that her food had arrived. That, she decided, was all she needed: eggs, bacon, toast and coffee. If she still felt a little out of it after a good meal, she'd buy some aspirin in the inn's convenience shop, just for insurance.

Lydia perused the local paper as she ate. ConCo's plant was open and doing well, she noted, with Great Oaks employment up and business in their commercial district booming. A local high school had finally let a woman join the football team, and a particularly grueling winter was expected across the area, the subzero temperatures predicted described, in droll New England style, as "a bit chillier than last year's."

Quite a change from the *Chronicle*, she noted, wondering idly what news she might be missing in San Francisco. It struck her suddenly that she couldn't imagine anything, short of an earthquake taking down the Pet Sanctuary, that would really get to her. Was she that bored with her West Coast life?

Sipping her coffee, she put down the paper and sat back, taking in her environment with a thoughtful gaze. It had been so important to her, as a teenager, to get out of backward old Greensdale and emigrate to a cosmopolitan city. Now, at the ripe old age of thirty-three, she wondered once again if she'd made the wrong choice. She had enjoyed the sophistication of Los Angeles, and then the Bay Area, but she'd always missed New England.

This, she mused, watching her waitress retack a sprig of dangling holly to the stained wood above the kitchen door, still felt like home. There was a quality of down-to-earth ruggedness, subtle but distinct, that permeated towns like Great Oaks and her own. The laissez-faire, laid-back atmosphere in San Francisco had always struck her as somewhat fantastic and unreal. She'd always wondered what some of the still barefoot, posthippie habitués of Golden Gate Park would make of a "chilly" Greensdale winter.

If the truth were known, she'd never fully accepted the Bay Area as her real home. Wasn't that why she'd initially jumped at the opportunity of opening an eastern Sanctuary branch? She'd sensed that by doing this, she'd at least be reopening the option of spending more time back here, near Katherine and Clarissa. And if she and Jake were to—

Hold it right there, she told herself sharply, aware that her wild imagination had just taken one leap too far. There was no "she and Jake." There were just some vague promises that were as yet unfulfilled. Clearing her throat, which persisted in feeling scratchy, she signaled to the waitress for her check.

"I CAN'T GET USED TO THIS," Katherine said, standing in the empty playroom. "And I don't intend to."

"We don't have a lot of choice just now," Lydia said, putting a sympathetic hand on her shoulder.

"It's kind of creepy, if you ask me." Emily Atchins surveyed the oddly silent room from the doorway. "It's like science fiction or something. There's some invisible thingamajig that's making people sick here, and we can't see it, we can't feel it...."

"And we don't even know for sure that it *is* here," Lydia reminded her. "Jake still isn't positive about the cause of the disease."

"You'd think they'd know by now," Katherine muttered. "After putting poor Carrie through all those tests..."

"I'm going over there with some of these things," Emily said. She'd been gathering a few dolls and coloring books from the shelves and putting them into a knapsack. "Those kids must be going stir-crazy in that hospital."

Katherine nodded absently, hugging the suitcase with her own clothing in it to her as she gazed around. Lydia had helped her move out some additional belongings after meeting her at Peter's that morning. Emily was here to do the same. The glow from the white snow outside filled the room with an eerie light that made its emptiness seem all the more unnatural.

"I'm glad Grammy's not around to see this," Katherine said.

Lydia nodded. "It'll work out," she said, knowing it was a useless sort of remark. "Have we got everything?" she asked.

"I think so. Your stuff's in the car?"

"Ready to go." After checking out Peter's couch and the funky, friendly but cramped surroundings there—sleeping under a giant swordfish just didn't have much appeal—Lydia had opted to take a room at the Four Corners Inn. The rates were reasonable, and until they knew more about whether they could return to Taylor House, it seemed like a good idea for the duration of her stay.

"Yeah, I'm set, too," Emily said, hoisting her knapsack. "Say, they're not going to rule out bringing these toys and things over there, are they? I mean, do they have to be disinfected or something?"

Katherine looked to Lydia and shrugged. "I sincerely doubt that a *Little Engine That Could* coloring book is some sort of bacterial menace," she said. "But I guess you should ask one of the doctors there. What else are you bringing?"

As Emily rustled through her sack, cataloging, Lydia turned away from the other women, stifling a sneeze, then strode down the hall to the kitchen. Luckily there was a container of grapefruit juice in the fridge. She'd downed a full glass with a couple of aspirin and was sitting for a moment at the kitchen table, fatigue catching up with her, when she realized that the dull throbbing in her head was turning into a full-fledged pounding.

Of course, she could've been feeling this way because of the emotional anxiety her night at the White Raven had engendered, or... Lydia got up from the table, feeling her forehead again, her hand a bit shaky. Sore throat, possible fever and a headache.

Didn't something about those symptoms sound ominously familiar?

"Emily," she called, coming back into the playroom. "I think I'll follow you over to Nathaniel. I'd like to see the kids, too. And talk to a doctor."

"WE'RE PAGING HIM," the nurse said, favoring Lydia with a quick smile.

"Thank you," Lydia said. "I'll be down the hall in Room 2011."

The nurse nodded, already picking up another blinking phone line at her busy station. Lydia walked away from the small reception area, wondering if she was doing the right thing. She knew Jake was exceptionally busy this afternoon but she also believed he'd want to know about it if Lydia was ill—especially if her illness was connected to the Taylor House bug.

It wasn't just her own health she was concerned about, she realized, heading back to the children's room, but his. What if she did have that bug, and it was infectious? Probably the last thing he needed was to come down with some awful illness, when he was in the process of trying to cure it.

Well, there was no sense in getting anxious about it yet. Jake would take a look at her and they'd go from there. Besides, her headache was down to a minor throb again after the aspirin, and a surreptitious temperature-taking upstairs at Taylor House had reassured her somewhat. She did have the barest modicum of fever, half a degree's worth, but that could've been due to any number of things.

And if the whole thing was psychosomatic, wouldn't she feel like an absolute idiot?

Lydia forced herself to put these thoughts aside as she reentered the room where the Carter twins were, Emily at their bedside. She hadn't even mentioned to Emily or Katherine that she was feeling ill, although Katherine had forced her to down some milligrams of vitamin C when she'd first shown up at Peter's, not liking Lydia's occasional sneezes.

"How are we doing?" she asked Michael, who'd been asleep when she and Emily arrived, but was sitting up now, playing with a toy car. The boy looked up at her, pale, his eyes red-rimmed, his expression forlornly solemn.

"I want to go home," he said softly, bit his lip and ran the car around his lap as Lydia gently smoothed his tousled hair.

"I bet you get to go home soon," she told him, looking over at Emily. Emily was helping Melissa Carter read one of the books, quietly prompting her past the more difficult words. She winked at Lydia in an encouraging way. Lydia knew that Emily was feeling particularly bad about the unfortunate turn of events at Taylor House.

She'd felt guilty enough having to leave in the first place, but her remorse over having to move away in the midst of this crisis had been their sole subject of conversation on the drive over. Emily kept asking Lydia for her assurance that she'd "pitch in" with Katherine in finding someone who could take on Emily's responsibilities. Even though she knew that Lydia herself wouldn't be there much longer, and the entire future of Taylor House was temporarily in limbo, she'd insisted on describing some of her various routines and duties as Taylor House supervisor to Lydia, as if to assure herself that someone in the family had this vital information on file.

"Lydia Taylor?"

Lydia looked up from her improvised drag race between two toy cars on Michael's bed. A doctor she'd never met, whose short blond hair and clean-shaven appearance made him seem too young to *be* a doctor, was leaning in the doorway. "Yes," she said, and hurried over to him, moving into the hall. She didn't want to alarm Emily unnecessarily.

"I'm Dr. Rayborne," the young man said. "Dr. Harrison is busy at the moment and I'm helping him out with some of the patients. What can I do for you?"

"Well, I just wanted to ask him..." She paused, trying to figure out the best tack. "My sister Katherine has been one of his Greensdale patients recently, for a kind of a flu—"

"I'm familiar with the case," Dr. Rayborne said. "I know Dr. Harrison's trying to get to the bottom of this problem. Is one of your children...?"

He was indicating the room behind her. "Oh, no," Lydia said hastily. "It's me. I mean, I'm not feeling well, and Dr. Harrison specifically asked me to get in touch with him if anyone connected with Taylor House was showing symptoms, so I thought—"

"I see. Here, why don't we move into Room 2030?" he said, already guiding her down the hall. "I'll take a look at you myself as soon as I'm done with another examination nearby, and in the meantime—" They were back by the nurses' station. Dr. Rayborne reached over the counter and got a batch of forms, which he handed to Lydia. "Why don't you fill these out?"

Lydia glanced over the many pages as she followed the doctor down the corridor, a thought striking her. "Dr. Rayborne, if it's any help, I have a file on my medical history with me."

He paused, eyebrows raised. "You always carry it?"

"No," she said, smiling. "But I was seeing a specialist in Boston only this past week, and I happen to have them here." Dr. Newcomb's manila envelope was still in her shoulder bag. She'd been carrying around the file for days, unwilling to look at it again but always intending to. "If they'd be useful..."

"Wouldn't hurt," he said. "And it would save you from having to get a finger cramp from penciling in all those boxes. Here we are."

He ushered her into a small examining room with the requisite small white table and medical trappings. An open door to the left revealed an outer room, where a nurse was visible at a desk. "Have a seat, take care of the forms, and I'll be with you in a few minutes. Just give my nurse the file with the other sheets when you're done filling in the essentials, okay?"

Lydia nodded, walking in. "Thanks."

"I'll try to track Dr. Harrison down, too, and let him know you're here."

Lydia followed the young doctor's instructions, and after handing her file and forms to the nurse, she paced the small room, nervously feeling her forehead and throat. At the moment she wasn't sure which would be worse, finding out she had some kind of meningitis—what a fearful-sounding word!—or that she was a perfectly normal woman with an overactive imagination.

After what seemed like an interminable time that was only five minutes by the clock on the wall, Dr. Rayborne returned via the other door, which he shut behind him. "Okay," he said. "Let's sit you down and see how you are."

It was just like having any routine examination, Lydia knew, but she couldn't help trying to read something more into every subtle expression, murmur or bit of idle chitchat that Dr. Rayborne uttered as he went over her throat, eyes and ears. After her temperature, pulse and blood pressure had been taken, she couldn't help asking, "What do you think?"

"I think you've got a mild sore throat," he said, "a bit of a low-grade fever, sinuses acting up... what would pass in unsophisticated circles as the signs of a common cold," he said, smiling. "But due to the circumstances, you were absolutely right to come in, and just to be on the safe side, would you mind if we took a little blood sample?"

"Not at all," she said, still uneasy. "You mean, I don't have anything to worry about?"

"That's a trick question," he said wryly. "From what I know of this Greensdale thing, worry is still an operative word. I wish I could tell you something more definite—" he shrugged "—chances are, you'll be fine. But if I let you out of here with only a superficial exam and a cheery word, Dr. Harrison would have my head."

Dr. Rayborne's nurse was efficient. The blood test didn't really hurt. By now, Lydia didn't know what to think. Maybe it was just as well that Jake hadn't—

"Lydia!" The door swung open again as Jake strode into the room. She'd never seen him with a white doctor's coat on and her first absurd thought was that he looked good in it.

"Jake, I'm so sorry. I probably shouldn't have come here at all, but I just thought—"

"Nonsense," he said firmly, and gave her shoulders a little squeeze, kissing her forehead before stepping back to look at her. "How's the head?"

Vibrating nicely, she thought, instantly warmed and touched by the concern she saw in his dark eyes. "It's not so bad, now, really," she said. "You know I never would've bothered you with this, but you said—"

"You did the right thing," he assured her quickly. "From what Dr. Rayborne tells me, you don't seem to be a sick lady, fortunately."

She was already feeling foolish, realizing that seeing Jake again in person, and sensing how much he did care about her was nearly balm enough to cure her. "I just got paranoid about the symptoms—"

"Stop, Lydie, it's really okay." He smiled. "Look, I can't stay for another second, this ward's gone into overdrive, it seems, and I'm late for another patient...."

But Lydia wasn't hearing a word he was saying. Suddenly she was transfixed, staring. Her file. He had it under his arm with her papers, on a clipboard. Had he looked at it? Did he know everything about her now, her condition? Why hadn't she thought of that? And what would *he* think?

". . . so I'll have Rosa give you a prescription."

He was looking at her expectantly, indicating the door. Lydia stared at him, momentarily confused. "Prescription?"

"Just as a precaution, I'm going to give you a little amantadine. It's something that helps in some adult cases of influenza. We couldn't give it to the kids, but Katherine took a little and it seemed to help. If it's only a mild cold that you've got, the pills won't do you any harm. And if it's something more serious, they may nip it in the bud."

She nodded dumbly, following him to the door, watching as he conferred with his nurse, dictating Lydia's prescription. Maybe he hadn't looked at the file yet. If she could get it back now, she could keep her problem to herself. But then, why was she so concerned about him finding out?

"I've got to run," Jake said, returning to Lydia's side. "I'll check in with you later. You're at Peter's?"

"No, I'm at the Four Corners now," she said, her eyes shifting to the file under his arm.

"Okay," he said, already moving to the door.

"Jake—"

Her voice sounded unnaturally loud to her and the nurse looked up. Lydia realized she was crossing some subtle professional boundary, but she wanted to get that file.

"I'll call," Jake said, smiled apologetically, and was gone.

Lydia stood helpless, staring at the empty doorway.

Chapter Eight

"What do you think?"

Dr. Calder pursed his lips thoughtfully, looking up from the veritable sea of data on his cluttered desk. "Jake, your guess is as good as mine."

Jake sighed. "Matt, you're the specialist. When it comes to infectious diseases, your guess is supposed to be *better* than mine."

Dr. Calder smiled, looking at Dr. Knowles, who was seated across the desk next to Jake. "How about the pediatric neurologist's opinion?"

Knowles adjusted his thick glasses, flipping through one of the many open files in his lap. "Oh, it's a piece of cake," he said sardonically. "We've narrowed it down to two main subclusters, with symptoms that match either in some ways, but neither entirely. That leaves us . . ."

". . . in limbo," Jake finished, turning back to Dr. Calder. "Matt, we've got half a dozen sick children on our hands. Common aspirin and a small dosage of acetaminophen has kept most of their fevers down, but none of them are fully recovered."

"And I'm afraid they won't be," Dr. Knowles interjected, "until we've got this mysterious microbe nailed."

"You're treating the symptoms, not the cause," Calder observed.

"Exactly."

"Let's go over it again," Calder said, picking up the stapled report Jake had had copied for him. "Blood chemistries. You've run an SMA6 and SMA12..."

"LFT for possible hepatitis," Knowles added.

"HCT hematocrit..." Calder went on. Jake rose and paced to the window, running his hands through his hair. He knew everything on those sheets of paper already, all the tests Carrie Lane and a few of the others had been subjected to. Everything was pointing toward an acute viral encephalitis or an aseptic meningitis. But they still hadn't been able to identify the isolated virus.

This wasn't entirely unusual in such cases, but what was disturbing Jake and Pat Knowles was a nagging suspicion that they might be on the wrong track. A few of the test results didn't jibe with the profile of either of the two probable diseases, and although the children's condition had been stabilized, there wasn't much the staff at Nathaniel had been able to do. And if Taylor House was the site of a possible epidemic, they could expect the amount of patients to double, at least.

Then there was Lydia. Jake stared down at the snow-dusted parking lot below, seeing not it, but the look in her eyes when he'd rushed by to see her hours ago. He didn't think she was sick with this thing, but the mere thought that she might've been had shaken him up in a way he wasn't used to being shaken.

You've blown it, he told himself, not for the first time today, a day that had seemed unreasonably long. After managing to hold out for what felt like ages, keeping his emotional life under wraps, he was opening himself up, making himself vulnerable. And now he'd have to pay the price.

Should've known better. Could've handled it differently. *But no.* It was too late anyway, he was already in too deep for his own good. Lydia Taylor was preoccupying his thoughts, her image seeping into the fabric of the day. He was in love with her. *Damn it.*

The timing was off, that was the thing. Not that he'd ever even thought about making time in his hectic life for romance, but now was especially tough, with Max at home. His son had made the adjustment from Sophee to Jacqueline without a hitch. But they were merely household help and companions. He wasn't likely to react as well if, after being separated from his father for so long, he suddenly saw him with another woman.

We'll have to cross that bridge if and when we come to it, he mused. Jake looked at his watch, knowing by the deepening purple in the sky outside even before he did so that night was fast approaching. His own work was so backed up, let alone this Taylor House problem, that even a few nights' running here at Nathaniel wouldn't put him back on the track. He'd been so lax over this past week, using every spare minute to be with Max—or Lydia. And now it was catching up with him.

That wasn't all, though; the feeling that had been creeping into his system all day was an old one, insidiously familiar. Guilt was catching up with him, and the kind of anxiety he'd had when he was with Judith. But Lydia wasn't Judith, he reminded himself. And this was a different feeling, wasn't it? Lydia wasn't making him feel this way, she wasn't demanding anything from him that he couldn't give her. This time the feeling was coming from him, and if he thought about it, it was entirely natural. When you cared about someone like that, you were bound to be concerned if they...

"Jake? You still with us?"

Jake turned from the window, disoriented. "Sure," he said, walking back to his seat. "You were saying?"

"I think you should send a sample serum along to the public health boys, as Dr. Knowles has suggested," Calder continued. "Wouldn't hurt to get their feedback on this. And the quarantine on this Greensdale house makes sense. In the meantime, maybe a second cerebrospinal fluid test on one of the more recent arrivals would show us something different...."

Jake nodded, unable to keep his mind from returning to Lydia. What was he going to do about her?

"WHERE DID WE PUT POPEYE?" Lydia asked.

"The rabbit?" Grady looked around him, squinting. "First aisle, near the front."

Lydia nodded, surveying her new domain. "Now, this is more like it, Bobbo," she said. "Listen."

Bob tilted his head, standing at her side at the rear of the main aisle. Most of their stock was in now, and the store looked more like a pet shop should look, but more importantly, it was sounding better. She had her puppies yipping, kittens meowing, and the bird cages in the back were rapidly becoming noisier as various whistles and caws rent the air.

Bob nodded appreciatively. "Yup. Sounds like a full house."

"Almost," she said. There was even the familiar hum and swish of fish tanks, one aisle over against the wall. "Beats the steady clamor of hammers and nails," she added.

Patty, the girl they'd hired just that morning to work the cash register and help with maintenance, was coming down the aisle with a tall man in an overcoat. "One sound still missing," Lydia reminded Bob as they approached. "Front door chime."

"Right," he said. "I'll make that phone call."

Lydia absently felt her forehead. Not too warm. She knew she was supposed to be back in Greensdale taking it easy, but with the store's official opening only two days off, she couldn't keep away. Besides, she was already convinced that her bit of fever had been more psychosomatic than flu-related.

She smiled politely as Patty and the man stopped in front of her. "Miss Taylor, this is Mr. Sanderson. He's here about the apartment."

"Oh! Great," she said. "Patty, why don't you just take him upstairs and show him around?" She handed the girl the key. "I'll be here when you've had a look," she told Mr. Sanderson.

The man nodded, following Patty into the back. Lydia crossed her fingers. So far, subletting the rooms above the shop had been an albatross around her neck. Maybe this Mr. Sanderson would finally take that weight away.

Buying the Sellars Street building on impulse had yielded this one unforeseen consequence. The second-floor apartment had come with the store below as a package deal. It was the former dwelling of the original owners, a couple of tie-dyed toga-wearing people named Godiva and Sunshine.

These peace-loving folk had run the Open Mind Center there, one of those New Age kind of establishments, with seminars on raising consciousness and craft work for sale. This accounted for the rather mind-boggling color scheme Lydia had needed to paint over, both downstairs and outside.

Although the Realtor had assured Lydia that renting out Sunshine's digs would be a snap, so far nobody in Cambridge seemed to be in a mad rush to inhabit a space above a pet shop that still smelled faintly of incense and sported psychedelic mandalas on the walls. This was turning into a problem, because Lydia had counted on making some money on the apartment to offset some of her major maintenance costs.

The other young man they'd hired, the one with the crew cut, was having trouble getting a cage open up front. Lydia went to his rescue. "You turn the catch this way," she instructed. The phone behind the counter was ringing.

"Somebody get that?" Bob called, busy with the final adjustments to the swinging door to the back rooms. Patty was upstairs with Mr. Sanderson, who, Lydia hoped, might be mad about Day-Glo trim.

"Here, I'll feed these guys," she told Crew Cut. "You answer that." He nodded and moved off, and Lydia tore off a lettuce leaf from the bunch he'd handed her. Watching the large brown rabbit gnaw on the leaf, she cleared her still-scratchy throat and wondered for the umpteenth time that day if Jake Harrison had read her file.

That was the problem with keeping secrets. She hadn't meant to make an issue of this thing. In a sense it didn't matter, did it? Why should Jake care whether or not Lydia was capable of having children? He had a child of his own. Who knew if he wanted another?

On the other hand, if she remembered correctly, years ago at Lame Gull Jetty he'd had very strong feelings about the subject. He'd talked about wanting a big family, and how he'd bend over backward to spend time with his children. Having lost a father at an early age, he wouldn't want a child of his to have to experience the kind of emptiness he'd had to feel. . . .

Lydia sighed, remembering. In that respect, Jake was like any other man she knew. And she, like most other women, wanted a child—with him. In fact, hadn't she always fantasized about having one with a man who'd never had one, either, who'd want it as much as she did?

There was no sense in getting upset about it, she thought grimly. With her medical history the whole issue was academic. Frowning, she went on to the next rabbit cage. What was bugging her was her own fixation on this subject. She shouldn't be dwelling on it, not when she and Jake had only the most embryotic of relationships.

Embryotic?

You and your subconscious, she thought ruefully. "Here you go, Popeye," she said. "Have a leaf." Lydia cleared her throat again. No, she wasn't coming down with the flu. She had a little cold, and a bad case of infatuation complicated by lovesickness, that was how she'd analyze it.

She was still watching Popeye when she suddenly had the distinct feeling that *she* was being watched, too. Lydia turned to the window. It was that little boy, Max, the one who'd been in earlier in the week. She smiled at him and waved a leaf. The boy nodded at her and then headed for the door, obviously misinterpreting her friendliness as a sign that he should enter.

"We're still not open," she told him as he joined her by the rabbit cages. He was dressed pretty much the same, with a V-necked sweater over jeans this time, the omnipresent baseball cap still backward over his dark brown bangs.

"I know," he said. "What's the problem here?"

Lydia laughed. "Many problems," she told him. "Getting a store open isn't a simple operation, you know." She looked past him to the street. "Misplace your date again?"

"I've got somebody else now," he said absently, large dark eyes intent on the rabbit. "I've decided, though," he announced. "I don't want any gerbils. I want a rabbit. Maybe this one."

"You like Popeye?"

Max nodded. "How'd he lose the eye?"

Lydia looked at the brown and white bunny, who was busily chewing at the leaf, his permanent squint facing away from them. "I'm not sure," she told him. "When he was a baby rabbit he must've had an accident and cut himself on something. But he sees fine out of the other one."

"Popeye," Max said. "Want to come to my house?"

The rabbit paused in midchew, fixed Max with a brief one-eyed stare, then returned to his meal. Max laughed.

"I think that might have been a yes," Lydia said.

"How much?"

"Well, why don't we discuss that with your . . . father?" she suggested, remembering that Max had said his mother wasn't in Boston. "When we open," she added.

"You can't sell Popeye now?"

"No, not just yet," she said. "Why don't you come back the day after tomorrow?"

"You won't give him to anyone else?"

"No," Lydia assured him. "I'll save Popeye for you."

"Promise?"

"Cross my heart," Lydia said.

Max looked at her a moment, evidently wondering if he should trust her. "Okay," he said, apparently satisfied. "You know what?"

"What?"

"You're the luckiest person I know."

"Really?" She smiled. "Why's that?"

He looked at her as if she were crazy. "You've got all of these," he said, sweeping his arm in the direction of her newly stocked shelves. "Boy, I'd love to live in a place like this!"

"Well, I don't live here, exactly," she began to explain, but Max had already turned away and was running for the door.

"Gotta go!" he called. "Bye, Popeye!"

Lydia peered out the window, but from her angle she could only catch a glimpse of a blond-haired woman approaching the corner with some grocery bags, who turned up the next block as Max joined her. Probably a sitter or a family friend, she mused, wondering what the boy was doing here if his mother was across the country.

"So I'm lucky," she told Popeye. "Do you think so?"

Popeye ignored her, intent on his meal. There was irony for you, she thought ruefully. She'd have given up all the many animal friends in her shop for one little boy of her own like Max. And Max's mom apparently didn't mind letting him go. Some people didn't know how lucky they truly were.

Patty and Mr. Sanderson were walking down the next aisle toward the door. One look at the tall man's face told her she hadn't gained a new tenant. Lydia stifled a sigh as Patty shrugged sympathetically behind his back.

"He said it wasn't what he had in mind," the girl told her, joining Lydia by the rabbits as Mr. Sanderson walked out.

"Oh, well," Lydia said. "Win some, lose some. Do me a favor. Go open that brown box under the counter and get me one of those new Sold stickers, okay?"

"HI, IT'S ME. I hope I'm not calling too late."

"Jake! No, not at all." Lydia put down the book she'd been reading, or trying to read, for the past hour, and glanced at the clock. It was after ten, and from the sounds of an intercom and other people's voices behind Jake, she assumed he was still at the hospital.

"I just wanted to see how you were feeling."

"Much better, thanks. My temperature never went any higher than it was this afternoon, my headache's gone," she said, feeling sheepish, "and I've got a sore throat. Period. But even that's not major."

"Good. Maybe the prescription helped."

"I guess so," she said, thinking, maybe I just wanted to see you. "How are you?"

"Beyond exhaustion," he said, with a rueful chuckle. "But it's a nice kind of tired, in a way. If you know what I mean."

"I think I do," she said, smiling. "Jake, it's good to hear your voice."

"And yours," he said. "I'm sorry I wasn't able to talk to you this afternoon, but you know how it is. I've been thinking about you. About this morning... I wish I'd been able to stay longer."

"Me, too," she murmured.

"You're okay?"

"You mean... about us?" Funny, she'd never used the word "us" in that way before. It gave her an odd feeling. "I think so," she said cautiously. "I mean, I had a wonderful time."

"Wonderful," he repeated, as if musing over the word. "Yes, so did I."

There was a pause. She could hear the quiet buzz of activity in the background. She wondered what he was thinking. She wondered, as she'd been wondering all day, if Jake had read her medical history and gleaned the truth about her condition from Dr. Newcomb's notes. And if he had, would it make a difference?

"Look," he said. "I'd love to see you, but there's no way I'll be out of here before midnight."

"I understand," she said, too quickly.

"Tomorrow's impossible, too, I'm afraid," he went on. "But if I can make it an early night tomorrow...will you be around?"

"Chances are good," she said wryly. "Other than a last-minute crisis that's bound to come up over at the store, I should be in Greensdale then, visiting Katherine."

"I'll call you," he said abruptly, and from the voices she heard in the background, she gathered he was wanted elsewhere. "I wish I had more to tell you and Katherine about this illness, but at the moment we're still in a holding pattern."

"Is there anything we can do?"

"I'm afraid not," he said. "Just sit tight and let Dr. Knowles know if anyone else shows signs of the same kind of illness. Lydie, I have to go."

"Okay," she said. "You take care of yourself."

"And you," he said. "I—" Jake paused "—miss you," he muttered. "Sleep well."

"So long, Jake," she said, and he was off the line. Lydia sat with the phone in her lap, looking blankly at the floral wallpaper of her Four Corners room. There was so much left unsaid, she felt, on both sides of that conversation. Was this what modern, mature adults did in such a situation? Tiptoed around the deeper feelings, respected each other's privacy, made no promises, expected no rewards...?

Restless, she paced the comfortable little room. She sensed that she was right about one thing; he cared about her. It was possible, much as she was wary of jumping to the conclusion, that he was as unhappy about having to leave their relationship in limbo as she was.

Relationship! Did they even have one? Lydia shook her head, looking out onto the quiet Greensdale streets, the curbs still white with frozen snow. The idea was to get done what she needed to do here and then go back to California, where she belonged. But this nightmare at Taylor House, and now Jake—it all made her feel as though her entire life was on hold.

So maybe she could have a little fling with him, and return to her normal life as she'd intended. She'd be a bit sad, yes, but soon the whole experience would seem like a nice, idyllic dream, not unlike the sensuous fantasies she'd harbored about Jake Harrison before. The only thing wrong with that was, she knew too much about the real Jake Harrison now. And settling for a fantasy was too depressing to contemplate.

Lydia sighed, moving back to her book. In a way it was out of her hands. If Jake wanted to make more of what they'd had together, it was really up to him. If he started backtracking, she'd know soon enough where she stood. Worrying herself silly over the whole thing was a waste of time.

"THAT WAS THE RIGHT THING to do," Katherine said, as they eased their way out of the crowd milling around the box office, waiting for the next show.

Lydia nodded. "Yes, we needed a good laugh." A new comedy starring Robin Williams, one of her favorites, had been playing in Great Oaks, and the sisters had decided that a night out would be a good idea. Peter was in bed with his cold, and Katherine hadn't been out on the town since her illness.

"What's next?" Katherine said, bundling her scarf about her neck. "How about some coffee, or hot chocolate, or? . . ." She looked at Lydia with a raised eyebrow.

"Ice cream!" both exclaimed in unison, and they laughed. Among other things, the sisters shared a love of eating ice cream in the winter. "I wonder if that place on Caroll Street is still open."

"I think so," Katherine said. "Come on."

Arm in arm, they hurried around the corner. The ice-cream parlor was at the end of the next block and open for business. Lydia got a butter pecan cone and Katherine a mint chocolate chip. Katherine devoured her concoction in record time, but Lydia was still savoring hers as they passed the bookstore on Main.

"I just want to run in and see if they've got this detective novel Peter was asking about," Katherine said.

"I'll wait out here and finish this," Lydia told her, holding up her cone.

Obviously one of the few places open for postmovie commerce, the store looked crowded from the street. Lydia wandered farther down the block, pausing at the picture window of an Italian restaurant. She liked the looks of it, not too flashy, with a neighborhoodlike air, and was checking the menu in the window for future reference when something beyond it caught her eye.

No, it couldn't be. It was obviously someone who *looked* like Jake Harrison. But Jake was busy with work at the hospital, and this man was eating dinner with a beautiful young blond woman. The man turned more toward her and Lydia instinctively took a step back, her heart beating furiously. It *was* Jake, there was no mistaking it.

Then she realized that there was a third person at the table. She saw the back of his curly dark hair and realized it must be Jake's son. And the woman was that au pair, Jacqueline.

Her jealousy subsided, replaced with an entirely different kind of envy. Lydia stood, unobserved, tempted to go in but feeling she definitely didn't belong there. Jake and Jacqueline were both listening attentively to the little boy. She couldn't see his face but he was gesticulating, telling them a story.

She wondered briefly why Jake hadn't told her he was taking his son out tonight, and why he hadn't invited her. *Come on,* she told herself, *it's none of your business. Why should he?*

He'd said he'd call. But he might have tried to reach her, she realized. She and Katherine had left earlier than she'd planned, to make the movie. Then again, maybe he hadn't felt the time was right for her to meet.... She didn't even know his son's name.

Jacqueline was laughing at something he'd said. Lydia stepped back from the window, her feelings in turmoil. She could go in, force the issue. But why? What was she doing, pushing her way into Jake Harrison's already complicated life?

Even as she watched, she saw Jake look surreptitiously at his watch. She recognized that look. He was thinking of the hospital, no doubt. Lydia turned hurriedly away, not wanting to be seen. She walked on, head down, feeling suddenly forlorn. Really, she should keep her distance from the whole situation. Jake had enough worries on his hands, with this all-important trial custody and some kind of flu epidemic on his hands. Wasn't she being selfish, wanting his time and his attention?

And after all, what did she really have to give the man that he didn't have already? With that wonderfully cheering thought, she rushed down the windy street.

"WHEN ARE THEY going to invent a way to add an extra hour to the day? That's what I want to know," Jake said, yawning as he blearily poured himself another cup of coffee.

"I think that comes after the inflatable car," Larry Baxter said, handing him the milk. "You know, on that big list They keep somewhere. Progress has its priorities, you know."

Jake looked at his watch again. "I can't believe it's already sundown and I'm still here."

Larry affected a deep, Godfather-type voice. "My son, this is the business we have chosen," he said. "How's the home life?"

"Okay, I think," Jake said. "This new girl, Jacqueline, she's great. Max loves her. We all grabbed a bite to eat in Great Oaks last night, and he seemed happier than he's been since he came."

"But you, you look like you haven't slept in a year."

Jake nodded. "Hey, just getting the hour to have dinner out with Max meant having to make it up here later, burning the midnight oil." He shook his head. "And I had to sacrifice seeing Lydia."

"Tough life," Larry said. "Tell you what, you guys should drop this bacteriological stuff and develop a good cloning process instead. What you need, Jake, is another Jake."

"Get us a table, okay?" Jake said, rolling his eyes. "I've got a phone call to make."

Lydia wasn't at the inn. He dialed Peter Bradford's with a heavy heart, and Katherine answered. "I'm still normal," she told him. "That's good, isn't it?"

"Yes, it is," he said.

"Good," she said. "Because I've got to get back to work. The folks at Hampshire College have been sympathetic, but I don't want to let my kids down any longer. Can I travel with a safe conscience, say, after this weekend?"

"I suppose, as long as you don't overexert yourself. How's Peter?"

"It's a head cold," she said. "No sore throat, no migraines, no high fever, just a real red nose. And the kids? Sadie tells me the twins are doing a little better."

"Pretty much status quo," he told her.

"Jacob, a Mr. Gaffney called us this afternoon. He's with the National Institutes of Health and he wants a public health caseworker to meet us at the house tomorrow."

"Yes, Dr. Knowles sent a sample to them. They'll probably just take some photos and look over the whole property for now."

"I guess it has to be done," Katherine said. "Right?"

"Yes," Jake said. "But they won't damage anything."

"You mean, until they start dismantling our renovations," she said ruefully. "Oh, Jacob, I'm sorry, I'm sure you want to talk to my sister."

"Yes, I thought she might be there."

"Hold on."

When Jake returned to the table he was absolutely morose. "What happened?" Larry looked up with alarm. "Lose a patient?"

"You and your live for the moment philosophy," Jake said, slumping into the chair.

"Shot down in the line of duty?"

"No, I might as well be shooting myself," Jake said. "I told you, me and commitment do not mix."

"Ah." Larry nodded sagely. "Young doctors in love. What did she say?"

"Nothing, practically. I apologized for not being able to see her tonight, and she hurried right off the phone. She was, I dunno, remote. Cold."

"She'll thaw," Larry said.

Jake shook his head. "I can't see her, she's upset, who can blame her, why did I get into this thing?" he muttered, listlessly stirring his coffee. "It was hopeless to begin with."

"Look, Mr. Sunshine," Larry said. "The other morning after your last date with her, you floated into this joint high as a kite. Give yourself a break, and her, too. You two are only getting started, right?"

"It's over already," he replied. "I told you, she'll be in California in another week or so, and I'll be in the dumps for another decade at least."

"That's what I like, a positive thinker," Larry said. "She wants to see you. You want to see her. Something'll give."

"I'm not sure she *does* want to see me," he said, remembering Lydia's evasiveness when he'd talked about meeting tomorrow. "I think she's already realized I'm too unavailable, and she's pulling up her tent. Which is what any self-respecting woman would do."

Larry narrowed his eyes at Jake, looking him over as a doctor might size up a patient. "We ought to take you upstairs and run an L.S.E. test on you, Harrison."

"L.S.E.?"

"Low self-esteem," Larry said. "Why are you taking all of this on yourself? Jake, there's nothing wrong with being a busy guy. If this Lydia can't accept who you are, maybe she isn't the right woman for you. Ever think of looking at it that way?"

"No," he admitted. "Because there's so much that's right about Lydia..." He sighed. "But maybe you've got a point. Maybe I should find somebody as wrapped up in her work as I am in mine. Someone who's not ready to rush into a major commitment. Someone who could deal with a casual, low-key kind of relationship."

"Now you're talking."

"There's only one problem."

"Which is?"

"I want *her*."

"Hopeless," Larry muttered, getting up for a coffee refill. Jake gazed past him, looking at the telephone outside. He wanted to call her back, but what could he say? In another few minutes he'd be immersed in laboratory work. And judging from Lydia's coolness on the phone before, he'd probably be best leaving her alone for now.

Maybe they'd both be better off if he left her alone, period. But that idea struck him as too horrible to contemplate. No matter whether there was any kind of future in it or not, a part of him was crazy to see her again, to see her as much as he could while she was still in Greensdale.

He'd make the time, somehow. Tomorrow.

THEY'D PARKED THE CAR in the driveway and somehow never made it into the house. Ten minutes after their arrival, Katherine and Lydia were still sitting in Katherine's Volvo, the motor no longer running but the car's interior still warm enough to be comfortable as they sat talking, looking at the house's exterior but in tacit agreement that there was no need to rush inside.

The people from the public health department were due within the hour. Lydia didn't feel like wandering through the depressingly empty day-care center, anticipating seeing the place taken apart, and she knew Katherine felt the same. Katherine was having an even harder time, being deprived of what had been her home for over a year now. So they sat in the car as if they were enjoying the illusion that all was well or at least normal inside Taylor House, as if what they couldn't see wouldn't upset them.

But then Lydia was upset enough as it was. Jake had called again this morning, saying he could swing an hour's lunch break if she could meet him somewhere between here and the hospital. And—though of course she wanted to see him—she'd turned him down.

"This still isn't making sense to me," Katherine said.

"Who said it has to make sense?" Lydia asked. "It didn't make any sense for me to get involved with him in the first place."

"But you did, and you wanted to, and you still want to," her sister said. "If you had gone to meet him, you wouldn't be here agonizing over it; you'd be talking things out with him. And that would make you feel better, wouldn't it?"

"Not necessarily," Lydia said. "First of all, there's no way I'd let you face this Mr. Gaffney and his merry crew by yourself. Second of all, what's the point? I've already decided."

"Decided to make yourself miserable, yes," Katherine said dryly. "That's the part that's not making sense."

"There's no room for me in that man's life," Lydia said.

"You don't know that. You're jumping to a lot of conclusions, Lydie. And hasn't he gone out of his way to spend time with you?"

"Even if he *had* been thinking about wanting to see more of me, after what he saw of me in that file…" She shook her head.

"Why didn't you just tell him?" Katherine asked quietly.

"Oh, sure. That would've been a great topic for our first date here. 'So, Lydia, what else have you been up to over the past few years?' 'Having a miscarriage, Jake, and one of my tubes tied.' 'Gosh, that's interesting, Lydia—'"

"He's a doctor," Katherine said. "He'd have understood what you went through and probably been very sympathetic."

"Exactly. I'm tired of men being sympathetic. First they frown and give you a compassionate look, and then they check their watches and start wondering who else they might start dating, next week.''

"Oh, stop it," Katherine said. "Not all men are like that. And I still don't see why you've made it such a big secret, especially since this Dr. Newcomb of yours—"

"Please, don't start on Dr. Newcomb," Lydia said. "Look, I didn't mean to have it turn into a big thing. This whole business is absurd, anyway. We haven't even...done anything.''

"Oh, you will," Katherine said dryly. "You should see the two of you in a room together. One can feel the heat."

"Besides, even if he hasn't read that file, and we did end up making love, I still wouldn't want to talk about—my problem.''

"Why not?"

"Sleep with the man once and *then* spring it on him? 'Jake, I know we're not planning to get serious here, so don't get me wrong about this, but I thought you should know I probably can't have children. I mean, just in case you did happen to have any thoughts about getting involved.'" Lydia rolled her eyes. "That's what I call subtle, right?"

"But if it's true that you don't have an interest in 'getting serious' with Jake Harrison, what difference does the whole issue make, Lydie?"

Lydia stared out the windshield, watching her breath form a little mist in the air. "Right," she said softly. "It shouldn't make any difference. Only it sure does."

"You're in love with him."

Lydia nodded. "That's what you call it, I guess. If thinking about him nearly twenty-five hours a day is being in love..."

"Sounds suspiciously like it."

"Kath, this wasn't supposed to happen, none of it." She turned to face Katherine. "I was going to keep my distance and so was he, because both of us knew there was no way anything could really come of us getting involved."

"And why's that?" Katherine asked mildly.

"Are you kidding?"

"Lydie, if you two really wanted to be together, you could work out a way to make it happen. Look at me and Peter. I never imagined I'd be moving back to Greensdale and commuting to Hampshire, but I am, because it was a way for us to be together."

"That's a little different from trying to commute from San Francisco to Boston, Massachusetts."

"You've just opened a store in Cambridge. You said yourself you were about ready for a change of scene. And doctors transfer to other facilities all the time. No, really, don't roll your eyes at me, it happens! Nothing's impossible."

"And then there's this kid of his. And an ex-wife lurking around somewhere...."

"Love finds a way," Katherine said. "Go ahead, make faces at me. But it's true."

"Maybe I don't want to have to go through getting my hopes up, getting involved in some precarious, problem-laden situation. Every time I meet someone I like, the stakes are higher, and this time, the risk feels huge."

Katherine nodded slowly. "I'm not saying that you and Jake would somehow magically sail through whatever conflicts you're already sensing on the horizon. But honey, are you sure you want to stop this thing before you really know how he feels?"

"I know he wants more children," she said, and bit her lip as she felt her eyes fill with tears. "And boy, do I. Everywhere I look I see women my age with kids. Every car I see has one of those high chair seats in the back. Every street has someone with a toddler in a stroller on it."

Katherine gently squeezed her hand. "Fifty-fifty," she said quietly. "Your odds are still even, remember?"

"I know." Lydia managed a smile, forcing back the tears. "Time's getting a little tight, though, you know? And you know what else?"

"What, hon?"

"I've always had this fantasy that the first child I had—
if I could have one—would be a new experience for both me
and the man I loved. You know, something wonderful that
we'd both go through for the first time, getting closer in the
most intimate way people can. A first-time mother and a
first-time father..." She bit her lip again. "It wouldn't be
the same if it wasn't as important to him as it would be to
me."

Katherine nodded. "I understand," she said softly. "But
you might be surprised at how important it *would* feel to
Jake."

"It wouldn't be the same," she repeated.

Katherine sighed. "Sometimes fantasies do have to go,
Sis," she said. "And reality can turn out to be just as wonderfully fantastic. The fact that Peter and I haven't had a
child together hasn't made us feel any less close."

"I suppose," Lydia murmured.

Katherine nodded again, and stroked Lydia's cheek. "It'll
all work out," she said. "Maybe not exactly the way you
planned it, but things always do work out."

"That's Grammy's line." Lydia laughed.

"Then it has to be true," Katherine said, and turned to
gaze back at the house. "She must be having a fit over this
business."

"The children? Yes, I'll bet," Lydia said. "She'd never
stand for some health inspectors coming in to tear the place
up. She wouldn't let them set foot in the house. Can't you
just see her bodily blocking the front door?"

Katherine looked at her. Lydia held her gaze, then they
both smiled, shaking their heads. "No," Katherine said.
"It's an idea, but I don't think we could pull it off."

"I'm not in the mood for getting arrested, anyway,"
Lydia said. "We'll have to let them in."

"I guess so."

They sat for a moment in silence, looking at the empty house. "They're only doing their job," Lydia said.

"That's right," Katherine agreed. But somehow that was little consolation.

Chapter Nine

Of all the things she missed about being home in San Francisco, not being able to talk to Duck Face the iguana was high on her list.

When the lizard first arrived at the Sanctuary, Herbie, amazed that an iguana could possess such a prominent flattened snout, had christened him Duck Face and predicted he'd be a hard sell. Sure enough, Duck Face had been residing in his little cage on the Sanctuary shelf for nearly two years, and although children seemed both frightened and fascinated by him, they never cajoled their parents into taking Duck Face home.

This was actually fine with Lydia, who enjoyed feeding the hapless iguana and having little chats with him when business was slow. She liked talking to Duck Face because he was a good listener. "What do you think of that Mrs. Kolker and her poodle problem?" she'd asked him, his first day in. Duck Face had stuck his long tongue out, an entirely appropriate response. He and Lydia had been friends ever since.

There were a number of other animals she missed, like Harriet the marmoset, an adorable animal that really did deserve a good home. Her problem was that people didn't know quite what to make of her, since she resembled nothing so much as, well, a marmoset. This confused customers, and so Harriet, like Duck Face, joined the ranks of

Lydia's special cases, longtime orphans and shop confidants.

On a morning like this, she would have loved their companionship, and she hadn't gotten to know any of the new East Coast pets as well yet. She needed to talk to someone who wouldn't talk back, necessarily, but merely lend a sympathetic ear. Katherine was good to talk to, but she knew too much. She'd say the things Lydia didn't really want to hear.

"I know," Lydia muttered to her absent sister, as she changed lanes. "I know what you'd say, so don't bother. You *are* right." If Katherine had been in the car, she'd have only agreed, so it was just as well she wasn't there. That was the advantage of friends like Duck Face and Harriet. They weren't judgmental.

"I'm being judgmental and paranoid and overdefensive," Lydia informed her steering wheel. "What's happening to me?" She glanced in her rearview mirror, and the creases she saw on her forehead were an instant confirmation of her worst fears.

Lydia signaled, cut over, and pulled to a stop in a service area at the side of the road, shocked and chagrined. She stared worriedly at her reflection again and shook her head. "Oh, no," she murmured. "This is terrible. You've lost your sense of humor!" she told herself.

The face that stared back at her was understandably distraught. "Lydia, how could you?" she asked. She bit her lower lip, hunching over the wheel as cars whizzed by, heedless of the psychic disaster in their vicinity. "Let's be methodical," she addressed her reflection. "Where did you put it? When did you last have it? Think, Lydia, think!"

She concentrated. When had she laughed last? Said something funny? Even *thought* humorous thoughts?

The answer was so obvious that she might've laughed, but having lost her sense of humor, all she could manage was a small wry smile. The last time she'd laughed, really chortled, was with Jake Harrison. The last time she'd made a good joke herself, he'd been there. Come to think of it, the last time her sense of humor had been very much in evidence had been...

"You left it in that room at the inn, that's where," she told the face in the mirror. "Your sense of humor's probably somewhere under that big four-poster bed."

Maybe a maid had found it by now, she mused. Lydia pictured a rather dour, matronly-looking White Raven maid, tucking fresh sheets under the mattress in that room and stopping short, suddenly convulsed in laughter over a joke that had flown into her head. The poor woman would be saying funny things to her fellow staff members with references in them that neither she nor they would understand. Now there was a tragic situation.

Perhaps she'd end up seeing a doctor. Maybe the doctor would refer her to his esteemed colleague, Dr. Harrison. And Jake, upon examining the maid, would experience an odd kind of déjà vu. "Wait," he'd say, "that skewed, delightfully absurd worldview...those sardonic, piquant comments...I've only encountered this sensibility once before—"

The face in the mirror smiled, dangerous forehead creases disappearing at last. But just as immediately they were back. Because in her fantasy, of course, Dr. Harrison's next step was to come running back to Lydia, to restore the misplaced sense of humor to its rightful owner.

The problem was, he wasn't likely to come running if she kept pushing him away.

It was time to face facts. There was still too much unresolved to feel okay about Jake, to feel okay about herself. And since she was meeting Sadie at the hospital, she might as well look up Jake as well. Even though her original intention had been to avoid him at all costs.

"The only way you're going to get your sense of humor back," she told her reflection, "is to talk to that man again." Then she shifted gears, signaled, and eased back into the flow of traffic.

"YOU KNOW ROGER," Sadie said, sighing.

"Yes, but how?—"

"He hates being cooped up in this little room. He had nobody to play rocket patrol with. So he got it into his head that maybe somebody in another room . . ."

"I thought he was running a fever," Lydia said.

"He was and is," Sadie told her. "But a four-and-a-half-year-old dynamo like Roger doesn't let temperature keep him down. So, he waited until the nurse had left the room, and he crawled out of bed and sneaked into the corridor."

"No one saw him? At noon, in broad daylight?"

"Apparently not. He didn't go very far, anyway. The next room over was a teenager with three of his limbs in a sling, so obviously not a proper playmate. Roger was checking out the next room when he got scared because he saw a doctor coming." Sadie sighed again.

"And?"

"And that's when he climbed into the linen closet."

Lydia stopped in her tracks. "He what?" A nurse passing them on the corridor held a finger to her lips, admonishing them. "How on earth—" Lydia began again at a lowered volume.

"It was an unlocked door right there around the corner, so he ducked inside and climbed up on the second shelf. Fortunately an aid opened the door only a few minutes later, but unfortunately, Roger was so freaked-out he tried to jump past the guy, and that's when he fell."

Lydia shook her head. "We're lucky it's only a fractured wrist."

"Yes, everyone's lucky," Sadie said. "Including the hospital, who Roger's dad has been threatening to sue since it happened. Here we are." She knocked at the next door, which was labeled Radiology.

A nurse informed them that Roger had already had his X rays taken and was with Dr. Baxter in the next room. When the two women were ushered into the dimly lit lab, Roger was seated on a counter amid an eerily lit display of skeletal parts, a rapt audience for a short, prematurely balding doctor.

"You see, the film paper only reads light where it can't get through," he was saying. "and with the special camera..." He paused, looking up at Sadie. "Hello, ladies." He turned to Lydia. "Roger's mom?"

"No," she said. "Just visiting. How's the patient?"

Roger held up his elbow, the forearm and wrist wrapped in a thick white bandage. "I'm gonna be set in concrete," he announced proudly.

"They'll need to put a small cast on that," Dr. Baxter said. "We were just waiting for Roger's exposures—"

"Larry? Have you seen Mrs. Morton's collarbone?"

Lydia whirled round at the familiar voice. Jake had appeared in the outer doorway. "I thought you had it," Dr. Baxter said.

"Jake," Lydia said quietly.

He peered in, his eyes adjusting to the dim light. "Lydia?" His face brightened.

"I came by to see Roger," she said automatically. *Oh,* there she went again, being cagey. And Jake was frowning.

"Oh, right." He turned to the boy. "How're you doing, little guy?" Roger shrugged. Jake smiled and nodded at Sadie. "Hi. Seen your kids?"

"They seem a little better," she said hopefully.

"Fever's down," he agreed. "Well..." He looked at Lydia for the briefest of moments, expression opaque, then turned to the other doctor. "Don't worry about it, Larry, I'll check back with you later."

He was about to make a hurried exit, she saw. Lydia moved quickly to the door. "Wait a second," she said.

Jake's face was a study. "You mean, you actually want to talk to me?" he asked warily.

"You forgot to introduce your friend," Dr. Baxter interjected, as if that was the proper answer. He was suddenly examining Lydia with great interest, though she didn't think she was acting that oddly.

Jake threw him a look. "Dr. Larry Baxter, Lydia Taylor And this is Sadie Travis."

"Hi," said Sadie.

Lydia moved with Jake to the doorway. "Well, if you do have a minute—"

"Don't wait on lunch for me," Dr. Baxter said. "You go ahead, Jake, you and Ms. Taylor."

Jake turned back to the other doctor with an ominous expression. "Do you mind?" he said pointedly.

"No," Baxter said, all innocence. "That's what I'm saying. I don't mind at all if you have lunch with your friend here. I was in the middle of a lesson on radiology, anyway." He smiled at Roger, who was ignoring all the adults, his attention on the display of X rays.

"You were about to take a lunch break?" Lydia asked.

"I guess I was," Jake said.

"Then I'll come with you," Lydia said. "For the length of a cup of coffee. How's that?"

"Sure," Jake said, clearly bemused by her behavior.

"Sadie, I'll meet you back at the kids' room," Lydia said. Sadie and Dr. Baxter were looking at them with encouraging expressions, both nodding.

"If I find Mrs. Morton, I'll let you know," said Dr. Baxter. The two of them looked like an unlikely pair of parents who were giving approval to their teenager's prom date.

ONCE THEY WERE SEATED at the cafeteria table, she wondered what it was exactly that she had to say.

She could ask him whether or not he'd read her medical file. She could ask him about their future, or rather, if he thought they had one. But none of these questions seemed to fall trippingly off her tongue.

For a moment they looked at each other in silence. It felt all the more unnatural that they were in such close proximity, yet so oddly distant. Shouldn't they be touching each other, shouldn't he be holding her, as he had just the other night? That was the only thing that would've made sense, it seemed, but they sat as if they were two strangers, regarding each other with mutual wariness.

"I've been getting the feeling you're avoiding me," Jake said. "I thought you didn't want to see me today."

"Oh, no," she said hurriedly. "It's just, you know, with the public health people coming and everything, I guess we're all a bit uptight." That much was true. She'd felt tense enough watching the public health people take a tour of Taylor House with their clipboards, tape measures and Polaroid cameras, their flashlights looking into every nook and cranny.

"Look, I'm really sorry I haven't been able to get away sooner," he said. "I hope you haven't gotten the wrong idea."

"And what would that be?" she asked.

"I've been wanting to see you," Jake said. "It's just been difficult these past few days."

"I understand," she said automatically. "Jake, you don't have to feel any obligation...."

"It's not obligation," he said, his voice suddenly loud in the quiet cafeteria. He shook his head. "Lydie, why are we sitting around talking like we barely know each other? What's going on?"

Lydia shook her head. "I don't really know," she said ruefully. "Look, you have your life to lead and I have mine. Maybe we're fated to have these brief encounters and not much else."

"You're tossing it up to fate?" His tone was ironic, and she heard the edge in it. She didn't want to be as defensive as she knew she was being, but all of her defense systems were up. She didn't want to show him how much she cared, how much he already mattered to her. That kind of vulnerability was only going to leave her open to getting hurt.

"Well, given the circumstances..." She shrugged helplessly.

"We can change them," he said. "I want to see you again."

Lydia gazed into his troubled face, wondering again if he'd perused that file. "Even knowing what you know about me?" she said carefully.

"I want to know more," he said. "Besides, I thought was the one with the low self-esteem problem."

Maybe he was still in the dark. That should've made her feel better, *but no*—if he was, that might make everything all the more painful. Why get the man's hopes up, and her own? "Jake, I'll be leaving soon," she said. "Maybe we're best off not making things any more complicated than they already are."

Jake frowned. "Is that how you see me? A complication?" He reached across the table to take her hand. Lydia felt herself warm to his gentle touch. "Lydie," he said softly. "It feels like we're both trying to pretend that nothing's been happening between the two of us."

"Right," she said, staring down at her hand, captive in his. "Tell me again, what *is* happening?"

Jake looked at her a moment. "We like seeing each other. There's a definite...attraction there. And we have a chance to get closer," he said. "Don't you think?"

"It's a possibility," she said.

"Maybe that's something we hadn't counted on," he continued. "So it's creating some, ah, confusion."

Lydia nodded. Here was a good opportunity to clear some of it up, but she hesitated. "Jake, look, if you've already got too many other...people in your life...."

"If you're referring to my patients, yes. And there's my son, true. But no, there aren't any other people," he said, frowning. "If you mean, people—women—that I'm interested in."

"I shouldn't even be asking," she said, embarrassed. "Jake, I don't have any right—"

"All I know," he interrupted, "is that each of us going our separate ways with a cheery handshake isn't going to leave me feeling good. Not at this point."

"Or me." Sitting at this small cafeteria table with Jake holding her hand, she could almost imagine, as Grammy might say, that everything would turn out all right. But how? "I do have to go back to California soon, though," she said.

"A lot can happen between now and then," he said significantly.

"You hope," she teased, and Jake smiled. She smiled back, pleased that her surmise about her missing sense of humor had been correct. Now that she was talking to Jake again, she was already feeling more lighthearted.

The sound of Jake's beeper was truly unwelcome, coming as it did just when she'd been starting to feel a moment's security with him. "Damn," he muttered.

"It's okay," Lydia said, checking her watch. "Jake, I'm glad we've had this talk, but I should be heading into Boston."

"No, sit. I've got a minute or two, at least." He smiled wryly. "I'll take any seconds I can get. Finish your coffee. And tell me, when can we get together?"

"You're the truly busy one," she said. "Which reminds me. Have you figured out what this illness is yet?"

He shook his head. "Still haven't isolated the strain the way I'd like to," he said. "Things are status quo. Sadie's twins are a little better and Carrie Lane's definitely improved. But the best thing I can say is, we haven't had any more cases."

"You still don't have a clue?" Although she knew it was irrational, especially after her own experience with the conflicting opinions of gynecologists, Lydia still harbored a naive belief that doctors, especially those who inspired trust like Jake, should have ready answers for any and every medical problem.

"Not exactly. There's still some details in the diseases's pathology that don't fit any specific profile of the encephalitis cases I've seen." He drummed his fingers on the tabletop, the frustration evident in his tone. "What happened with Gaffney?"

"It went pretty much as you said," she told him. "They just looked the house over from top to bottom, but they haven't started taking any rooms apart. It's just as well," she added, remembering what had happened as the men were leaving. "Bruce might try to take them apart first."

"Bruce?"

"He's the day-care center dog. He's really upset because all the kids have disappeared, so he's been refusing to eat and acting out of sorts. So yesterday, when those men were at Grammy's he suddenly made a dash for the choicest ankles."

"He attacked them?"

Lydia nodded. "Nobody got hurt, but it was quite a scene. One of those guys sure took off in a hurry. He's probably still running." She smiled, remembering. "I know I shouldn't be defending Bruce, but . . ."

"Isn't that a little like killing the messenger?" Jake asked. "Gaffney isn't responsible for the situation at the house."

"I know," Lydia said. Jake's beeper beeped again. "That's my cue," she said, as he got up from the table.

"You haven't answered my question," he said. "Our next date?"

"You tell me, Doctor."

Jake rubbed his chin, frowning suddenly. "Well, I'm . . . let's see . . ."

"Uh-huh," she said.

"Please," he said. "Don't take this the wrong way. But just now, in terms of a time and place—" he sighed "—can I call you at the end of my day's shift?"

"How did it go?" Larry Baxter looked up briefly from his batch of X rays as Jake reentered the radiology lab.

"I feel much better, thanks," Jake said, plopping himself down on a nearby stool.

"You talked things out with her?"

"Sort of. I think I convinced her not to give up on me just because I'm too busy to breathe."

"Excellent. An understanding woman."

Jake nodded soberly. "She seemed pretty understanding when I told her about Max."

"You gave her the whole history?"

"The lurid details, yes." Jake rubbed his eyes. "And it was a relief coming clean about the whole mess. It was when she started avoiding me that I thought she'd had second thoughts. If I could only spend more than five minutes with the woman . . ."

"Call in sick."

"You're hilarious." Jake sighed. "Well, at least I'm still in the running. Not that we've reached any conclusions about anything."

"Join the rest of us," Larry said. "I've been practically married to my significant other for years, and we still haven't reached any conclusions. That's normal."

"At least you two live in the same state."

"That also has its disadvantages," Larry said.

Jake laughed. "Come on, you love living with Teresa. You love fighting with her, too. Admit it."

"I admit to nothing without my legal counsel present," Larry muttered. "But did I actually hear you emitting a laughlike noise?"

"Guilty."

"That's a relief. Now maybe you'll start acting like a human being again."

"I'll do my best." Jake leaned in to look over Larry's shoulder. "Is that Roger Bartlett?"

"Yes, here are the little tyke's hairline fractures," Larry said. "And here . . ." His voice trailed off suddenly, and he flipped the desk light under the X ray to a higher intensity.

"What is it?"

"Something weird," Larry muttered. "Look."

He was pointing to the bones in Roger's arm, and for a moment Jake couldn't understand his colleague's reaction. "Chipped bone?" he asked. "Looks okay to me."

"No, no, not the contour," Larry said excitedly. "The shading."

Jake stared at the X ray, following Larry's finger. The skeletal white under observation did seem discolored, with a kind of gray banding pattern across the bone. "What is that?"

"Good question," Larry said, pacing maniacally in a small circle. "I'll tell you what it looks like to me: lead."

"Lead?"

"Either lead or some other deposit, say, a heavy metal. This is the kind of banding pattern that shows up when you run an FEP sometimes."

"Free erythrocyte..."

"...protoporphyrin, yeah." Larry stopped in his tracks and stared at Jake. "What does that suggest to you?"

Jake's mind was already abuzz. "Of course," he said, getting off the stool. "Poisoning. What else would give us the kind of symptoms—"

"Get that kid back in here," Larry said. "In fact—"

"Get 'em all in, absolutely," Jake said, hurrying for the door. "If that pattern shows up in all the X rays—"

"Save the eureka," Larry admonished him. "We've got some tests to run."

"MORE TESTS?" Mrs. Carter looked incredulous. She hovered between the two beds where the twins sat up in their matching pajamas, looking as if she might put a body block on any doctor who tried to come near them.

"Tammy, it's okay, really," Katherine assured her. "The doctors want to check a few things, and Michael and Melissa will be fine. It'll only take a minute."

Mrs. Carter looked from Katherine to Dr. Knowles. Jake was standing restlessly nearby as Lydia looked on. Michael was watching Dr. Baxter's restless trajectory, his head moving back and forth. "Is it going to hurt?" he piped up.

Jake paused. "No, Mike," he said. "And if you're both brave enough to help us out, I have a feeling there might be some ice cream coming as a reward."

Michael swiveled round to look hopefully at his mother. Mrs. Carter folded her arms. "Is this going to get us anywhere?" she asked.

"We think we're onto something," Dr. Knowles said. "Mrs. Carter, if we could step outside a moment, I'll be glad to fill you in on all the details."

Mrs. Carter made a little noise of regretful acquiescence, moving with Dr. Knowles to the hallway. While they conferred in subdued voices, Jake returned to Lydia's side. "I'm glad you got here," he said. "We need your help."

"Anything," she said quickly. She'd called Katherine from Cambridge, casually checking with her before driving back to Greensdale, and luckily caught her just as she was about to leave Taylor House for the hospital.

Katherine told Lydia that Jake had made some significant discovery and wanted her assistance at Nathaniel, so Lydia had changed her plans and driven back to the hospital instead. Once there, she learned that Jake and Dr. Knowles were investigating the possibility of the children's illness being caused by some kind of toxic poisoning.

"Katherine filled me in on the basic scenario," she said. "But I'm still not sure I understand. You saw something in Roger's X ray...?"

"Deposits of lead or some other heavy metal in the marrow," he said. "Which means we've been trying to cure the wrong disease. You see, that would account for the discrepancies in the symptom patterns we'd been finding," he'd explained. "Something like this is really hard to recognize for what it is unless you have a firsthand knowledge of the cause."

"You mean, it looked like meningitis but it's...food poisoning?"

"Not food, necessarily. These kinds of nephrotoxic disorders can have their origins in any number of inorganic agents. It could be paint, a fiber in the plasterboard, something in the water."

"And this is good news?" she'd asked, confused. "It sounds as problematic as the virus."

"It's not infectious," he answered, with a grim smile. "Don't you see? There haven't been any more cases because we've got them all right here. If it's not an encephalitis we're dealing with, at least we don't have to worry about a small-scale epidemic."

She nodded slowly. "You mean, it's only these six children who've got the...who've been poisoned?"

"Hopefully, yes. Now the only problem is finding out how it happened. X rays we took of Carrie Lane and Sarah Fine showed the same evidence of a lead or metal buildup, so we know we're in the ballpark. But now we've got to get specific, if we want to make sure we can apply the right cure."

"And you *can* cure them?"

Jake nodded. "The treatment's going to depend on the exact toxic agent we're dealing with. But judging by the way these kids have already reacted, the damage to their systems hasn't been lethal or even major—"

"Thank God," she murmured.

"—and we should be able to reverse whatever damage has been done, given the proper therapy. Which brings us back to the same challenge. We have to figure out what caused the thing."

"You're putting the twins through more tests."

"Yes, but if we can talk to all the children, maybe we can find a link just by some simple detective work. Maybe there's an area they all played in together, or a game that involved some substance the other children didn't come in contact with."

She nodded. "I see."

"But I don't really have time to talk to each of the kids, so if you and your sister can do some of the questioning . . ."

"But what *about* Katherine?" she asked.

"How do you mean?"

"She was the first one to get sick, wasn't she?"

Jake nodded. "Yes," he said slowly. "But with this new information, we can rule out a relationship between her flu and what's afflicted the children. I guess you'd call her getting sick a kind of red herring."

"What do you mean?"

"It misled us into thinking that we were dealing with the same illness. Once we got onto the encephalitis thing, Dr. Knowles's logic was that she had a more common flu that developed into an encephalitic infection by close contact with the kids. Though if you remember, we were confused by some dissimilarities in their symptoms.''

"And now . . . ?"

"We need to rethink the entire scenario," he mused. "And I think what your sister had was a bad case of flu, no more and no less."

"Well, that's a relief."

He nodded. "We don't have much time to feel relieved now, though, Lydie. We need to see what sort of clues we can get out of talking to these kids."

"No problem," she assured him. "I'll start right now, if you want."

"Great." He put a hand on her shoulder, his gaze holding hers for a moment. "I'm glad you're here," he said.

She smiled. "Me, too." She could see the excitement in his face, a new and hopeful cast in his eyes that had replaced the worried and preoccupied look she'd almost become accustomed to seeing there. That more than anything buoyed her own spirits.

"Let's get going," Jake said.

Katherine was seated by Melissa, inspecting one of her coloring books. Lydia and Jake joined her at the little girl's bedside. "I have a new book," Melissa told Jake. "You want to see?"

"Sure," he said, standing by patiently as Melissa pulled another book from under the covers. Michael was staring at Lydia.

"Where's Emily?" he asked her. Lydia sat down on the end of the little boy's bed.

"She couldn't come to visit today, honey," she said. "But I know she's thinking about you." She glanced over at Jake, hovering by the other bed. "Michael, would you like to play a little game?"

He nodded vigorously. "Yeah, I'm bored."

Lydia smiled. "I don't blame you, being cooped up in your bed all day. It was much more fun being at the Taylor House, wasn't it?"

"You bet."

"Why don't we pretend you *are* there for a little while?" she said. "You know, just for fun."

"Am I going to get ice cream?"

"I think you might." she smiled. "So, let's start. Pretend it's the first thing in the morning and your mom just dropped you and your sister off at the house."

"Aunt Deborah drops us off. My mom's sister."

"Okay," Lydia said. "So what's the first thing you do when you come in?"

Michael thought, making a great show of concentration by knitting his little brow. "Play on the swings," he said. "First one on the swings always gets to stay on a little longer."

"Swings," Lydia said, and looked to Jake, who was already removing a lined pad of paper from his clipboard. "Here," he said, handing it to her with a pencil. "You'd better take notes."

"Thanks," she said. Jake nodded, and gave her shoulder another encouraging squeeze as he passed the bed, heading for the door to join Dr. Knowles and Mrs. Carter, who were still animatedly talking outside.

"I'll check back in here as soon as I can," he said, and left the room. Lydia watched him go, feeling a kind of happiness she hadn't felt before about him. It was subtle but significant. For the first time, she sensed that she was actually a part of his life. She was really participating in Jake's work, and he was obviously appreciative.

Suddenly she was hopeful, almost convinced that her fears and anxieties had been overreactions, after all. Now wasn't the time to dwell on all that, however. She had an important job to do.

"Okay, Mike," she said, pencil poised. "How many of you use the swings at once? And is it just you and Melissa, or does everybody take turns there?"

Chapter Ten

"So, what've we got?"

"We've got a woodpile, we've got back steps, we've got swings, we've got old baking tins, we've got Grammy's garden...." Lydia flipped over the first few sheets of the yellow pad. "We've got a lot of specific toys. There's the paints. There's the carpeting...."

"In other words, about everything in the day-care center."

"Everything in it and outside it," Lydia amended.

"Isn't this the turnoff?"

"Yes. Follow Katherine." Katherine was signaling a few lengths ahead of them on the turnpike. Jake signaled and eased over behind her, glancing at the pad in Lydia's lap.

"I was hoping we'd find something more, ah, conclusive."

"Me, too," said Lydia, staring at her pages of scrawled notes. "But according to these kids, it could've been just about anything."

"There's nothing the six of them did that none of the other children did?"

"Well, it's a little hard separating fact out from fantasy," Lydia mused. "One day four of them apparently saved Greensdale from an alien invasion."

"That's it," Jake said wryly. "Just what we need. An alien heavy metal. Maybe something never seen before by our backward earth scientists, threatening to cripple the country...."

"...until you discover it and with the help of NASA and the CIA, make the world safe for democracy, right," Lydia finished. "I like this. Maybe we could sell it to the movies."

"Sounds like a good story for Steven Spielberg," Jake agreed. "But in the meantime, what've we got?"

"We've got a lot of seemingly harmless activities," Lydia said, putting the pad aside for a moment and rubbing her eyes. "I'm sorry, I'm not going to make a great private eye."

"You've done fine," Jake said, following Katherine's car down the winding road that led through Greensdale to the house. "We just have to sift through the stuff more carefully, look for links."

"Look for links," she repeated. "Well, they all spent a lot of time outside the week before they got sick, for one thing. There were a couple of unseasonably warm days before it rained. That was the day before I got here."

"I remember." Jake looked over at her. "Was that only a few weeks ago?"

"Believe it or not," she told him. "Seems longer, doesn't it?"

"I don't know," he said. "The funny thing about you being here is, it feels like you've always been here."

"I don't know if that's a compliment or not."

"It's an observation," he said. "Something I've noticed about being with you. You make me feel..." His voice trailed off and he shrugged, looking self-conscious as she shot him a curious glance.

"Feel what?" she prompted him.

Jake frowned. "Feel like it's perfectly normal," he said, eyes fixed on the road. "You being there, I mean."

"Oh. Like, I'm dull?"

"Dull? Not a chance," he said, smiling.

"Familiar as an old rag?" she teased.

"Forget I said anything."

"Okay," she said, but she wouldn't. She was touched by this observation of his, especially because she'd had the same feeling herself. When she was with Jake, it seemed absolutely natural that she should be, that they should be together. Maybe that was why she was having such a hard time trying to convince herself that this would never work out. Whatever "this" was.

"Outside where, specifically?" he said.

"Hmm?"

"Where did the notorious Taylor House Six, defenders of Greensdale from alien invasion, play outside together?"

She was glad he'd taken this bantering tone. The grim atmosphere at the hospital and all those technical terms he and Dr. Knowles had been tossing around had alarmed her. The fact that Jake could be so good-humored about a potentially frightening subject set her more at ease.

"On the swings. On the jungle gym. Around the garden. At the back of the property, where we stock the wood. And by the back steps."

"And what sorts of games did they play?"

"Nothing really well-defined," she said, looking through her notes again. "One thing they did on their own for a couple of days was run their own bakery. That's where the tins come in."

"Tins?"

"Emily gave them some old baking stuff to play with that wasn't being used in Grammy's kitchen anymore. I thought maybe there was a possibility there. You know, rust, or flaking metal particles or something like that."

Jake ran a hand through his hair, slowing for the stoplight at the bottom of the town green. "We'll look into it. But you see, these heavy metals aren't necessarily in metal as we know it. It's chemical traces, usually not visible to the naked eye, that could show up only microscopically, as part of something you wouldn't think of as 'metallic.' Like drinking water."

"I've thought about the water," she said. "That's the confusing part. We—at least, Katherine and Peter and Em ily—drink it all the time. Emily and Tucker do a lot of cooking, and none of the adults, let alone the other kids, have gotten sick before. Besides, most of the kids drink juices and sodas at the house."

Jake nodded. "So that implies another source."

Lydia tapped the pad. "Something in here we haven't seen yet."

"Or something at the house."

They were almost there, turning onto the road that crested over the hill. The trees that lined the road as they sped past seemed bare and cold. Even Taylor House looked a bit forlorn as they turned into the driveway and parked behind Katherine.

At least they were spared the sight of the public health cars parked there. Lydia had half expected to see a fleet of men in rubber suits with face masks deployed all over the property, pickaxes, chain saws and other implements of destruction in hand as they began their systematic search.

But Jake had already gotten in touch with Gaffney, alerting the powers that be. For now the health officials were sitting tight, awaiting the doctors' word. So there were just the three of them, bundled against the cold, breath visible in the air as they huddled together on the front porch.

"Katherine, maybe you can collect these things," Jake suggested, handing her the list Lydia had prepared in the car.

"Paint boxes, erector set pieces..." She scanned the list, nodding. "What do I do with them?"

"Just make a pile for us to go look at. We're going to walk around the backyard and see if there's anything obvious that bears investigating."

Katherine went into the house and Lydia followed Jake around to the back. She closed the gate to the fence they'd had put up to ring the property—a state requirement for any day-care facility—and stood with him at the southwest corner of the house, surveying the grounds.

Again, she was struck by the emptiness of an area that only days ago had been filled with activity and noise. The swings creaked softly as the wind lifted them. Jake walked slowly over to them. Lydia inspected the outer frame for some telltale sign of paint chips or . . . what?

"I'm not sure what it is we're looking for," she said.

"Hard to say," Jake mused. "Anything unusual . . . that's subtle enough to have gone unnoticed."

"Great," she said wryly. "That sounds simple enough."

"I know." He shook his head, gazing around him with an abstracted air. "How old is that jungle gym?"

"We bought it before we opened, about fifteen months ago," she remembered. "You think maybe there's something funny about this material?" She tapped one of the bars. "But all the kids play on it, not just the six in the hospital."

"Maybe our six don't just play on it. Maybe they've got a secret jungle-gym-bar-licking club."

"Are you serious?"

"I don't know," he said. "Did aliens really try to attack Greensdale? We're dealing with a bunch of very active imaginations." Jake idly kicked at the bottom of the jungle gym. "I wish we had something more concrete to go on." He turned back to her. "What was that you said about a woodpile?"

"Down there." She pointed past the mass of vegetation farther down the lawn, ringed by a low wooden fence, which was Grammy's garden. "It's at the very edge of this yard. I'll show you."

They strolled down the sloping lawn past the garden. By the back fence in the distance they could see the piles of firewood, some of them cut decades ago, which formed an extra wall just before the property turned into more free-flowing forest.

"What we own goes on for another few acres past the fence," she explained as they drew closer. "But this is as far as any of the kids are allowed to go. The rest of it's fairly overgrown, as you can see."

Jake was looking intently at the fence, following its winding line to the side. "I'm sure they've already checked the fence for breaks or holes," he said. "But we should look anyway."

"Emily swears up and down that if any of them had wandered off she'd have known about it."

"Kids can be wonderfully devious," he reminded her, and turned to look back at the house. "Unless they were literally right under one of the women's noses, I don't see why a few couldn't have sneaked off. With that garden in the way..."

Lydia nodded, but she wasn't really listening, her attention caught by something odd at the side of the woodpile. Unless she was mistaken, wasn't that Bruce? She whistled and called the dog's name, but he didn't move, apparently fast asleep.

"That's strange," she murmured. "Bruce?"

As she got closer, she saw that the retriever was awake, watching her with bloodshot eyes and a weakly wagging tail. His mouth was frothy and he was breathing hard. He tried vainly to rise as she approached, then gave up, settling back with a stricken look and the barest of husky growls.

"Jake, come here," she called, worried. As she stepped closer, Bruce made a vague snapping gesture, but his heart wasn't in it. The poor dog was breathing hard and his coat looked damp. "He's sick," she said, as Jake joined her by the woodpile.

Jake knelt down by Bruce's side. Again the dog raised his head long enough for a desultory warning bark, then gave up, lying back with his front paws splayed out. Jake carefully petted the dog behind the ear, putting a gentle hand on its stomach. Bruce emitted a pitiful groaning sound.

"Definitely," Jake muttered. "When's the last time this fella was fed?"

Lydia was about to answer when she saw something that made her heart skip a beat, a glint of metal in the high grass past the woodpile's edge. "The pump," she said. "Jake!"

He joined her as she knelt down, inspecting the rusty, old and old-fashioned pump. She'd almost forgotten it was there. "Look," she said excitedly. "There used to be a toolshed out here, and before that a barn, I think," she went on. "This pump draws on well water that comes from a stream about a half mile off the property."

Jake looked at her. "A working well?"

"I wouldn't have thought so," she said. "I mean, when I was a kid I don't remember anyone using it—because the house draws water from the town's supply."

Jake looked back at Bruce, stretched out in the grass a few yards away. "Maybe there's still water down there," he said. "And maybe—wait a second. What's this?"

Lydia followed his gaze. Just behind the pump, a round black pie pan lay in the dirt, filled with water. "That's one of ours!" she exclaimed.

"Of course it could be rainwater, or melted snow, but..." Jake stood up abruptly and stepped over to the pump. He grasped the handle and pulled it down. The old iron was rusted and complained noisily at first, but it moved. Soon it was fairly noiseless, just emitting a quiet wheeze as Jake cranked at the handle.

Lydia knelt by Bruce, gently petting the stricken animal as she watched Jake, her eyes riveted on the nozzle of the old pump. He'd only been at it for a minute when a trickle of water splashed to the ground. He pumped harder. Another trickle, and then a steady little stream.

"Not much," he said, breathing heavily as he stepped away. "But there it is."

Lydia got to her feet. "Wait, this is making sense," she said. "The kids created a make-believe bakery, right? They were making mud pies with soapsuds for toppings, the first day I was here."

Jake's eyes widened. "And eating them?"

"No, I'm sure they couldn't have, but that's not the point. When Melissa was telling me this before, and she mentioned making the pies and cookies, she said they'd served tea and coffee, too. Well, of course I assumed that meant one of the women had made it for them, if at all...."

"But what if they'd made their own batch?" he inquired, staring at the pie pan at his feet.

"I'm sure Emily or Sadie would've known," she said quickly. "But maybe it got by them somehow. I mean, what if it was pretend tea, like the pretend pies?—"

"Pump water tea?" Jake said. They stared at each other. "If Bruce has been drinking this water and looks that ill—"

"He was acting so strangely over the past few days! Remember, I was telling you—"

"I've got to get a sample of this well water, pronto," Jake said. "Let's not jump to any conclusions, but let's jump into action," he said, already moving up the lawn. "You know the number of the local vet?"

"WHY DID THEY have to do this?" Katherine was standing in the hallway outside the kitchen foyer, hands on her hips as she gazed at the foot-square hole in the wall by her feet.

"I guess it was a preliminary something or other," Lydia said. "Look, at least they didn't take the wall down."

The main day-care room had been a maze of taped-off areas, chalk markings and seemingly haphazard disarray when Katherine walked in. Gaffney's co-workers hadn't done any major damage to the house, they saw, but they'd obviously been prepared to.

"It could've been a lot worse," Katherine murmured, and Lydia realized she wasn't talking about the wall.

"Kath, stop," she said gently. "You can't keep blaming yourself. How were we supposed to know that the old pump still worked, let alone that there might be something wrong with the well water?"

"We went over everything so carefully," she said. "The fence gets checked every week for repairs—"

"I know."

"—and that morning, Barbara had her eye on those kids the whole time, I'm sure of it. She was with them when they brought the pies to the back steps...."

"It's nobody's fault, really," Lydia assured her. "And when we reopen Taylor House, we'll just have to double up on the supervision."

"If they let us open," Katherine said grimly. "I'm sure our reputation's in great shape as it is."

"We'll persevere," Lydia said. "Let's look on the bright side. If Jake's right about this, the children will be on the road to a faster recovery."

"When did Jacob say he'd call?"

"He didn't, exactly," Lydia said, taking her sister's arm. "Kath, all we can do is wait, for the time being. Let's brew up a fresh pot of coffee."

"We'll all start to levitate." This from Peter, leaning out of the kitchen doorway. "Katherine, have you been taking coffee-making lessons from Emily?"

"You said you liked it strong," she grumbled, heading back into the kitchen with Lydia close behind.

"How about my sister-in-law makes another one of her famous fruit pies?" Peter suggested, munching on a carrot as he took his seat at the kitchen table.

"Don't talk about pies," Katherine said, glancing fearfully out the window, where dusk was overtaking the yard.

"I'd love to, Peter," Lydia said, since she was, in fact, itching to get her hands into some dough. A little baking would be just the thing to take her mind off things during this worrisome vigil. "But we don't have the right stuff in the house just now."

"All right," he said. "How about a few hands of poker?"

Lydia looked at her sister, who rolled her eyes. "I'll go to the store," she said. "How about I make another batch of those oatmeal cookies with raisins?"

"Now we're talking," Peter said, slapping his hands together. "Here's some grocery money. And while you're at it, a few beers wouldn't hurt. There's nothing I hate more than sitting around waiting for somebody to—"

Lydia lunged for the phone on the first ring. "Jake?"

"Yes, it's me, and yes, we've got it."

"You do?!" Both Peter and Katherine rose at the sound of her excited voice.

"We're not equipped for anything too complicated at the lab here," Jake went on. "But Marvin—he's been analyzing that sample—and he's found traces of something that's definitely heavy metal-like.''

"Like what?"

"I'm not sure I can pronounce it," he said, with a laugh. "Wait, I'm being coached. Sodium ethyl mercurithiosalicylate? Similar to. And definitely tetraethyl."

"You've lost me."

"Inorganic lead." He sounded positively euphoric, which Lydia found comforting but a little confusing.

"And that's good?"

"Well, it certainly hasn't been good for these poor kids," Jake said. "But it's good news for you, in a way."

There was a click as Peter picked up the receiver in the hall. "We're all on the line now, Jake," he said. "Go ahead."

"I was about to explain to Lydia that this isn't the kind of chemical composition that develops organically. It has to come from some place—an unnatural source."

"You mean, the well itself isn't the problem?"

"I doubt it. The water's bad, Lydie. And that means somewhere upstream, something's going on that shouldn't be."

"You mean, we're not responsible?" Katherine chimed in.

"Peter, are you following me?" Jake asked.

"Yes," Peter said. "In my language what you're saying means the chances are good Taylor House won't be liable if there are any lawsuits."

"Lawsuits?" Katherine exclaimed.

"You never know," Peter said. "Jake, what's in the well water, exactly?"

"We're still trying to define the different traces. But the point is, with inorganic heavy metals, we're talking about some kind of man-made culprit."

"Chemical pollution?" Peter asked.

"That's a possibility. Do you have any ideas where the well draws its water? The main source?"

"'Fraid not," Peter said. "Katherine?"

"We should ask some people in town," she said. "Sadie's friends the Markhams live down the road a piece, with the back of their property on the same forest line. Maybe they would know."

"I'll get to work on it," Peter said.

"And we're going to get to work here," Jake said. "Now that we finally know what we're dealing with, we can alter the kids' medication and treatment accordingly. How's Bruce?"

"Dr. Bass says his chances are fifty-fifty," Lydia told him.

"I'll give him a call," Jake said. "Can you folks get in touch with all the parents? Dr. Knowles has managed to reach the Carters and the Lanes so far."

"We'll be glad to," Katherine and Lydia said almost simultaneously, and they both laughed. It was a welcome sound of nervous relief. For the first time in days, they could call a Greensdale parent with some good news to report.

"A TOAST," Katherine suggested, raising her wineglass. "One last toast before we leave."

"Another?" asked Lydia.

"Why not?" said Jake.

"Who to this time?" Peter asked. "We've already toasted the good doctor, the beautiful Katherine, my stunning legal mind and Lydia's bound-to-be-successful store opening tomorrow. What else is left?"

They had just finished up a celebratory dinner at the Four Corners Inn, the first truly festive meal Lydia had been to since her arrival in Greensdale. Further tests had confirmed Jake and Dr. Knowles' preliminary diagnosis, and the children were already undergoing treatment for the kind of low-grade toxic poisoning that the doctors believed was reversible.

"What's left is a toast to teamwork," Jake said, looking around the table. "We never would've been able to lick this thing without everybody's help."

"I haven't really done my part yet," Peter interjected. "But when I do find out how those chemical by-products managed to get into our well water, someone's going to have legal hell to pay."

"Believe him," Katherine said. "He's already got phones ringing from here to the state line, trying to find out what factories might have access to that stream."

So far, it had only been determined that the underground stream that fed the old well surfaced a mile or so away on the border of the neighboring county, continuing north above ground for another twenty miles. It was one of the many little tributaries of Watermill Lake, a turn of the century ice-skating spot that was now more of a backwater bog outside Great Oaks.

"First thing tomorrow, I start canvassing the other towns," Peter said. "If there've been other incidents of this kind of toxic thing—"

"Okay, but let's gulp the last of this second bottle down first," Katherine said. "My arm's getting tired."

"I second that. Cheers," Jake said, and they clinked their glasses. He smiled at Lydia as their glasses touched. Peter had been making plans like this throughout the meal, his intensity increasing with each glass of wine. His stubborn zeal to launch a crusade against what he now called the Toxic Taylor Monster was beginning to appear comic.

"Did we drink to Lydia's store?" he asked.

"Twice," Katherine told him. "I think that's the last toast for you tonight, sweetheart."

"Can't imagine why," he said, with a lopsided grin, then nuzzled his wife's neck as she leaned to whisper some gently reproving words into his ear.

"How are you holding up?" Jake turned to Lydia.

"I'm giddy," she told him, "with relief."

"I know what you mean," he said, leaning back in his seat. "It's been quite a day."

Lydia nodded, thinking that she'd have to draw upon some unknown reserve of energy for the *next* day. "I'd better make it an early night," she told him.

"Oh, that's right, you've got your opening tomorrow. Are you as ready as you want to be?"

"Of course not," Lydia said. "But at twelve noon tomorrow, we open the doors, come what may."

"I won't be able to come to the official opening," Jake said. "You know, I've been meaning to stop by and at least look at the place, but there hasn't—"

"Please," she said. "Don't apologize. I know how it's been. Besides, you can take a look at it tonight, if you like."

"Tonight?"

"You're driving me home, aren't you?" Jake nodded, puzzled. "Well, I'm not going back to Greensdale. I'm staying over at the Sanctuary."

"Is this some kind of superstitious ritual?"

Lydia smiled. "No. But there are some final deliveries coming at six tomorrow morning, and with all the work that's still left to do there, I figured I might as well sleep on the second floor. There's an empty apartment up there."

"Really? Are you keeping it?"

Lydia shook her head. "Just haven't found a tenant yet. But it's a perfect crash pad."

"Crash pad?"

Lydia laughed. "You'll see."

"WHAT YEAR IS THIS?"

Jake and Lydia stood at the foot of the stairs to the second floor. She'd flipped on the light switch to reveal the stairwell's mural, a panoply of angels in many phosphorescent colors that ascended to the landing.

"Oh, I'd say about '67 or '68," she said wryly. "Bring back any groovy memories?"

Jake chuckled. "I was a little young to be groovy," he admitted. "Is the upstairs all like this?"

"Even more fantabulous," she said. "Come see."

He followed her up the stairs, chuckling. "Actually, this kind of environment should make a Californian feel right at home." He sang: "'If you're going to San Francisco, be sure to wear some flowers in your hair...'"

"Stop," she said. "I'll have you know that no one in my hometown wears flowers anymore." She flicked the light switch at the top of the stairs, but no light went on in the hall. "Whoops," she said, gazing up. "I've never been up here at night before, and I have a terrible feeling..."

Her suspicion proved to be correct. None of the upstairs rooms had light bulbs in their sockets. Fortunately, she'd thought to stock some candles in the storeroom below. While she went to get them, Jake went out to his car and returned with a paper bag.

"You know, the place looks great," he said, indicating the store behind them. "You've done a good job."

She'd given him a cursory tour when they first came in, Lydia leaving most of the lights off so as not to disturb the non-nocturnal residents. "Still needs some adjustments," she muttered, finally locating the box of candles under some stacks of fish food on a bottom shelf. "But thanks. Any words of praise are appreciated. What did you get out there?"

"This," he announced, pulling a small champagne bottle from the bag. "I meant to send it over here tomorrow, but I figured, as long as we're here..."

"I like the way you think," she said. "Sure, let's call this a preopening—"

"—celebratory—"

"—nightcap," she finished. "I'm too wired to go straight to bed, anyway."

A few minutes later, Jake was popping the cork while she deposited the pile of sheets, blanket and pillows she'd brought with her on the perfectly serviceable bed that was still in the bedroom upstairs. For glasses they had two of the coffee mugs that came from the office downstairs, and for illumination the storm candles.

"Actually, the decor's much improved by candlelight," Jake noted, looking around at the swirling clouds and planetary symbols that adorned the walls.

"True," she agreed, holding out her mug. He poured the champagne. They clinked mugs.

"To your new home," he said.

"Well, you mean, my new franchise," she corrected.

"Slip of the tongue," he said. "Wishful thinking, I suppose."

Lydia smiled. They looked at each other a moment in the soft light, then sipped. "Umm," she said. "Delicious."

"Yes," he said, his eyes holding hers, and she had the distinct impression he wasn't necessarily praising the champagne. The affection she saw glittering in his eyes made her self-conscious, and she turned away, crossing to the bed. She put the mug down by the foot of it and began to unfold a sheet.

"You will be visiting, though, won't you?" Jake asked behind her. "To see how it goes here, I mean."

"For little short trips, yes," she said. "But Jake, I still have my other store to run."

"But it's not as if you're going away and never coming back."

"No," she said, wondering what he was driving at.

"Well, then." Jake sauntered over, mug in hand. He set it down next to hers and grabbed one end of her unfolded sheet. "There's some hope here. We can date."

"Date?" She laughed. "You mean, like go out to dinner a few times a year?"

Jake tucked in his corner as she smoothed out her end. "Some kind of a future is better than no future at all," he said. But he didn't sound particularly thrilled at this prospect, and in truth, neither was she.

"I guess," she said. There was a silence between them, one of those pauses where she could almost swear she heard Jake's thoughts swirling around in the air, mixing up with her own. Much as her good humor had returned, she had to fend off a wave of deep depression. Confronted with the realities of his life and hers, what could they really do?

She unfolded the next sheet. Jake automatically took an end. "Look," he said, as they spread it out between them. "We want to see each other again. We tried the old 'ship that pass in the night' scenario and it didn't work. So now let's see what we can come up with. A long-distance kind of thing..." He shrugged.

"Kind of thing," she echoed. "Yes, that's what we've got, don't we? A sort of a kind of something or other."

"What can we call it? I'm sort of getting attached to you, Lydie," he said quietly. "In a serious kind of way."

She felt a little thrill of excitement ripple through her as he said that, his dark eyes intent on hers. She stared at him across the bed, the blanket gathered in her arms. Naturally, her old demon fears chose that moment to join them at the bedside, perching around Jake's shoulders with crooked-toothed grins.

He's in for a surprise, said one. *How attached is he going to be when he finds out that little medical detail you haven't mentioned yet?*

A classic Fear of Commitment fella, crowed the other. *The guy's found a perfect nonmate mate—someone he only has to take to the movies when she happens to be on his coast!*

Lydia shut her eyes a moment and when she opened them the demons had had the good grace to disappear. "What's wrong?" Jake asked.

"Just thinking," she said.

He shook his head disapprovingly. "What do you say, just this once we don't think."

He came around to take the end of the blanket from her hands. Then his hand was taking hers, the blanket discarded. And then, as if they were both participating in some prearranged plan, they sank to the bed together, arms slipping around each other in an embrace that took her breath away.

The bed was soft, his touch softer, then more urgent. For once she followed his suggestion, and suspended all judgement and rational thought. That wasn't too hard. The feelings his lips and hands were conjuring up in her were overwhelming in intensity. They rolled back across the bed together, breathless in the candlelight, suddenly unwilling to take their time.

His kisses grew more fervent, mouth moving from hers to savor the softness of her neck, his fingers hurriedly making a path for his hungry lips, unbuttoning the pale pink sweater. She heard herself make a sound she'd never heard, a half moan of happy anticipation, and Jake stopped, his eyes seeking hers.

"You can tell me to stop anytime now," he whispered.

"I know," she whispered back.

"There's a lot we *should* talk about," he said, his face suddenly grave in the dim light. "I'm not letting you fly out of Greensdale too easily, Lydie."

"Who said it would be easy?" she said, and smiled. Thinking about Dr. Newcomb's file, or any of the questions and fears she had, seemed absurd at a moment like this. That dam of wanting and needing was threatening to burst. It had been such a long time. And it felt so good to be with him like this. She refused to let herself be deprived of a feeling that felt so good.

"Do you want to talk?" he whispered.

In answer she reached up, her hand gliding around his neck to pull him closer. "No," she murmured, and kissed him again. "No more talking. Please."

"I was hoping you might say that," he murmured. "Because I've been wanting to kiss you like this for the longest time. Here...and here...and here..."

His lips sought and then found the rounded fullness of her breasts. The cardigan slid back over her shoulders as his warm lips tasted the trembling pale softness of her skin. She felt transported by the sensuous magic of his touch, but too impatient to lie back and be disrobed.

With another sigh of pleasure, she sat up against him, gently halting his hands' eager progress as her sweater fell to the bare wooden floor. "My turn," she murmured, pulling at the knot in his tie.

It was resisting her, and she tugged at it, impatient fingers fumbling. For a moment both of them were transfixed in concentration on her efforts, until finally, with a muttered oath, she merely yanked it to one side and started hastily unbuttoning his shirt.

Jake chuckled, and they rolled together on the bed, Lydia playfully struggling in his powerful grasp, a laugh bubbling out of her at the exhilarating release of such unbelievable tension. Pinning him beneath her at last, she tore at his blue gabardine shirt with eager fingers, ready to rip the material if it resisted her.

Now she covered his chest with a fiery trail of kisses, her fingers playing with the curly thatch of hair, then fumbling at his belt. Her long hair raked across his face as she struggled to undress him, her white skirt billowing around them like a little tent.

"After . . . fifteen years . . ." she muttered, yanking at his tie again. "I refuse to be thwarted by a strip of silk. . . ."

Spluttering in mock suffocation, Jake came to her assistance. At last the tie was undone, and soon his pants and underwear were discarded on the floor, the white skirt pulled past her knees and free of her. Now a soft sheet crumpled beneath their nakedness. Jake gathered her tightly to him and she moaned again with pleasure at the feel of his lean, taut body enfolding hers.

Each kiss gave way to another. "I thought you were tired," he teased her, coming up for air. His voice was a husky rasp when he finally lifted his lips from hers, his night-black eyes glittering with amused affection as he slid his supple hands over her body in a ceaseless, eager exploration.

"Not now," she countered in a whisper. "This is a treat I'd given up on waiting for," she murmured, as he nibbled sensuously at her earlobe.

"Me, too," he breathed. "But I'm already absolutely sure that it was worth the wait. Don't you think?"

"We're not thinking," she whispered. "Remember?"

"Yes," he said. "Do you like this?"

"Umph," she gasped. "Yes . . . yes . . ."

And that was all she remembered them saying as passion overtook them. Except once, as he was hovering over her, as she was hungering to feel his body merge with hers. "Lydia," he murmured, and something else, just before his mouth ravished hers, one hand sliding behind her head, fingers knotting the silken tresses, and they joined together.

What had he said just before that ecstatic merging? That he loved her? Or had she only imagined it, wanting to say it to him? But spoken or unspoken, that was the word, and as they loved each other, bodies twisting and dancing in the white sheets, the candles seemed to flame brighter and the room was filled with an ecstatic, blinding light.

Chapter Eleven

"This is it. I'm absolutely... positively... mmm..."

Lydia, stretching provocatively against his warm body beneath the sheets, smiled as Jake's words died away into another murmur of contentment, his arms encircling her again.

"You were saying?" she murmured, nuzzling his neck.

"I'm getting up," he said, his voice muffled in her hair. "Honest. This time I mean it."

"Mmm-hmm," she said, smiling as he made no move to support this claim, but idly stroking her shoulders instead as his lips nibbled at her ear.

They hadn't really slept at all, only falling into what were essentially short exhausted dozes between bouts of playful snuggling, lovemaking, and sleepily intimate conversation. Throughout, the flickering candles had been dimly illuminating the room, but now the sky was already brightening with the first light of dawn.

Jake had been threatening to get out of bed for quite a while, but one more hug, caress or kiss had invariably kept him where he was, which was fine with Lydia. She hadn't felt so contented to the core and yet needful of even more affection in as long as she could remember.

It wasn't just that he was such a wonderful lover, sensitive, gentle but forceful in ways that left her breathless with excitement. It was the sense she got that while Jake was here with her, he was showing her the best of him, all of the hidden surfaces revealed, from his funny little expressions to his most serious inner thoughts. When he looked at her, touched her in the darkness, or even merely listened, she felt she was receiving the full extent of his energy, concentration and interest.

The time they'd spent together here had seemed magical to her. Though she'd made fun before of the constellations painted on the ceiling, the room's mystical trappings had seemed oddly appropriate to their long night of love. The rest of the world had simply vanished beneath the intensity of their absorption in each other.

If the earth had disappeared for good, she wouldn't have cared, as long as they could stay adrift in a gentle limbo in this bed. That would be fine, really, because while he was a city, a entire state himself, she was a country with her own peaks and valleys; between the two of them they were continents, a world unto themselves.

But regrettably, that regular, normal old world had refused to take a vacation from existence. From the way Jake stretched upward and away from her she knew he was checking his watch again. "We've entered the danger zone," he muttered.

"You mean true lateness approaches?"

"On winged feet, yes," he said, frowning as she tactfully moved away, easing away her arm from his wonderfully muscular torso. "But that doesn't mean..."

"What, you're taking me with you?" she asked playfully. "There's an idea. I'll just drape myself over your shoulders while you go on your rounds."

"'Good morning, Dr. Harrison, and who is your papoose?'" he said, chuckling. "It would certainly shake up a lot of patients. But, no, much as I'd like to..."

"Isn't it awfully early to have to go to the hospital?"

"I need to stop home first, see how the kid's doing, see how fast I can wolf down some breakfast and become reasonably functional for a very long day," he said.

"Must be terrible to have to work after missing a night's sleep," she said. "Now I'm starting to feel guilty."

"Guilty? Oh, come on," he said, his frown deepening as he gazed down at her. "Just stop looking so beautiful, will you? You're going to ruin my career here."

"'Scuse me," she said, covering her face and breasts with her hands. "But you must be sleepy if you call this beautiful."

"I don't get sleepy when I look at you," he said, removing one hand to kiss an erotic circle around one breast. "I get..."

"Mmm, you certainly do," she murmured, feeling him move against her. "But I'm not going to take the rap for destroying your professional credibility." Once again, she forced herself to roll to one side, much as she wanted to curl right up into the shelter of his warm embrace. "Go!" she cried, with a mock tearful tone.

There was a muffled curse behind her, and then the springs sang and she felt his weight move off the bed. Lydia turned back, sitting up in disbelief. "Hey," she protested. "You actually went."

"I know, it's a criminal act," he muttered, rummaging around on the floor for his clothes. "But another minute and I actually would've let the world and everyone else in it fend for themselves."

She could detect a bit of true surprise and annoyance beneath the lightness in his tone. "I'm sorry," she said.

Jake straightened up. "Don't you be sorry," he commanded. "*I'm* sorry. Any other man who had half a brain in his body wouldn't leave that bed, no matter how many people needed his attentions...." He shook his head, leaned forward and kissed her lightly on the lips, lingering for a moment to smile into her eyes and then abruptly retreating. "Too dangerous. I'm going to have to keep my distance for a few minutes or I'll never get dressed."

Lydia settled back against the pillows, watching his every move with great interest. Funny, but it had been so long since she'd spent the night with a man that everything about it was enjoyably novel. And she liked to watch his body in motion as he donned underwear, socks, shirt and then trousers.

It was the sort of intimate act she found oddly touching, seeing him put together his face-the-world-self. Now that she knew so much more of him, knew the other expressions that could inhabit his features, this more restrained appearance he was fashioning had a different resonance for her. She felt a rush of such affection for him as he got down on all fours, searching for something below the bed, that tears actually filled her eyes.

Uh-oh, she thought, *you're over the edge.*

"Where did we put my tie?" he queried, his face suddenly looming at the bed's edge. "What's wrong?" he added, looking at her more closely.

"Nothing," she said, and smiled. "I'm just having a good time, that's all." She turned to look behind her. "I think it might be down under the headboard here...." She reached down past the mattress, her fingers encountering the striped silk. "Here you go," she announced, holding it up. "Not severely damaged."

"Thanks," he said, taking it from her, his hand lingering over hers a moment before departing.

Lydia watched him hurriedly put the tie on, her chin resting on her drawn-up knees. "How busy a day do you have?"

"Oh, only one of the busiest of the week," he said, wincing as he tightened the tie's knot. "Six hours at Nathaniel, four hours seeing some local people here in Great Oaks, and then I'm back at the hospital into the evening for some research work. Tonight's the one night this week we have free run of the lab."

"Oh," she said, "so then I won't—" She stopped herself, embarrassed. She wanted to see him, of course. She still wanted to meet his son, to stop feeling like an intruder in his life. But she'd purposely avoided making any mention of possible future plans for the two of them, feeling they'd have to play all of that by ear and not wanting to attach too much significance to what had happened between them.

Too much significance? It wasn't until he turned to look at her with an expression of uneasiness and guilt that it finally hit home: she was already involved with the man in her heart, and if he were to indicate that spending the night together hadn't meant as much to him as it had to her, it would hurt her, badly.

"No," he said. "I won't be able to see you tonight." Jake sat down on the edge of the bed, reaching over to hold her feet beneath his hands. "Lydie, I didn't know what might happen with us, you know that—"

"Of course," she said quickly. "Jake, I didn't think—"

"So there really isn't any way I can suddenly turn my schedule around for us, even though I want to. And I want to, believe me."

"No, really, Jake, I wasn't expecting that you'd—"

"But you should expect," he interrupted, his voice suddenly raised in emphasis. "You have every right to expect things from me, Lydia—like time and attention. That's the problem." His face had turned grave, that hint of sadness in his eyes again.

"Jake, I'm okay about it," she said gently, though she could sense she wouldn't be, in a matter of minutes, perhaps immediately after he'd left the building. "Honestly, I understand."

One of his hands moved up to stroke her cheek. "You know that's the main reason I've been...holding myself back," he said. "I knew that if we spent time together like this, I'd want to be with you, more...and with the kind of work load I've got right now, and this Taylor House thing, and my situation at home—"

"Stop," she said, and kissed his hand. "Jake, we're big boys and girls here. I knew what I was getting myself into when I let you stay the night." She forced a smile. "After all, I'm the one who's going to be hightailing it back to the West Coast in a matter of days. Call *me* irresponsible, if you want."

Now, that was a good speech, wasn't it? She almost believed it herself. Jake was gazing into her eyes, as if trying to assess what she'd said against the vulnerability he must've seen there. "I'll make time to see you," he said softly. "Not tonight, but certainly tomorrow. Lydie..."

"You don't have to make any promises, Jake," she said softly.

"I want to," he said. "I want us to spend some real time together before you leave, and talk about things. I wish we were able to do that right now, but you know how crazy things are."

"I know." She nodded, thinking that she had at least one sensitive thing she needed to talk about with him. Giving her hand a last squeeze, he was rising from the bed. Lydia put her chin back on her knees, trying to fend off the first pang of withdrawal she was already feeling. Big girl, indeed. For a moment she felt like a child about to be deprived of her favorite...everything, and she shook off the feeling, dismayed.

"And I'll call you, later in the day. You'll be here?"

Lydia yawned. "Absolutely," she said. "I wonder if a pet store run by a zombie has ever opened in Cambridge before."

"Your deliveries aren't due for another hour or so," he said. "You could go back to sleep." He cast a longing look at the rumpled sheets. "What a temptation."

"No, I'm up," she said. "And I don't want you to be any later than you already are," she added. Wrapping the sheet around her, she took him by the hand, leading him across the bare floor to the door. "Out," she commanded.

He smiled, took hold of her bare shoulders and pulled her to him for a last kiss. It was a pretty long kiss. By the end of it, her sheet had slipped to the floor. When Jake finally pulled away from her he shut his eyes tightly. "Put that thing back on," he said, "or I'll never be able to get out of here."

Lydia smiled, scooping up the sheet. Jake opened his eyes, smiled, and gave her a wave as he bounded down the stairs. "Good luck today!" he called.

"You, too," she called after him. She watched his long, lean frame disappear around the landing below, and then, without even consciously planning to, she found herself drifting to the windows to see if she could get a glimpse of him getting into his car on the street.

"Sap," she muttered, when she realized she couldn't see, but only hear his car engine from this angle. "You've turned into a total saphead."

She'd finally fulfilled a long-cherished romantic fantasy—sleeping with Jake Harrison. And remarkably, it had lived up to, no, been even better than her imagining. That in itself was a stroke of luck. The downside was, she hadn't counted on caring so much.

But she did. She cared about him, the him she'd gotten to know so well, it seemed, over a mere week. And suddenly, the thought that last night was all the two of them might share in the way of a real intimacy was a horrifying one.

THE PARAKEETS never arrived.

The lights of one of the fish tanks weren't functional. A shelf bearing heavy boxes of kitten litter and dog food crashed to the floor, narrowly missing Patty, and Crew Cut was having major problems with the cash register. Then there was the Scottish terrier pup that ate too much food and threw up all over his nice clean cage.

All in all, it was very much exactly like what Lydia was used to from the West Coast store. But the main reason she was able to take all of it in stride was that her feet were still a few inches off the ground.

She wasn't dazed or in a fog, or any of the other predictable cliché conditions that might normally accompany a Morning After. No, her hours with Jake upstairs had left her in a state of unusual calm and clarity. She felt as if her normally anxiety-ridden, perpetually driven nature had been caressed and kissed into a welcome tranquillity. Nothing short of the ceiling's collapse would have really fazed her today.

So at noon, even though things in general showed no sign of becoming less chaotic, Lydia went to the front door of the shop and prepared to unlock it. She turned to face her staff. They all smiled hopefully at her, Bob Grady in particular trying to look anything but apprehensive.

"Are we all ready?"

A chorus of cheerful assent mingled with the barks, meows, chirps and burbles that filled the store. Lydia nodded, turned the CLOSED sign around and unlocked the door. She even opened it about a foot and stuck her head out into the crisp midday air. "Hi, Cambridge," she called. "We're here!"

The only passing pedestrians, a nurse wheeling an old woman in a wheelchair, looked at her blankly and went on their way. But Lydia was undaunted. She checked to see that the red and blue flags they'd hung from the store awning hadn't been blown away by the wind, and stepped back inside.

"Pet Sanctuary East is now in business," she announced.

For about an hour nothing happened.

She hadn't expected a steady stream of customers, as it was a weekday, after all, and Thanksgiving vacation was just a few days away. But still, it was a little daunting to have knocked herself out and end up with a store completely devoid of people.

Finally, the little bell they'd installed over the front door did tinkle. Lydia heard it from the back room, where she was instructing Crew Cut and Arlene, the new girl, in the care and feeding of mice. Though she supposed she should have let Bob or Patty take care of it, she leaped up and rushed out into the store to see who the first official customer might be.

"Lydie, it's beautiful!"

She should have known. Katherine and Peter were strolling down the aisle, oohing and ahing. "Can I interest you in a menagerie?" she asked. "I happen to have my entire stock available."

"No sales yet?"

"Well, we did just open," Lydia explained. "You really like the look of the place?"

"Nice paint job," Peter commented. "Say, that reminds me. Client of mine may stop by here later to see your hippie commune pad upstairs. His daughter's looking for an apartment."

"Oh," she said, surprised to hear a note of disappointment in her own voice.

"I thought you were dying to get rid of it," Peter said.

"Oh, I am," she said, realizing as she feigned enthusiasm that she suddenly wasn't in a hurry to. Sentimentality was already setting in. She didn't like the idea of someone taking the upstairs away when it had just become "hers" somehow, hers and Jake's.

"Tell her," Katherine was prompting Peter, giving him an excited nudge.

"Tell me what?"

"We've made some headway on the well water mystery," he said.

"Peter's traced that stream over two counties," Katherine said. "And that lake that's the source—"

"You wanted me to tell her," Peter interrupted. "What famous corporation do you suppose has recently opened a new facility with chemical waste dumping grounds that are within yards of the lake?"

Lydia stared at him. "Not ConCo," she said.

"Yes, ConCo," said Katherine. "Can you believe it?"

"We haven't been able to get any solid evidence, let alone straightforward information from the ConCo people yet," Peter went on. "That's to be expected. It's Runaround City over there. But the fact is, the most busily operative part of that new building is a research laboratory, and they've already done their share of spilling and dumping over the past four months."

"You mean they're allowed to just dump chemical waste in that lake?"

"No, they're not," Peter explained. "They've got some sanitary landfill space that's absolutely legal, but seepage from their buried waste is a possibility. Theirs is certainly the only facility that deals with industrial chemicals anywhere near the source water. So what we're trying to determine is the specific content of their waste material. If we find the same heavy metal traces..."

"This is too much," Lydia said, looking at Katherine. "It's like ConCo's revenge!"

Katherine laughed. "You mean, getting even for us not letting them use our land? The thought occurred to me," she said. "But I'm not *that* paranoid."

"I'm sure they didn't do it on purpose," Peter said. "But if they are responsible, it's going to give me great pleasure to nail their corporate butts to the wall. It's precisely this kind of neglect that drives me nuts. Companies like ConCo pay lip service to Environmental Protection Agency regulations and then bust them through sheer ineptitude or sloppiness every day. And they think all they have to do is look contrite in the press for five minutes and it blows over. But not this time."

"No, not with the great crusader on their case," Katherine said, putting her arms around Peter. "Go get 'em, tiger."

"Defending Taylor House against suits from irate parents would've been one thing," he said. "But suing Conco? Now, that's my idea of a good time."

"Boy, things are certainly looking up," Lydia said.

Peter grinned. "Why don't you tell her the other good news?"

"They say Carrie Lane should be out of the hospital in a few days," Katherine said. "The em...emetics, I think Dr. Knowles calls them, have been really working, with all the children. Now that the doctors know what the problem is they're able to treat it much more effectively."

"That's fantastic," Lydia said. "And the house?"

"We'll be back in business tomorrow," Katherine told her. Her brow darkened for a moment. "Minus Emily, unfortunately. I still haven't found someone to take over the reins full-time.''

"At least there's a job to fill," Lydia reminded her. "A few days ago we didn't think there would *be* any day-care center, remember?"

"Point well-taken," Katherine said.

"Will you look at the size of that guy!" Peter was wandering among the snake tanks.

"I'd rather not, honey," Katherine called. She took Lydia by the arm, leading her a little farther up the aisle. "Speaking of fantastic," she said quietly. "What's going on with you?"

"Me?" Lydia looked at her. "What do you mean?"

"I mean you're positively radiating," Katherine said wryly. "Come on, I happen to know you just a little bit," she said, smiling. "Where did you and Jake go last night after dinner?"

"Oh, nowhere in particular," Lydia said airily, then laughed. "What, you mean it shows?"

Katherine nodded. "You look happier than I've seen you since you got here, that's all I know," she said. "What's the scoop?"

"Lydia, phone for you!" Patty was brandishing the receiver from behind the counter.

"News at eleven," Lydia told Katherine, as the door to the shop jingled and two teenagers, obviously customers, came into the store. "I'll stop by after work."

"Okay," said Katherine. "We're back in the house now. Peter moved in the stuff yesterday."

"Good," Lydia replied. "See you later."

"Hey, Kath, you interested in a nice iguana for the garden?" Peter asked.

"I better get this guy out of here," she said. "Good luck today!"

"Thanks." She waved goodbyes, noting that as they opened the door to go, a mother with two kids in tow came in. Apparently when it rained, it poured. After an hour of inactivity, the store was starting to come alive. She took the phone from Patty, motioning her to go out and be solicitous. "Hello?"

"Am I speaking to the owner of Pet Sanctuary East?"

"Yes."

"The one with the small round birthmark on the inside of her upper left—"

"Jake!" she said. "Hi."

"How's it going?" he asked.

"We only just opened, and there was nothing for a while. But they're starting to trickle in," she told him.

"How are you holding up?"

"Oh, fine," she said. Her reflection in the silver of the counter's chrome showed her a mushed face with a mile-long grin plastered on it. "Really fine," she said, softer "And you?"

"I think I left a part of me in that bed upstairs," he said

"Mmm," she said. "A good part? 'Cause if you did, I'l go up there right now. Patty and Bob can run the store."

He chuckled. "You're a wanton woman."

"I'll take that as a compliment," she said. "Oh, hey Doctor, congratulations."

"Hmm?"

"I hear the kids are doing well."

"They are," he said. "I think we've found the righ combination therapy of chelates and diuretics."

"Whatever you say, as long as it works."

"So far, so good," he said. "Are you okay?"

"Okay?" she echoed. "Actually, I feel great."

"Me, too," he said. "Although I may fall over if I sto moving."

"Do you have a lot to do?"

"Too much," he said ruefully. "As a matter of fact, I' be working into the evening...."

"Which means I shouldn't count on seeing you. Dor worry; I didn't think I would," she said quickly.

Jake chuckled. "You're a very accommodating person

"To a point," she said. "When *will* I see you?"

"At around four o'clock."

"Really?!"

"I have to give you an official pet store opening day kiss, don't I?" he said.

"Jake, I'm flattered, but as busy as you are—"

"Actually, there's an ulterior motive. My son's been after me to get him a pet, so I thought I'd zip over there on my break and pick one out, with your expertise as guidance."

"I'd love to," she said. "What does he want, specifically?"

"I think a rabbit. Are they hard to take care of?" he asked. "Because if feeding them is a problem, it might not be a good idea."

"Oh, no," she said. "They're a lot easier to take care of than many. Dogs, for example."

"Well, help me pick out a nice one, will you? When it comes to rabbits, I trust your taste implicitly."

Lydia laughed. "You're just full of compliments this morning."

"Hold on a sec...I see a nurse's aid headed this way with a pile of paperwork I've been trying to avoid."

Lydia hesitated, then took the plunge. "Oh, Jake, you know that medical file that I gave to your nurse?"

"Which?"

"When I thought I was sick," she hurried on. "I had some papers with me from a doctor in San Francisco, in a manila envelope. Do you think I could get that back now?"

"No problem. I'll bring it with me."

"That would be great," she said, worried that he might look at it en route. But why would he? She'd have to take the risk. "If it wouldn't be any trouble—"

"None," he said. "Okay, I gotta go. I've been missing you," he added.

"I miss you, too," she said softly.

"Stay warm. See you in mere hours," he said, and the line clicked into silence. Lydia hung up the receiver, realizing she was smiling again. *You're getting a little mushy,* she told her distorted reflection. But then, how often did she get to feel this happy? A little mushiness wouldn't do her in.

BY FOUR O'CLOCK she'd sold a kitten, a puppy, a pair of gerbils and a parrot. For a first day that was quite all right. The main thing was, they were establishing themselves as a presence on Sellars Street. Word of mouth and the ads she'd taken out in two local papers should do the rest.

"Someone here wants to put a down payment on a rabbit," Bob said, leaning into the back room as Lydia looked up from her crouched position on the floor, 3-in-one oil in hand. The portable scrub unit they used had squeaky wheels.

"Down payment? Can't you take care of them?" she said.

"He only wants to see you."

"Me?" Lydia straightened up, puzzled. "Oh, wait, I know who that must be," she said. "I'll be right out."

Sure enough, the top of a backward baseball cap was visible over the counter's edge as she approached. Max was standing there with a paper bag in his hand. "Hi," he said.

"Hi, Max," she said. "Have you come for Popeye?"

"Kinda," he said. "I don't have all the money for him yet, but I thought if I gave you some, maybe I could take him home with me today."

"Well, we can't really do that, Max," Lydia said gently. "But you don't have to worry. No one else is going to be able to buy Popeye. I'm saving him for you."

"Wait, look," he said impatiently, and before Lydia could stop him, he was emptying the contents of his paper bag on the counter, a mound of change, largely pennies, with some dollar bills mixed in. "Over ten dollars," he announced.

"That's impressive," she agreed. "But Max..."

"I've been saving," he told her. "And I'll get the rest from my dad."

"Tell me something. Did your father know you were coming here today?" Max shook his head. "Does he know you want Popeye?"

Max nodded. "Yeah, I told him. But he says he has to think about it."

Lydia had figured as much. "Well, until he makes up his mind, it wouldn't be right for me to take this money, Max. Let's put this back in, okay?"

Max sighed as she started to scoop up some of the change from the counter and into his bag. "Okay."

"We'll just wait until you and your dad can come back with all of the money at once."

Max frowned, grudgingly holding the bag open for her. "He's busy all the time," he said.

"That's a shame," she said, sliding off the last few pennies. "But I bet if you tell him that we're holding a special rabbit, especially for you, on sale," she added, as an afterthought. "He'll make the time to come in. Maybe this weekend," she said hopefully.

"Maybe, maybe, maybe," Max said with a little sigh. "That's what he says."

"What does your father do?" she asked.

Max shrugged. "He runs around," he said vaguely. "Some times he comes home late. Last night he didn't come home at all."

Lydia shook her head, taking an instant dislike to Max's absent father. She had an urge to give the boy Popeye, gratis, but knew that hasty act might create trouble and backfire. A mother at the other end of the country and a father who ignored him—again she found it difficult to fathom such parents.

"Well, if your dad has any questions about rabbits, you have him call me here, okay? I'll tell him how easy it is to keep Popeye at home, and how inexpensive."

Max nodded. "Can I go say hello? Have you fed him yet?"

"I think he's had lunch," Lydia said. "But come on, you can give him an extra lettuce leaf, so he'll know you're his friend. How's that?"

Max smiled. As he ran down the aisle toward the rabbit cages, Lydia moved around the counter, thinking: what I wouldn't give, for a smile like that in *my* home... She

shrugged off the too-familiar melancholy. Today had been
too good to give into it now.

Someone was waving at her through the store window.
Lydia peered out, her heartbeat accelerating as she recognized Jake. She hurried down the aisle to the front door. No
sooner had she opened it then he pulled her into his arms.

"Looks great," he said, smiling.

"You haven't seen it yet," she protested.

"I'm talking about the look in your eyes," he said, smiling. "Have a congratulatory kiss."

His lips closed over hers and she closed her eyes, enjoying the surge of pleasure as his arms pulled her even more
tightly to him. The now-familiar taste of him was delicious
to her, and the feel of him so exciting that she nearly forgot
she was supposed to be the proprietor of a respectable pet
shop before she gently eased her lips away.

"One kiss will have to do for now," she said, her breath
a little shaky. "I'm a working woman. Come inside."

"Does that mean I have to let go of you?" he asked with
a mock frown, his arms still encircling her waist.

"I think it would be a good idea," she said, and then
suddenly he did let go, abruptly, an odd, startled look on his
face as he stared over her shoulder.

"Jake, what's the . . . ?" she began, and turned to follow
his gaze.

Wide dark eyes stared up at them from under a backward baseball cap. Max's face held a confused and hurt
expression as he looked from Jake to Lydia.

"Max," Jake said. "What are you doing here?"

The little boy still clutched a piece of lettuce in his fist. As
Lydia looked on astonished, he hurled it at her, then ran
past them to the door. "Max!" she called, but he was already scrambling down the sidewalk, his father running after him.

"STOP APOLOGIZING," Lydia said, pacing the Taylor House
kitchen floor. "It's nobody's fault."

Jake sighed at the other end of the phone. "I should've had you meet him sooner," he said. "I was planning on it. How was I to know Jacqueline would be dropping him at your place when she picked him up from his tutor's?"

"It's nobody's fault," she repeated.

"I was nervous about the two of you meeting," he went on. "I thought he might react, you know, defensively, seeing me with . . . an unfamiliar woman."

"Well, let's just say we've hit this issue head-on," Lydia said dryly. She shook her head, thinking over what Jake had told her about Max's temper tantrum the night before. "He really said that? About Popeye?"

"Afraid so," Jake muttered. "But I know he really wanted that rabbit."

"Of course he does," Lydia said. "He just wants me to know that he doesn't want . . . me."

"But you were getting to know each other fine," Jake said. "That is, before you knew—who you both were. And that's a good sign, because he's hard to get to know. For a nine-year-old, he's still kind of antisocial. Actually, I'd been worried the two of you might not hit it off. Which would have been terrible."

"Only now the situation's just as bad," Lydia said.

"He seemed a little better this morning," Jake said, but she didn't hear much conviction in his voice. "Oh, listen, with Max flipping out, I forgot to give you that medical folder of yours. Should I just messenger it over?"

Lydia stiffened. She'd forgotten, too. One more sensitive issue to deal with. "Yes, why don't you send it to the store?"

"No problem. Look, I've got to get back to the floor. I'll call you later, all right?"

"All right," she said resignedly.

"Don't worry about anything," he added.

"Worry? Oh, no," she said. "Take care."

When she got off the phone, Katherine came in the back door, looking pink-cheeked from the cold but radiantly happy.

"The kids are having fun out there," she said, hanging up her coat in the foyer.

"Well, at least something's going right," Lydia said ruefully.

"Yes, this is more like it." Katherine turned to gaze out the kitchen window, watching the kids laughing and yelling from the swings outside.

"How many are back today?" Lydia asked.

"We've got a dozen," Katherine said. "Tucker's been calling everyone and letting them know, and with Carrie and the twins getting out of the hospital any day now, we should have a full house by next week. More coffee?"

Lydia nodded. Even though she'd gotten a decent night's sleep, back in the guest bedroom upstairs, she was still feeling exhausted. Her romantic night with Jake, the store's opening yesterday, and the traumatic scene with Jake and Max had taken its toll. Even a full cup of coffee prepared "à la Atchins" had barely cut through her early-morning haze.

Sadie came bustling through the back door. "I think today's the last day for this kind of outdoor play," she announced. "Even with all their mittens and earmuffs, I start to worry."

Katherine nodded. "I don't even want to see a runny nose," she said dryly. "Did Tucker have any luck with Mrs. Hopper?"

Sadie nodded, chuckling. "You ought to ask her yourself when she comes inside. Apparently Mrs. Hopper was still nervous about the water in the house. You know how people are. Anyway, Tucker told her she'd drink three full glasses of it in front of her when she brings little Susie back, just to prove the point."

Katherine laughed. "Sadie, have you spoken to her yet? About our idea?"

"I felt her out about it. We think Tucker might be the ideal candidate to fill in for Emily," she explained to Lydia. "She knows how the place runs, inside and out, and she was basically Em's right arm over the past few months."

"Well, what did she say?"

Sadie grinned. "Nothing! You know Tucker. She just sort of lit up, quietly, and nodded. I think she's really excited."

The phone rang and Katherine grabbed it. "Taylor House," she said. Lydia watched, sipping her coffee as Sadie poured a small cup for herself and doused it with milk and sugar.

"Emily may be gone, but her caffeine lives on," she said, smiling, gulped some down and headed for the door.

Lydia was glad to see everyone in high spirits again. It almost, though not quite, lifted her own sagging ones. Yesterday, when Jake hadn't returned to the store with Max, she'd felt as though fate was determined to keep her from having any kind of simple, uncomplicated happiness. He'd phoned later to apologize for his son's behavior and she'd said she understood, but she was already feeling the return of her uncertainties and misgivings.

And that infernal medical report! Or rather, her own infernal internal problem—it was one more reason to extricate herself before she suffered another disappointment. She was beginning to think that a retreat to California was the smartest solution to the whole messy situation. She walked listlessly to the window and looked out at the obliviously happy children, envying them.

Katherine's phone call was evidently from Clarissa. She could tell that by the certain tone Katherine took on when she talked to her daughter sometimes. "Fine," she was saying now. "Whenever you want." Clarissa was due up for Thanksgiving. Lydia wondered what change in plans was in the air. One thing about Clarissa was consistent—her absolute inconsistency when it came to sticking to any given social agenda.

Lydia returned her coffee cup to the sink, trying to shake the blues that had been dogging her all morning. She'd tried so hard to take this thing with Jake for what it was, an isolated incident, a nice romantic interlude, no more, no less. But that was turning out to be harder than she'd imagined.

"She's coming early," Katherine announced, getting off the phone. "Well, that's better than canceling out." She peered at her sister. "What's wrong?"

"Oh, nothing," Lydia said. "I guess I should head into work."

"Not so fast, little sister," Katherine said. "What did Jake have to say?"

"Max is still upset, and who can blame him?" Lydia said. "He doesn't even want his rabbit now."

Katherine shook her head in sympathy. "He'll get over it."

"Sure, after I'm gone," Lydia said. "Which is fine, I guess, because after all, I'm leaving Greensdale within a week, and I know this isn't anything serious between Jake and me—"

"Only you'd like him to spend every waking hour of the next five days with you," Katherine said. "That's not serious."

Lydia smiled wanly. "Of course it is," she said.

"Well, I'll tell you when you can see him, and his sulky son," Katherine said. "Thursday. Invite them over for the big turkey."

"Maybe," Lydia said. "But he'll probably be working at the hospital."

"Kidnap him," Katherine said. "And I'll hide his hospital beeper under the couch or something."

Chapter Twelve

"I hate to say 'I told you so,' but I told you so."

Larry Baxter shot Jake a quizzical look as he emptied their trays. "What, Harrison, you were right about something? Good Lord, what's this world coming to?"

"I just called Lydia Taylor again," Jake said. "And she's definitely giving me the brush-off."

"You're paranoid." Larry held the door open for him as they left the cafeteria. "You mean, she gets on the phone and says, 'I won't talk to you'?"

"No, but she was too busy to talk."

"She's at work, right? Try talking to you when you're doing one of your marathon days," Larry said.

"But she's leaving after this weekend," Jake said. "Our only date is a Thanksgiving dinner tomorrow. We haven't had a moment alone together since the pet shop disaster."

Larry nodded thoughtfully as they waited for the elevator. "So what did you do wrong?"

"Nothing other than be myself," Jake said glumly.

"Oh, well," Larry said. "Then who can blame her?"

"Very funny." Jake sighed. "This is what I mean about 'I told you so.' I told you that no woman would want to get involved with a man who's as involved with his work as I am with mine, because that's one involvement too many, let alone my other ones."

"You said that? And I understood it?" Larry shook his head. "Boy, we've been hanging out together too long."

"I need at least two of me." He jabbed at the floor number on the panel inside the elevator.

"Well, I guess you've got a point," Larry allowed. "But something isn't making sense here."

"Yes, why I let myself get into this mess in the first place."

"No, not that part, idiot," Larry said. "According to you, the two of you had a magical night together, just a few nights ago. And the next night you were still on good terms, even after your son sort of put a damper on things."

"Yes, and then I had to cancel a lunch date," Jake said. "Which was probably one cancellation, one unavailability too many. So her understanding must've run out. You know, like I was overdrawn at the sympathy bank."

Larry shook his head. "No, you're missing something."

"Since when did you become an expert on the vagaries of feminine psychology?"

"I'm not. But that female is in love with you. No, don't look at me like that, I know it when I see it. And I saw how she was looking at you when I met her here. That is not a woman who would give up on you so easily."

"But apparently she has."

"There's more to it," Larry persisted. "But you figure it out. I gotta go look at a cracked vertebra."

Jake had been worried enough by Lydia's behavior not to merely shrug off his friend's opinion. Probably there was something he'd overlooked or misunderstood. But what? Troubled, he headed for the room where Roger Bartlett was still convalescing. Four of the other Taylor House patients had already gone home, and Roger was next in line for clearance. "Hey, Roger-Dodger," he said, coming into the boy's room. "How's the pitching arm?"

Roger Bartlett sat up in bed, scowling at the doctor as he held up his cast. "It itches," he complained. "When does this come off?"

"Couple of weeks," Jake told him, taking Roger's chart from the end of the bed and looking it over. "But look o the bright side. You're feeling better, and you get to go home tomorrow.''

Roger nodded. "My mom says she baked me a cake."

"I don't blame her," Jake murmured, examining the chart, pleased to see that the therapy had worked well. The last blood test revealed a much healthier system on the mend. "In a way, you're kind of a hero, you know."

"I am?" The boy grimaced.

"Well, if you hadn't broken that wrist of yours, we might not have figured out what was wrong with you and Mike and your other friends."

"Huh," Roger said, pleased. "See, I'm not just a troublemaker, like Mrs. Travis always says."

"Doesn't mean you should've gone off crawling into closets, though," Jake was quick to add. "Now lie still while we take your temperature one last time."

Jake's nurse was just hanging up the phone as he returned to the office. "Want your messages?" Jake nodded absently, his mind returning once again to Lydia's behavior. *Was* he being paranoid? Or was Larry right, and had he done something or said something that had put Lydia at a distance? He tried to concentrate on what Daphne was saying.

"...and we never did reach Mr. Walsh about his chemotherapy, but we called in that new prescription for Mrs. Kranston," the nurse continued, checking her ledger. "I had that folder messengered to Ms. Taylor, and the file on Thelma Cale sent to Dr. Hoffsteader. That's the update."

"Ms. Taylor," he repeated. "Thanks, Daph."

Walking down the corridor to continue his rounds, he wondered if that was the issue. Maybe Lydia assumed he'd read the folder. In fact, he had stolen a quick glance at it, just to verify what he already knew from Dr. Newcomb's inadvertent admission the week before.

Was it possible she was avoiding him out of some sort of misplaced embarrassment? Did she think that his knowing she was possibly infertile would affect the way he felt about her? It didn't seem right, but then, anything he had to go on was better than being in the dark. Embarrassment or not, he had to confront Lydia, soon.

"YOU REALLY DIDN'T have to do this, Lydie," Clarissa said. "You must be totally pooped after working all day."

Lydia shook her head, easing away from the curb at the shuttle terminal. "It wasn't that busy," she said. "Unfortunately," she added wryly. Clarissa's flight from New York had gotten in at six-thirty, and since Lydia was only a fifteen-minute drive from the airport, she'd volunteered to pick up Katherine's daughter there before returning home to Greensdale. "That's your only bag?"

"I'm traveling light," she said. "So, are you going to take me by the store now? I'd love to see it."

"It would be faster to take the turnpike," Lydia told her. "Why don't you visit tomorrow?"

"'Kay," Clarissa said, settling back in her seat. "So! Mom told me the good news. About the house. Everything's okay now, isn't it?"

"Yes, we're open again," Lydia said, navigating the loop out of the airport proper.

"And the store's opening was a success?"

"Pretty much."

Clarissa turned to face her. "Then why are you so down?"

"Am I?" Lydia shrugged. "Not really." She glanced over at Clarissa, who had a watchful expression. "I like your new hairstyle."

"I've just been letting it grow," Clarissa said, giving her head an impatient toss. "Don't change the subject, Aunt Lydia."

Lydia smiled. Clarissa only addressed her in that formal fashion when she thought Lydia wasn't being informal enough. "I'm not changing the subject," she said. "There *is* no subject."

"Not according to Mom," Clarissa said.

Lydia sighed. "What did she say now?"

"She said you were in the throes of a traumatic love affair," Clarissa said.

"She couldn't have," Lydia said. "That doesn't sound like Katherine at all."

"I'm paraphrasing," Clarissa admitted. "But that's the gist, isn't it? And you look totally unhappy, so something's gone wrong. Right?"

"It's really not worth going into," Lydia said.

"It's the *only* thing worth going into," Clarissa declared. "Now, either you tell me everything that's going on, or I just won't talk to you the whole time I'm here. So, out with it, all the details!"

Lydia knew she didn't have much choice. It was traditional that she and Clarissa have major heart-to-heart talks the few times a year that they got to spend time together, and she didn't want to both hurt Clarissa's feelings by clamming up, or deprive herself of the pleasure of letting her hair down with Katherine's daughter.

In a way, over the past few years she'd begun to feel more at ease talking things out with Clarissa than with her sister. Clarissa tended to be less judgmental than Katherine, who was inclined to be older-sisterly, not that she could help it. And Clarissa sometimes found it easier to confide things to Lydia than to her mother, for similar reasons.

So on the turnpike that led from Boston past Great Oaks and into Greensdale, Lydia told Clarissa about Jake Harrison and the rather problematic package his life presented. "No wonder you're worried about it," Clarissa said. "But there's nothing you've said that can't be talked about and dealt with, if he wants to be with you as much as you want to be with him."

"You sound like your mother," Lydia said. "But no, some things can't be talked around. Like the fact that I probably can't have a child—and I know he wants more than one."

"If he wants you . . ." Clarissa began.

"Look, there's no point in my further embarrassing myself by having this out with him," she said resignedly, giving her horn a short toot as a car cut in front of them.

Clarissa considered this in silence a moment, then shook her head. "If it was me," she said, "I'd tell him what was on my mind. At least I'd know where I stood for once and for all."

Lydia shot her a look. "Hey, kid," she said. "Since when did you start sounding more grown-up than your aunt?"

Clarissa smiled. "I've been a good listener for years now," she said. "I'm only telling you what you'd tell me."

"ONE POUND of new potatoes, six garlic cloves, two sprigs of fresh rosemary...cheesecloth," Lydia muttered, consulting her list. She paused, thinking. The cheesecloth for the turkey would require a separate trip.

"I bet that gourmet food shop at the other end of Sellars carries it," Patty volunteered.

"Right, the one where a head of lettuce costs five bucks," Crew Cut commented.

"Oh, you wouldn't know the difference between quality food and that crud you eat in a million years," Bob Grady said. "But the ladies have discerning tastes."

Lydia put down her list. "Why is three-quarters of the staff of Pet Sanctuary East standing around here giving me a running critique of my Thanksgiving shopping?" she asked. "According to my watch, we'll be open for another hour."

"Just in case someone wants to eat rabbit instead of turkey tomorrow," Crew Cut said, then ducked out of the way as Bob tried to swat his rear.

"I'm not amused," Lydia muttered, folding her list and putting it into her coat pocket. "All right, everybody, you are hereby on your own. A preview of the days to come. So when I come back before closing time, I want to see...oh, half the inventory sold, how's that?"

"Is this an excuse to pink-slip us, just before the holidays?" Bob groaned. "That's cruelty to humans."

Lydia smiled, hoisted up her shoulder bag, and headed for the front door. She and Katherine had divvied up the shopping tasks that morning. With Emily gone, Katherine was too busy at Taylor House to do it all, and it was actually Clarissa who'd be doing the legwork for her. Peter had already shouldered the turkey responsibility, picking up two gargantuan fowls to accommodate the crowd they were expecting for the Taylor House feast.

So Lydia would be bringing in a few bags of necessary foods from Cambridge, and had purposely set aside this time at the end of the day for the job. She was glad to have such a task. Things at the store still weren't busy enough to keep thoughts of Jake out of her mind.

She still hadn't convinced herself that avoidance was the right tack to take. Clarissa and Katherine were still persisting that Lydia was using any excuse to extract herself from a relationship she'd been scared to get into. And though it irked her, Lydia knew there was truth in that.

She *was* scared. Some survival instinct of hers was on automatic pilot. She hadn't wanted to face needing him, becoming dependent on him, when the circumstances already practically dictated a no-future scenario. Thinking about leaving Greensdale when they'd really started to get close had given her anxiety attacks.

In fact, in a wild moment of romantic fantasy, she'd contemplated not renting out the second floor above the shop, on the outside chance that she herself might use it as an East Coast home base. If she and Jake had gotten more involved. If she had wanted to deal with his almost guaranteed disappointment when he found out about her medical history. If he'd overcome that . . .

A lot of ifs. Well, she'd probably have to deal with them, finally, when she saw Jake at Thanksgiving, and with Max, too, if he agreed to come. Thinking about Jake so much made her fancy that the man heading down the street toward her was him. Lydia slowed. It was.

She stopped short, a few paces from the Sanctuary. Jake was striding up the block to meet her, only yards away. She was going to have to deal with the man a lot sooner than she'd thought. In a panicked moment, Lydia considered going back inside the shop and bolting the door. But he'd seen her, and he was already by her side.

"Lydia." His dark eyes sought to hold hers, but she was determined to look anywhere but directly into them. "Where are you going?"

"Out," she said. "Jake, what are you doing here?"

"We've got some talking to do."

"Oh." She nodded, apprehensive, and started to walk. "Well, I've got some shopping to do...."

He kept stride with her. "I have a feeling you've been avoiding talking to me, lately," he said. "What's going on?"

"I just thought I'd let you be," she said. "I mean, with Max and everything."

"I don't want to be let be," he said. "I want to be with you, Lydia."

She bit her lip, pulling her coat tighter against the wind. "Are you really sure about that?" she asked. "I mean, your life is full of enough conflicts as it is."

"You're not a conflict," he said firmly.

"I seem to be, with Max," she said. "And Jake, there's..." She paused, her heart pounding, not knowing how to say it. "Look, Jake, we want different things."

"Such as?"

"Well, you want to raise a big family, and me, well, I'm busy with my pet shop—two pet shops, now," she hurried on. "And with my career and your career, well—"

Jake put a hand on her arm and stepped in front of her. "Lydia, don't," he said.

"Don't what?" she said, not wanting any arguments, not wanting to have to explain.

There was a pained look in his eyes as he gazed at her. "I know about your situation," he said quietly. "Your problem with childbearing."

Her eyes widened. "You read my file?"

"The file? No. I knew before that, before we even met for dinner the first night. You see, Dr. Newcomb is an old friend of mine," he said. "It was an entirely accidental disclosure, so don't get the wrong idea, but I heard about your visiting him."

Lydia's throat was so tight that the words seem to squeak out. "You saw Dr. Newcomb? And you—you knew all along...." Her voice trailed off. A kind of emotional numbness was setting in. Without even thinking about it, she was walking again, quickly, and Jake was hurrying along beside to keep up with her.

"Wait," he was saying.

"I have to get some cheesecloth," she announced, stepping into Raul's Gourmet Foods. She was suddenly feeling so exposed that the warm store with its overflowing aisles of produce and imported goods seemed a haven just now.

Jake followed, his voice an urgent counterpoint to the bright baroque music that was being piped out through the store's speakers. "Listen," he said. "I knew it was a sensitive issue with you, Lydia. I mean wanting kids, and not being sure you could have them. And since the subject hadn't really come up that night, I avoided it."

"I see," she said, though she didn't, really. "To spare my feelings?"

"I was about to bring it up," he said. "But I saw how you were reacting when we talked about children, and I sensed it was a raw nerve for you. You were practically crying when you saw that little girl at the other table."

Lydia remembered. That had been the day she'd seen Dr. Newcomb, and it was true she hadn't wanted to really talk about kids with Jake. Her feelings were in turmoil. She felt both relieved and angry at the same time. "I don't see why it's any of your business," she said. "I mean, why are we even discussing this?"

"Because it's important," he said. "I would've brought it up sooner, but you obviously didn't want to confide in me, so..."

He was right and he was wrong. She *had* wanted to confide in Jake about her miscarriage and its repercussions, but she hadn't felt "the right time" had arrived to talk about it. And now that the truth was out, what did it mean? What did he think?

"Did I do the wrong thing?" he asked.

She put her items down by the cash register, not really seeing or thinking about what she was doing. "Yes. No! Jake, I guess I can appreciate your being sensitive to my feelings. But in a way, it all doesn't matter much. Does it?"

"How can you say that?" he demanded. "Everything matters, especially when it's your feelings at stake, and mine. There's something you're not understanding here, Lydia, something basic. Maybe I haven't said it straight out enough before, but I'm telling you now: I don't care what kinds of problems we have to deal with—whether it's me being able to be with you while I do my job, or you living three thousand miles away, or what my son thinks or what your fears are about children—" He paused just long enough to take a deep breath. "The point is, I love you, Lydie! So whatever I have to do to make it work, that's what I'm going to do."

He stopped abruptly, suddenly looking as sheepish as he was winded. And Lydia could only stare at him, speechless. She'd almost given up hope that she'd ever hear a man say that sort of thing to her, a man she could love the same way in return. "But I'm not . . . you want . . ."

"I want you," he said. "All of these things we're up against, we can work them out. We love each other, you know it. And isn't that the only thing that really counts?"

"Oh, Jake," she murmured. "I . . ." She was getting too choked up to make any coherent reply, as he stroked her cheek with the soft palm of his hand.

"That's what counts, all right," said the gray-haired woman behind the cash register, who had been listening to this exchange, rapt. "If you don't kiss him, miss, I will."

A FEW KISSES, hugs and rounds of Kleenex later, they walked back to the Sanctuary, arm in arm, Jake carrying her groceries. "From what I understand, though it's not my area of expertise," he was saying, "no doctor's going to tell you that you *can't* bear a child."

"True," Lydia allowed. "There are some dangers, sure," he went on. "If you did get pregnant, you'd be taking a risk. And I can understand your not wanting to take that risk. But you could try, if you wanted to."

"That's what Dr. Newcomb said," she told him.

"And he's not the only doctor we—you could talk to," he said. "I know some specialists here and in New York, if you wanted to pursue this. I'm not pushing, you understand," he added hastily, as she looked at him. "I mean, it's really your choice. Except I'd love for it to be ours," he added.

"And if, after everything, I can't?..."

"We'll do whatever both of us want," he said. "If we think Max needs a little brother or sister, we can adopt one."

Lydia let out a deep breath. "I suppose," she said. "But I do want to try, Jake."

He nodded, turning to face her as they approached the door to the Sanctuary. "I'm glad to hear that. Lydia, do you really have to go back to San Francisco?"

She looked up at him, startled. Jake kissed her again, the shopping bag dangling from his hand as he pressed her to him. "I do live there," she murmured, when she was able to take her lips from his.

"It's time for you to go bicoastal," he said, his hand caressing her cheek. "You've got free room and board any time you visit. With me, I mean."

"Interesting offer," she said, smiling, and kissed him again. It was also interesting that she'd held off renting out the second-floor apartment. Obviously a part of her had still wanted to hold onto it and her hopes for a future with Jake.

"We've got a lot to talk about," Jake said. "That's why I wanted to see you now, before tomorrow."

She nodded. "Is Max coming?"

"He says he doesn't want to, but he'll come," Jake said. "I think if he sees you again, maybe you two could pick up from where you left off before."

"I'd like that," she said. Looking at the cheerily lighted windows of the pet shop, a thought occurred to her. "And maybe I could come up with a little something to help us along...."

"FIVE MORE MINUTES," Katherine pronounced, shutting the oven door.

"Smells fantastic," said Clarissa.

"Stuffing's ready," Lydia noted.

"We need two more chairs." Peter sauntered into the kitchen, Jake behind him, both men sniffing the air with looks of anticipation as they approached the stove.

"Try the pantry room," Katherine said. "Uh-uh," she said, swatting her husband's hand. "Keep away from those cranberries."

"The natives are restless," he commented, nodding in the direction of the convivial din that was coming from the other rooms.

"We can sit down in a few minutes," she said. "Got your carving knife sharpened?"

Jake leaned past Lydia to look at the bubbling gravy she was stirring, and slipped an arm around her waist. "How's it going?"

"Just like Katherine said," she told him. "Dinner's nearly ready."

"I was talking more about..."

"Ah," she said. "Right. Now's a good time, I think. Maybe you could ask Max to come in here."

Jake nodded, gave her shoulder a reassuring squeeze and left. Lydia moved over to the huge wooden salad bowl. Gazing out the window at the little hutch she'd constructed by Grammy's garden, she uttered a brief prayer.

After a fairly sullen "Hello," upon his arrival with Jake Max had avoided her, and Lydia had followed his lead by leaving him alone. But now she was pilfering some choice lettuce leaves to take outside, and she had a feeling Max wasn't going to mind giving her a hand.

"Hey, what are you doing to my artfully constructed su-persalad?" Clarissa exclaimed.

"Pretend you didn't see," Lydia said, then smiled a welcome as Max appeared in the doorway, wearing his baseball cap and a wary look. "Hey, Max, you got a minute? There's someone outside who wants to see you." He shrugged. "Come on, we'll put our coats on," she said, walking to the pantry. She didn't look back, but heard him fall into step behind her.

Coats on, they went outdoors, Max following a yard or so behind. But when one white and one brown ear emerged from the hutch, he ran forward to catch up with her. "Hey, Popeye," Lydia greeted the rabbit, kneeling in the grass. "I brought a friend of yours for a visit." The rabbit sniffed nervously at them, nose twitching madly. Lydia turned to Max. "Here," she said, and handed him the lettuce. "I think he'd like it if you gave it to him."

Max took the lettuce from her and sat down in the grass, unable to keep a smile from creeping over his face as the rabbit grabbed at the leaf in his hand, nibbling away ferociously at it. "Guess he's hungry," he muttered.

Lydia felt relief surge through her. Finally, a few words! "I guess," she said cautiously. Max continued feeding the rabbit and she bided her time until he spoke again.

"What's he doing here?"

"Waiting for you," she said. Max turned to look at her directly for the first time since he'd come over.

"What's that mean?"

"It means I took him home from the Pet Sanctuary so nobody else would take him," Lydia said. "I thought maybe if he—if we waited long enough, you might come around."

Max shrugged, and concentrated on Popeye. Then he looked at her again. "My dad talks about you a lot," he said, with that faint air of distaste boys his age often evince when the conversation involves girls.

"Oh?"

"Yeah, he must think you're pretty neat."

Lydia cleared her throat. "I think *he's* pretty neat," she ventured.

Max nodded. "He's smart. He may not be around all the time, but when he's there, we have a pretty good time."

"I'm not surprised," she said.

Max studied his leaf of lettuce, avoiding her eyes again. "So, you like him, huh?"

Lydia nodded. "I like him a lot," she said. "Is that a bad thing? Would you rather I didn't?"

Max frowned at the leaf. "I don't know."

"I like you, too," she said quietly. Max made a face. "I liked you before I knew you were your dad's son," she went on. "So you know I'm not making it up."

Max nodded. "Yeah, maybe," he said. "Did you really take Popeye home so I could have him?"

Lydia nodded. "Your dad said he's going to speak to your mother about Popeye going back to Seattle with you, if you want."

Max's face lit up. "Really?"

"Really."

Max looked at Popeye, clearly excited. Then he turned to her again. "I guess it's okay," he muttered.

"What is?"

"What you asked before," he said, with a grimace of annoyance. "You know, about my dad."

"It's okay that I like him?"

"Yeah." Max turned his attention back to Popeye. "Wow, look at that! He ate the whole thing."

"Well, give him this one, too, then," she said, smiling. She had to overcome a temptation to whip off his baseball cap and tousle his hair. Instead she just watched, wondering why she should be feeling the beginnings of tears in her eyes.

"There you go, Popeye," Max was saying. "You get a big meal today. After all—" he looked up at her with a crooked smile "—it's Thanksgiving."

THEY'D HAD TO PUT three different tables together to accommodate everybody: Katherine, Peter, Lydia, Jake, Max, Clarissa, all the ladies from the Alliance and a dozen children. It was arguably the largest Thanksgiving celebration Taylor House had ever seen. No doubt Grammy would've fussed and fretted over the somewhat unstylish appointments of the feast.

For one thing, the furnace had picked this day of all days to go on the fritz and had finally broken down altogether an hour before dinnertime. There was now a motley collection of space heaters lining the dining-room walls, and many a guest was bundled in extra sweaters and scarves. The dining room itself, having been converted into play space, wasn't looking like a proper dining room anymore, but none of these details really mattered. What mattered was that they were all together.

All in this case included Emily and John Atchins. Katherine had made a point of inviting them so they could have the kind of family Thanksgiving they were used to, with old friends. "Next year you guys come to our place," Emily announced.

"Sure," said Marsha. "You'll have to knock down a wall or two, but that's okay, right, John?"

Tucker sat at Emily's side, looking as pleased and proud as any promoted soldier who'd now taken command of the troops. Her husband sat beside her, looking equally proud with their baby in his lap, and talking a blue streak to Barbara Wainright on his left. Katherine leaned over to Lydia. "I get it," she whispered. "He talks enough for both of them."

"Hold still," said Clarissa, a camera raised to her eye. The baby put a chubby little hand over her father's mouth as the flashbulb went off.

"Right," Tucker said, smiling at the child, and Lydia and Katherine couldn't suppress a giggle.

Max was seated at the head of the children's table, having volunteered, as oldest, to keep his younger peers in line. Lydia could hear him bragging to Roger Bartlett. "It's big-

ger than most *dogs* are," he said. "And it's only got one
eye!" Roger looked properly impressed.

"That's the last, I think," Katherine announced. There
were so many serving dishes on the table that Lydia feared
people's plates would slide off. The whole downstairs was
filled with delicious aromas, the room with laughter and
conversation. Peter stood up, tapping his spoon against a
pewter mug, but it took a while to get some semblance of
quiet.

"Okay," he called. "We'd like to say grace. Hey, order
in the court! You want to eat, don't you?" After many false
starts, the guests finally did fall silent. "Clarissa, sit down,
will you? Let's all hold hands."

Lydia took Katherine's with her left and Jake's with her
right. Jake smiled across the table to where Max's group was
seated and he gave them both a jaunty wave. Clarissa, camera in hand, hurriedly took a flash photo of the kids holding hands before returning to her seat opposite Lydia.

"I'll be brief," Peter said, and was answered by a muttered chorus of encouragement. "Well, we've certainly got
more than enough to be thankful for this year," he said.
"Taylor House did even better than we'd hoped it would.
And we managed to get through what could've been a pretty
grim crisis with no one much the worse for wear." He
paused, and looked at his wife. "Katherine, why don't you
take it from there?"

She smiled, and still holding his hand, leaned forward to
address the others. "Well, the main thing is... we're all
here!" she said.

"Exactly!" Sadie cried, and laughter ran around the table.

"And we've all got our health," Katherine went on.
"And the house is still standing." She looked up at Peter.
"Does that cover everything?"

"I think so," Peter said. Jake gave Lydia's hand a little
squeeze and she held his gaze as their host added: "So let's
give thanks for all those blessings."

"Amen!"

Lydia was still gazing into Jake's eyes, and when the others took their hands away to eagerly attack the many platters, the volume in the room almost deafening, she still held his.

"You know what I'm thankful for?" he murmured. "You."

She squeezed his hand. "Ditto, Doctor," she said.

"YOU'RE NOT LISTENING," Jake chided her gently. "I'm planning our entire future together for the next decade or two, and you're not hearing a word."

"Sorry," Lydia said, and she took her hand down. She'd been examining the ring, set with its tiny but glittering diamonds, for an hour now. "I just can't stop admiring it," she said.

Jake smiled. "Good," he said.

"I can't wait to get back to Greensdale," she said, snuggling up against him under the covers. "I mean, I can," she added, caressing his shoulder. "But I want to see the expression on Katherine's face when we tell her."

"If they're at the house," Jake said. "I don't know if Peter was able to get the furnace fixed."

Earlier this Saturday afternoon, after they'd taken Max to the airport, Jake had spirited Lydia off to a bed-and-breakfast place in Stockbridge. He'd done the next-to-impossible, wrapping up all of his professional obligations so that they could spend the rest of the weekend uninterruptedly alone.

And he'd had an ulterior motive.

"We're being reckless and impulsive, aren't we?" she murmured, her eye still on the ring as she ran her hand over the warm contours of his chest.

"In the best possible way, yes," he said, capturing her hand in his and deftly kissing each fingertip.

"Although we've left ourselves an out," she mused.

"How's that?"

"We haven't set a date yet."

"Don't get any ideas," he growled. "You said you'd marry me. We're engaged. We've been engaged for—" he checked his watch "—an hour and five minutes."

"Mmm," she said. "And it's been a *fun* hour and five minutes, hasn't it?"

Jake grinned. "Fun is too simple a word for the kind of experience this is," he said.

"But amid all the fun," she murmured, putting her head on his shoulder, "we haven't set a date."

"That's just a logistical wrinkle," Jake said. "Among other things, we have to talk to Max about his school schedule."

"Max likes me," Lydia said.

Jake shook his head. "He only wants you for your rabbits."

"Stop," she said. "No, not that," she added, as his fingers paused from their goose-bump-raising exploration of her bare back. "Stop teasing."

"And you like Max?"

Lydia nodded. "He's tough on the outside," she noted. "But sweet and mushy on the in. Not unlike his father." She raised her head to look at him. "You know what he told me?"

"What?"

"He said if you and I stayed together, it would be okay with him if we made him a younger brother. Not a sister, he specified. A boy he could 'mess around with.'"

Jake chuckled. "He said that?"

"He did."

Jake kissed her forehead, sliding her back against the sheets, gently turning her until she was beneath him. "Well, then," he whispered, his voice husky as his dark eyes glimmered above her. "We'd better get to it."

"Now?" she asked, playfully wary.

"Just practice," he suggested, hugging her closer to him.

"Ah," she said, closing her eyes and smiling as he fitted his body to hers. "Well, they do say practice makes perfect...."

Epilogue

Taylor House was empty again. It sat, huddled on its little hill against the cold, silent but for the sound of shutters creaking under the eaves in the wind and the quiet ticking of the old grandfather clock downstairs. But the familiar rumble of the ancient furnace was gone, and as the wind rose, it seemed to find new nooks and crannies to fly into. Anyone who had been inside would've been chilled to the bone.

The wind was fierce. A squirrel that had been huddling against a windowpane balked as the gnarled branch of an elm rope-tied to the shutter swung precariously close. The shutter squeaked louder. The squirrel stood up, tiny nose quivering in fear.

The wind gave a little howl of triumph as the rope, decades old, finally snapped. The squirrel bolted just in time. The tree, suddenly loosened, twisted toward the house, and the elm branch smashed through the windowpane, shattering it.

Inside, the heater propped upon the sideboard by the broken window fell over in the sudden gust, but its cord was still plugged in. When its face hit the wooden sideboard, a dial twisted. The heater whirred to life, the edge of the window curtain fluttering around it in agitation.

Only minutes later, the frightened squirrel returned, peering into the broken window at the sudden light within. A tongue of flame was flickering at the curtain's edge. But no one else was there to see it as the wind whistled onward, chasing a stray loosened piece of slate around the gables on the old roof.

Taylor House shivered. And the flames, emboldened by the mischievous wind, grew brighter....

Harlequin American Romance

COMING NEXT MONTH

#273 TAYLOR HOUSE: CLARISSA'S WISH
by Leigh Anne Williams

Clarissa Taylor Cartwright was determined to rebuild the family home. But architect Barnaby Rhodes's terms were unusual. Make Clarissa fall in love with him. Don't miss the final book in the TAYLOR HOUSE trilogy.

#274 A FINE MADNESS by Barbara Bretton

Billionaire Max Steel's Florida island was so secure that even he couldn't come and go as he pleased. While Kelly plotted to rescue him, he and an island of PAX operatives plotted a riskier mission. A mission that was destined to make heroes of Kelly and Max—if it didn't kill them first.

#275 GIFTS OF THE SPIRIT by Anne McAllister

Chase Whitelaw wanted a wife and family—but he wasn't prepared to give Joanna another chance to fill the role. Five years ago she had left him at the altar; now she wanted back in his life. But this time, was *he* ready?

#276 WISH UPON A STAR by Emma Merritt

Along with her three children, Rachel March was finally making it on her own—until Lucas Brand demonstrated his devastating tenderness and Rachel realized she was up against a master. How could she resist the irresistible—and more importantly, did she even want to anymore?

**There was no hope in that time and place
But there would be another lifetime . . .**

The warrior died at her feet, his blood running out of the cave entrance and mingling with the waterfall. With his last breath he cursed the woman. Told her that her spirit would remain chained in the cave forever until a child was created and born there.

So goes the ancient legend of the Chained Lady and the curse that bound her throughout the ages—until destiny brought Diana Prentice and Colby Savagar together under the influence of forces beyond their understanding. Suddenly each was haunted by dreams that linked past and present, while their waking hours were fraught with danger. Only when Colby, Diana's modern-day warrior, learned to love could those dark forces be vanquished. Only then could Diana set the Chained Lady free. . . .

Next month, Harlequin Temptation and the intrepid Jayne Ann Krentz bring you Harlequin's first true sequel—

DREAMS, Parts 1 and 2

Look for this two-part epic tale, the

Temptation

"Editors' Choice."

Harlequin Temptation dares to be different!

Once in a while, we Temptation editors spot a romance that's truly innovative. To make sure *you* don't miss any one of these outstanding selections, we'll mark them for you.

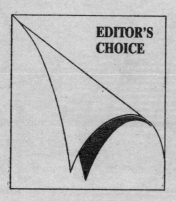

When the ''Editors' Choice'' fold-back appears on a Temptation cover, you'll know we've found that extra-special page-turner!

THE

Temptation

EDITORS